BEACH CAT BLUES

Alison O'Leary

RED DOG
UK

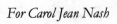

For Carol Jean Nash

CHAPTER ONE

TOBY GLANCED AROUND him with an air of studied nonchalance. He flicked his lighter across the end of his cigarette and drew in a lungful of smoke. A prickle of sweat dampened his armpits, and he inhaled deeply as the gratifying swirl of nicotine hit his brain. To the left of him stood the small, nondescript red brick office. Tucked away among the court buildings, he had almost missed it. He leaned back against the wall and watched for a moment as a small elderly woman walked around the corner and entered the building, her head bowed and her shoulders hunched against the light wind that had sprung up.

He hadn't needed to come today, in fact he almost hadn't, but at the last minute he had changed his mind and now he was glad that he had. He wanted to be ready when the time came. He pulled out his phone and ran quickly through the list again. He'd done his research. Medical certificate, birth certificate, NHS number, his own ID. As long as nobody poked their nose in and started asking questions, the plan was practically foolproof. The only weak point was the witnesses, but he'd find somebody. There was always somebody who would help out. For a price.

Tossing his cigarette end to the ground, he walked slowly back towards the town centre. It couldn't be much longer now. And once he'd registered the death, he could make a start on probate. All he had to do was keep his nerve.

"SO HOW DID it go today?"

Molly put down her iPad and looked up as Jeremy entered the room, stepping sideways to avoid tripping over Aubrey and Vincent, who ran across to greet him. Apart from the fact that they loved him dearly, he had the endearing and always to be encouraged habit of carrying a few cat treats in his pockets.

"Very good." Jeremy sat down and leaned back with his hands behind his head. "Although I must admit, it feels quite weird. Poacher turned gamekeeper." He smiled suddenly. "Her Majesty's Inspectorate. It sounds like a tune from a Gilbert and Sullivan operetta. Or a contagious disease. Oh, doctor, I think I've caught a touch of Her Majesty's Inspectorate. I can't think where I got it from."

Molly smiled.

"It'll feel different once you start doing your first inspections. Have they given you any indication yet?"

Jeremy nodded.

"Yes, today. They're sending me out as part of the team to inspect some posh private school. They think that it will be good experience."

"I didn't realise that private schools came under the umbrella of Ofsted?"

"Well, they do and they don't," said Jeremy. "They come under the auspices of the Independent Schools Inspectorate, but it's still overseen by Ofsted. So how was your day?"

"Fine. It was good. I'm still feeling a touch of the new girl syndrome, but it's wearing off. One of the residents had a bit of a meltdown, but other than that it was mostly sorting out a load of admin. Oh, and a new admission. George. Nice old bloke, but very ill. According to his medical notes, he probably hasn't got much longer. He told me that he misses his cat. The Lodge has got a visiting pet scheme so I might take Aubrey in to keep him company for a bit."

Aubrey glanced across at her. He hoped that she didn't think she was going to start farming him out to all and sundry because, much as he adored Molly, there were some things up with which a cat should not put. On the other hand, if this George was lonely, he supposed it wouldn't kill him to lend a helping paw. Also, there might be benefits involved. He couldn't think what exactly, but he'd often been surprised, usually in a good way.

"No regrets?"

Molly shook her head.

"No. So far so good."

"How are you getting on with the manager?"

"Well, he's a bit different from Gavin. At least he doesn't think he's starring in an episode of L A Law. Honestly, how Gavin managed to wring drama from a routine conveyance, God alone knows. Anyway, Thomas is very friendly. Helpful." She thought for a moment. "A bit bumbly, like the sort of school teacher that the kids would have laughed at but the first one they'd go to if they were in trouble. He wears those chunky cardigans with football buttons. In the old days he would have had a pipe. He told me that he spends his days off fishing."

Jeremy smiled.

"He sounds rather nice."

"He is. Actually, he's good company. He's got a kind of dry wit. Apparently, he was a mental health nurse, over at the old asylum before they closed it down."

"Good experience for the dementia wing then?"

Molly nodded.

"He's always very calm and he does really seem to care about the residents. In fact, if he spent as much time on paperwork as he does sitting around and talking to them, he probably wouldn't need an assistant manager."

"It must seem strange after Donoghue's."

Molly nodded.

"It does. But in a good way. At Donoghue's it was all pretty much routine. At Lilac Tree Lodge I have no idea what's going to happen—every day brings its own surprises.

They were silent for a moment and then Jeremy said,

"Do you think that you'll miss working in a legal office?"

Molly shook her head.

"No, not really. I did enjoy it, but after everything that happened at Fallowfield…"

The silence returned. The murder that had taken place in the village of Fallowfield, and the dreadful story that had unfolded as a result, had shaken everybody. The charming cottage that they had been living in as part of Jeremy's exchange year at Ferndale School had started to feel distinctly less than charming, and they had all secretly longed to get back to their old house.

Molly continued.

"I really wanted a complete change. I think that we all did. And what could be a nicer change than living by the sea?"

Aubrey agreed. When they'd first started talking about this sea side business, he had been totally bemused. It felt like no sooner had they got back home and he'd settled in again with his mates, than Jeremy had started applying for jobs and they'd been on the move. But it had been great.

The beach thing that he had been secretly dreading was less than ten minutes stroll from their new house and it was like one huge garden, only with that sand stuff instead of grass. And the rock pools were a thing of joy. The first time he'd spotted one he had spent all morning just dipping his paw in and out and nobody had even tried to stop him. And there were the caves, too. Big, dark cavernous spaces tucked below the cliffs. Perfect for a cat to go hunting and exploring. There were even scraps to be had from the people in the beach huts who seemed to spend a lot of time eating outside on their little verandas.

But the greatest thing about the move, the best of all, was that they had taken Vincent with them. He glanced across at his friend who had draped himself across the window sill, his sleek black fur glossy in the early evening sun, ostensibly asleep but in reality, clocking everything that went on outside.

They didn't ever talk about it, but he knew how shaken Vincent had been that night when his owners didn't return. For three consecutive days, Vincent had waited patiently for the sound of his owner's car. And for three consecutive days it had failed to appear. The house had remained empty. Nobody had come in and nobody had gone out. At first, he had refused Aubrey's offer of a shared food bowl, but eventually hunger had driven him to it. Molly, catching him in the kitchen one night, had started putting down two food bowls. To this day, Aubrey wasn't sure what had happened to Vincent's owners but he had overheard the word 'tragedy' and while he wasn't quite sure what it meant, he had a fairly good idea.

When the time for the move came, it was obvious to all concerned that Vincent was coming with them. His only regret was that they hadn't been able to take little Moses too, but Moses was happy enough chasing butterflies and eating as much, and sometimes more, than his round little tummy would take.

He looked up as Carlos came into the room. Even taller now, and showing every sign of turning into a handsome youth, he loped across the room and scooped Aubrey into his arms.

"How'd it go today, Molly?"

Carlos flopped down next to Jeremy on the sofa and leaned back, one hand rhythmically running the length of Aubrey's back.

"I was just telling Jeremy. So far, so good. How was college?"

Carlos dipped his head and tickled Aubrey's neck.

"Good. Yeah, good."

Aubrey and Vincent exchanged glances. A good friend to both of them, particularly when it came to extra rations and allowing them to sleep on his bed, it was a matter of some relief that Carlos had settled in so well. Although having left school and now, in theory, being of an age where he might live independently, the issue of him setting up home elsewhere had never been raised. As far as Molly and Jeremy were concerned, they had taken him in after Maria, his mother, was murdered and his home was with them.

CHAPTER TWO

TOBY PAUSED OUTSIDE the door and looked around him. Every time he came here, he was struck again by the subtle comfort of the place. With its plushy carpeted corridors and subdued lighting, the heating constantly on at a warm soothing temperature, this place was more like a luxury hotel than a residential home. His mouth tightened. George had all this, while he was still living in a shitty little borrowed caravan on the Happy Campers Caravan site. And he only had that until the season started up again in the spring. God knew what George was paying for this place, it must be costing a fortune. A fortune that should have been his. Well, some of it anyway. Without bothering to knock, he grasped the door handle and walked in.

"George, how are you? Settling in okay?"

The elderly gentleman turned and looked at him, his pale blue eyes cold.

"What are you doing here again?"

From their position on the end of his bed, Aubrey and Vincent stared across at the visitor. Initially slightly reluctant to accompany Molly to work, they had quickly discovered the up side to the arrangement. There were plenty of residents to give them treats and always somewhere warm to stretch out, and George was turning out to be a top bloke. Some of the other residents were, it had to be said, slightly less accommodating. As they had discovered when they had been forcibly ejected from two of the most comfortable chairs in one of the residents' sitting rooms. However, as Vincent had said to Aubrey after their first outing as part of the visiting pet scheme, you had to take the rough with the smooth and by and large it looked as though they were on to a winner. Especially after they discovered the run of small balconies attached to all the rooms. As long as a window was open, it was Access All Areas.

The visitor looked back at them with obvious dislike and then glanced up at the display of photographs on the wall, pushing down a spike of irritation as he did so. The framed images of jolly family holidays with golden sands and buckets and spades, and tinsel-lit Christmases with roaring fires and wall to wall Christmas cards, all dating from well over half a century earlier, was a world away from the endless run of soon to be condemned council flats and damp rented rooms of his own childhood. And it was difficult not to notice that there were no images of himself among the family groupings. Not so much as a school photograph. But much as George might try, he couldn't just airbrush him out of existence. He was here, whether George liked it or not.

He stared for a moment at the pictures of George's mother, with her stupid little frilly apron, standing smiling over the Christmas pudding, all stiff permed hair and frosty blue eyeshadow. Who could blame their father for wanting a bit on the side? Any man would if he had to go home to that old bag every night. And that ugly little troll with the gingham dress and ribbons—the spitting image of her mother—she was a nasty piece of work too. Last he'd heard, Beth was in America having fallen out with both her parents and George, although she hadn't despised them so much that she felt able to refuse the money that their father had continued to send her right up until he had died. George had put a stop to that as soon as he came into the estate.

That was typical of George. Never willingly do a good turn. But it wasn't like he hadn't done well out of the old man. He'd seen the will. Their father had left almost his entire estate, including the business, to George. Beth had received the small holiday cottage on the Isle of Wight and a hundred grand while he, Toby, had received only a paltry twenty thousand pounds in recognition, as his father had expressed it, of his younger son's existence. What the fuck did that even mean? And George would have had that off him too, if he could have. Anyway, how far did twenty thousand pounds get you? Not far, was the answer. By the time he'd paid off a few debts and taken a holiday, it was gone.

He moved further into the room and sat down opposite his half-brother, leaning forward with his hands resting on his knees.

"So, George, how are you settling in?" he repeated.

George remained silent; his face impassive.

"How are you feeling?" he persisted. "Is there anything you need? Anything that I can get you?"

George screwed his face into a scowl of contempt.

"No. And I don't want you coming here again. The neighbours should never have told you where I was."

The younger man paused and then, with what was clearly an effort, assumed an amiable expression. "George, we are brothers. Half-brothers. And let's face it, we've only got each other now. We could at least try to get along."

"I don't see why." George's tone was clipped, his eyes hard. "You're only here because you want something out of me. What is it this time?" George continued without waiting for an answer. "No, don't tell me. The same thing that you always want. Money. Are you still, what do they call it, resting?"

Toby bit back the retort that threatened to erupt. The last proper job he'd had was a sofa commercial, and that was months ago. He'd long since spent the fee. He was reduced to buying own brand vodka in the supermarket and if he wanted anything new to wear, he had to go to the charity shops. But he was worth more than that—he knew it. He had no intention of spending the rest of his life bumping along the bottom of society and being grateful for the odd voice-over. It was only a matter of time before he got some decent work. A soap, maybe, or one of those historical dramas. He had nice legs; he'd look good in tights.

He swallowed hard and pinned a smile across his face. George was his best chance for now and all he had to do was be patient and do his best not to antagonise him in the meantime.

He took a deep breath.

"I've been thinking, George."

George sneered.

"Don't strain yourself."

Toby swallowed. He was having difficulty not leaping out of the chair and fastening his hands straight round George's scrawny neck.

"As I said, I've been thinking."

"About what?"

"Well, we're both on our own. Nobody to help either of us. And, let's face it, you are getting on a bit."

"And?"

"You're not in the best of health. You might need somebody to make decisions for you. You know, to kind of act on your behalf. Somebody to make sure that you get everything that you need."

"I see. And what are you proposing exactly?"

"I've been looking into it. If you, that is, we, had a lasting power of attorney…"

The elder man laughed. A surprisingly vigorous noise that started in his emaciated chest and rumbled its way up to his throat.

"And you honestly think that I'd trust you? I'd sooner trust a rattle snake. You seem to forget that you still owe me two thousand pounds from last year."

"And I intend to pay you back, George, you know that. As soon as I get another job."

"Fat chance. I only lent it to you because, for some reason that totally escapes me, father seemed to be fond of you. God alone knows why. When I think of how my poor mother suffered…"

George stopped and passed a hand over his face, his thin fingers trembling slightly. Toby watched him; eyes narrowed. Oh yes, she'd suffered all right. If you call it suffering to live in a big detached house with a wealthy old man, posh holidays and a new car every year. He doubted that the old bitch had ever done a hand's turn in her life. Whereas his mother had scraped along on bar work and cleaning, when she could get it, occasionally supplemented by a hand-out from his father when he was feeling generous. Which wasn't often. As he was forever telling them, he had a lot of commitments and he had to prioritise. Which, roughly translated, meant that he and his mother were always at the bottom of the list. About the only thing he'd ever really done for them was to acknowledge himself as father on his birth certificate, so at least he'd carried his name. Which, he had to admit, was very handy in the current circumstances.

George dropped his hand and continued.

"Anyway, if you've turned up thinking that you can get round me again, you can forget it. There'll be no more where that came from. Even if I wanted to, which I don't, I've got this place to pay for now."

They both looked up as the door opened and a care worker put her head around the door.

"Lunch is ready, George, if you'd like to come down."

Toby glanced across at the big heavy marble clock which had been given to George by the other directors on his retirement. He had always hated that clock. Expensive, opulent and given to George as a gift, it was representative of everything that George had and he didn't. When the time came, God alone knew what he'd do with it. Nobody in their right mind would want to buy it, and he was damned if he was going to lug it all the way to a charity shop. They probably wouldn't want it anyway. Besides which, what had charity ever done for him? He'd chuck it away, or just leave it. Let the Lodge sort it out.

He watched while the care worker helped George to his feet. Leaning on her arm, he looked pointedly at Toby.

"After you."

Toby held the door open for them and then followed them back down the corridor towards the lift, noting the frailty of his brother's frame beneath the clothes that were starting to hang on him.

"I'll take the stairs."

He walked to the head of the stairs and waited until the lift doors closed. Running quickly back towards George's room, he tried the door. As he'd thought, like most of the residents when they left their rooms, George hadn't locked it.

CHAPTER THREE

AUBREY AND VINCENT looked up as George's door opened again. With one accord they dived out of the window and on to the balcony. That look the man had given them earlier had been distinctly hostile. They watched as he moved towards the small chest of drawers and began to pull open each drawer rapidly, stirring the contents with one hand before slamming it shut again. He paused and looked around him, and then let his gaze settle on the bedside cabinet. A slow smile spread across his face. With one eye on the door, he crossed the room and opened the cabinet door. Crouching down, he pulled out a small leather document case and flipped it open. Aubrey and Vincent watched as he rifled through the contents, his hand lighting on two sheets stapled together. He read the contents rapidly—his small eyes, the same shade of pale blue as his brother's, moved swiftly across the words. When he spoke, they had to strain to hear the sibilant whisper, but his anger was obvious from the bulging of his eyes.

"I knew it. The old bastard. Fucking cats and dogs. What about family?"

Whipping his phone from his inside pocket, the man held it over the document and snapped the contents. Shoving the folder back in the cupboard, he pulled out some more papers and began quickly scanning them. He jumped as the door opened again. Shoving the papers back in the cupboard, he straightened up and turned to face the door. A small woman, her dark hair tied neatly back, hesitated on the threshold, her expression wary. One hand gripped the big laundry trolley.

The man smiled, an easy lop-sided grin, and crinkled his eyes. He lifted his hand and swept his blond highlighted fringe from his forehead.

"I was just checking that George has everything he needs. He's my brother," he added.

The woman nodded and remained on the threshold.

"Toby," said the man, walking towards her, one hand extended. The woman backed away slightly and he let his hand drop. He studied her for a moment. "So," he continued, "it all seems very nice here. Lucky old George. Must be expensive though. Crikey, I've stayed in worse hotels than this." He gave a light deprecating chuckle and crinkled his eyes again.

The woman remained silent. She looked, Aubrey thought, nervous. He wondered why. She worked here; he knew. She was one of the staff who always dealt with the laundry. He'd seen her wheeling the big laundry crates around on a number of occasions, although she never stopped to talk to them or stroke them like lots of the other care workers did.

Toby looked directly at her, opening his eyes wider and his face wearing a mask of amiable openness.

"So, how is he doing? I mean, I know that he's ill…" He adjusted his expression to mournful, a slight downturn of the mouth and his head tipped to one side. He blinked slowly, to add to the effect. "It's so sad to see poor old George in this state. I'm guessing that it won't be much longer?"

The woman looked back at him, her eyes blank.

"I don't know."

Aubrey and Vincent both knew, though. It surely wouldn't be long now. They had known that George was dying. They had known from the moment that they had set eyes on him. It was something to do with a very faint odour, almost a tang, that brushed the air when he moved, and the papery whiteness of his skin that seemed more translucent with every day that passed. It was always George that they visited first on their days at the Lodge, before any other resident, and they both checked back on him at regular intervals. They crept closer to the open window and leapt lightly on to the sill.

Toby continued.

"I'm surprised really, that he's not in hospital?"

It was posed as a question rather than a statement.

The woman tightened her grip on the laundry trolley and thought for a moment before speaking.

"We have visiting nursing staff."

Aubrey looked at her. Unlike most of the care workers who always stopped for a chat with visitors, she was obviously economical with her words. Her face still wore the wary expression it had displayed when she had opened the door and seen Toby Carson in the room.

Toby nodded, his expression morphing now into one of gentle query.

"I can't quite recall now; he did tell me. How much is he paying?"

"I don't know."

"Roughly?" persisted Toby.

"Twelve hundred pounds."

"Per month?"

"Per week."

From the balcony, Aubrey and Vincent watched as Toby's mouth tightened and he swallowed hard.

"And worth every penny, I'm sure."

CHAPTER FOUR

AUBREY SHUDDERED AND turned to Vincent.

"Vin, what is this place?"

He looked around him as he spoke, at the grim forbidding trees dripping rainwater on the patchy grass, their branches festooned with dead fairy lights that hung like lifeless spiders. Spaced along the dark narrow pathways were shapeless lumps, a number of them showing a dim light inside. It looked to Aubrey very much like a place where bad things happened.

"It's a caravan park. People stay here. I've been to one before. The people that I used to live with, they took me with them to their caravan every year. I liked it. Nice change."

Aubrey looked at Vincent admiringly. The things that Vincent knew. Vincent continued.

"I'm not so sure about this one, though. I came over exploring that time when Molly took you to the vet for your injections. I should think it's better when the sun's shining," he added.

Aubrey nodded. Most things were better when the sun was shining. He followed him warily along a narrow path, darting swift glances to right and left. This place was making him uneasy.

"Where are we going?"

Vincent looked back over his shoulder and grinned.

"The bins. They're packed."

He nudged Aubrey suddenly and dived into the shadows as a figure wove its way unsteadily up to the caravan next to them, the wavering light from his torch playing around his feet. They watched as Toby lifted the wine bottle that he was carrying and took another swig. He wiped his mouth with the back of his hand and dropped a greasy chip wrapper to the ground, kicking it in front of him with the toe of his trainer. He pulled open the door of the caravan and stared for a moment at the inside. From the shadows, the cats stared with him. At the window, the little flower-patterned curtains hung limply, their grubby edges brushing the narrow metal frame. The bed, a sour faded quilt dumped on top, took up most of the space and was still rumpled from the morning. In the distance a dog started barking, a low continuous yapping pitched at maximum annoyance level.

Climbing wearily up the little step, Toby went in and shut the door. He lifted the bottle to his mouth again and looked around him. If he stretched his arms out, he could almost touch every wall. God, this place stank. Not just the caravan itself, but the whole site. It reeked of despair. And the toilets in the shower block were blocked again. It was like some giant sewage works over there—you had to put your hand over your nose every time you went near it. Hard to believe that some poor sods actually came here on holiday, although by the time the season came around the toilets would be magically fixed, the caravans buffed to a gleaming finish and the windows and curtains freshly washed. It was only at this time of year that the squalor set in.

He reflected on the few holidays that he had taken as a child; his expression morose. Unlike George and Beth who had holidayed in posh hotels with swimming pools and games rooms, he and his mother had been lucky to get a few days in a Bed and Breakfast, and that was only when his father was able to get away for a few days to join them. It had never occurred to him to pay for them to go away by themselves. The only time he ever put his hand in his pocket was when there was something in it for him. The rest of the time they had spent summers sweltering in the heat of the town, venturing out only to the nearest pub. His mother to the bar, and him to the garden with a packet of crisps and instructions not to wander.

He smiled, his grim mood dissipating slightly at the memory of his mother, with her constantly changing hair colour and short tight skirts and her open affectionate nature. Too open and affectionate, he'd often thought. Much good it had done her. She'd done her best by him though, he had never doubted that, albeit a very limited best. But then, to be fair, she did what she could with what she had. And mostly his memories of her were good ones. Some of their happiest times had been when she'd been between boyfriends and they had huddled up together in front of the telly with the old gas fire popping and a glass of gin for her and a giant size bar of chocolate for him. It wasn't her fault that she was over-fond of the squash and was too easily taken in. They all had their weaknesses. He, if anybody, should know that.

He climbed on to the bed and rolled on to his side. Reaching across, he lifted the curtain slightly and peered out into the gathering night. Vibrant and cheerful in the season, with children running around splashing in and out of the pool and bouncing their beach balls off the grass verges, in the winter the camp site was dank and depressing, the pool drained and covered over, the club house shut and the caravans occupied by those who had nowhere else to live and no choice. The Happy Camper site had become a convenient place for the local housing department to park their problem families, if only for a few months of the year. If he'd known that, he wouldn't have taken the place when Mike had offered it to him. But who was he kidding? After Arlene threw him out, he didn't have anywhere else to go.

He sunk his chin onto his chest and wrapped himself in self-pity. If he had any money, he'd go out. Stroll down to the pub and have a few pints, escape for a few hours and forget all this squalor. But he didn't have any money, he'd spent the last of it in Bargain Booze in town and he'd have to take evasive action tomorrow in case Mike came round asking for some rent. He'd get up early to avoid him and go into town. It was market day tomorrow; he still had some bits and pieces left. He'd see if he could sell some to a couple of the traders that he knew. At least it would get him out of this shit hole for a few hours.

He brooded sullenly on his half-brother. There was old George, living the life of Riley, whoever Riley was, swilling around in the lap of luxury at that lodge place, waited on hand and foot, while he was reduced to this. And what had George ever done to deserve it? Nothing as far as Toby could see. After university he'd worked in the business and then simply taken the old man's place on the board when he'd retired and raked in the money. And he hadn't even left home, just lived with the old bag until she died and then he had the house as well, a big four-bedroomed detached property near to the golf course. Well, all that was about to change.

Thrusting his hand into his pocket, he pulled his mobile out and began scrolling through the images. There it was, in black and white. The last will and testament of George Carson, lately of Lilac Tree Lodge, and dated just before he had gone to live there. Written on one of those will forms, of course, the kind you buy from a stationer. George was far too tight to engage a solicitor. And witnessed by two of his former neighbours, neither of whom was likely to take any further interest. Especially if he didn't inform them as to when the funeral was.

The executor was named as some bloke he had never heard of, but his address was given as somewhere in Yorkshire, but that didn't matter anyway. By the time he got to hear of George's death, if he ever did, a new will would be in place. As evidenced by the care home staff who had witnessed all his visits, George and his brother had been close at the end of his life, and he had simply had a change of heart. As a plan, it was simplicity itself. All he had to do was get a fresh form, make a few changes, get it witnessed, and then substitute it. If he was feeling generous, he might even include a small gift for those bastard cats and dogs that George was so fond of. Because, after all, he was a nice bloke.

CHAPTER FIVE

JEREMY DROPPED HIS leather briefcase, a present from Molly and Carlos when he'd landed his post with the Inspectorate, and strode through to the kitchen, loosening his tie as he walked. Weaving in and out of his legs, Aubrey and Vincent marched ahead of him.

Molly looked up from the label on the jar that she had been reading and propped her reading glasses on her head.

"How did it go?"

Jeremy reached across the work surface. Pouring himself a glass of wine from the open bottle, he leaned back and took a mouthful.

"Okay. I think. Difficult to tell on the first day." He smiled. "A bit different to Sir Frank Wainwright's though. Talk about children of the rich. It's a completely different world. Honestly Moll, you should see the paintings hanging in the staffroom. I swear that they're genuine. Not like those horrible plastic prints of Russian winters in shades of black and black that the last head of Sir Frank's bought in as a job lot. As if the staff didn't have enough to be depressed about."

Molly smiled as Jeremy continued.

"And the students' common room is something else. All squishy sofas and matching china mugs. They've even got coffee machines. You know, those pod things. Not like when I was at school. The closest thing we got to any kind of luxury in our sixth form common room was a few battered armchairs that someone had donated and an electric kettle." He paused and thought for a moment. "Although there's something about it that makes me feel slightly uneasy." He ruffled the back of his head and frowned. "I don't know, I just get the feeling that there's something not quite right there."

"What?"

Jeremy shrugged.

"That's just it, I don't know. I can't put my finger on it. But it's like my mother would say, it's that back of the neck feeling. I didn't take to the headmaster, either."

"Why not?"

"I don't really know. He's got one of those sort of sharp haircuts, if you know what I mean, and these really cold green eyes. He seemed very watchful, like he was hiding something."

Molly burst out laughing.

"Well, that's hardly surprising. Nobody likes being put through the mill. You remember what it was like when Sir Frank's was inspected."

"Don't remind me. But at Sir Frank's we really did have something to hide. Like half the staff going off sick as soon as we got notice that Ofsted was on its way. God, you couldn't have cleared the building quicker if it had been on fire."

"So, what did you see today?"

"Not that much," Jeremy admitted. "I had a meeting with the management team and met some of the teaching staff. Later this week I'll get to do some actual lesson observations."

"You'll get a better feel for things then."

"I expect so. It's probably just my prejudice. When you've taught somewhere like Sir Frank's where you have to keep sellotaping the binding on the text books and there's only one between three anyway, it kind of sticks in the throat a bit. But the stuff that they've got there is amazing, I've never seen anything like it. They've got a film club."

"Lots of schools have film clubs. What's wrong with that?"

"Most schools don't have their own cinemas. Note the plural. Not one cinema, three. Three cinemas and all fully kitted out. And they have school trips to places like the Louvre, not a coach outing to Southsea, like we did at Sir Frank's."

Aubrey smothered a smile. He remembered the day trip to Southsea. Or, more specifically, he remembered Jeremy staggering back home after midnight, swearing that he would never do it again. Apparently, three of the boys had started a running fight on the sea front with some of the locals, six of the girls decided to relieve the local Boots of the contents of the cosmetic counter and one boy disappeared altogether, only to be discovered reeling around drunk and shouting abuse in the amusement arcade.

"But the school is compliant, isn't it? I mean, they're doing everything that they should?" said Molly.

"Oh yes, so far as I can tell at this stage." He paused. "It was fine this morning. All polished shoes and posh biscuits. The headmaster couldn't have been more charming, but in a queasy sort of way. Like a politician before an election. His name's Jake Wade. Dr Jake Wade. Though he was all 'call me Jake' and big cheesy smiles. But there's something not quite right there. I just know it. Ah well, no doubt it will reveal itself."

He put his glass down and leaned towards her, suddenly anxious.

"Moll, what's up? Are you feeling all right?" He peered more closely at her. "You look worried. Has something happened?"

Molly put down the jar she was holding and pulled out a kitchen chair. She sat down and rested her chin on her hand.

"You remember me telling you the other day about some things going missing from residents' rooms?"

Jeremy nodded.

"So far they've all been small things," she continued. "Some items of jewellery, nothing particularly valuable. A small carriage clock. But yesterday, one of the residents, Gerald, reported his phone as having been stolen and today another one claimed that her purse has gone from out of her bedside cabinet. She said that there was only some loose change in it, but it had her wedding ring in it too. It's too tight for her now, so she keeps it in her purse. Oh, and her address card was in there as well, of course."

"Her what?"

"Address card. We encourage all our residents to keep a Lodge card in their purse or wallet so that if they get taken ill or something when they go out then there's something on them to say where they live."

"Right." Jeremy looked thoughtful. "Good idea. This phone that was taken, was it locked?"

Molly nodded.

"But you know as well as I do that it takes nothing to get them unlocked."

"True. Half the kids at Sir Frank's were running it as a side-line." He took another mouthful of wine. "You're sure that the residents haven't just imagined it?"

"Jeremy, please." Molly sounded reproachful. "They're old, not stupid. All right, some of them might be a bit hazy as to what day it is, but not Clara. Especially not Clara. She's the one whose purse is missing. She used to be a magistrate. If she says that her purse has gone missing, then her purse has gone missing."

"Yes, right. Of course. Sorry, Moll." He smiled apologetically. "What does Thomas say about it?"

Molly gave a half-smile.

"Not a great deal. Thomas prefers not to think about it. He says it will sort itself out. Although how, I don't know. But he doesn't want Mrs. Randall to be upset."

"Who?"

"Mrs. Randall. She's the owner."

"What's she like?"

"I don't know. I've never met her. Apparently, she's a wealthy widow with a number of business interests. The Lodge is just one of them. Thomas says that she lives abroad most of the time. She never visits anyway. Funny though," she mused. "Thomas always seems a bit jumpy whenever I mention her."

"Why?"

"I don't know. He does a good job at the Lodge. When residents come to us, they tend to stay until they, well, until they die. Our last report rated us as outstanding. In fact, we've got a waiting list for our rooms so I can't see that Mrs. Randall has anything to complain about."

"Maybe he just doesn't like the thought of anyone interfering?"

"Maybe. Anyway, his view is basically that all the stuff that's gone missing will just turn up eventually, that the residents have just forgotten where they put things. They do sometimes," she added. "I guess we all do. But now, well…"

"You don't think it's that simple?"

CHAPTER SIX

MOLLY SIGHED AND rubbed the side of her head.

"I don't know, maybe it is. I suppose that it could be a resident, probably not even doing it with any malice. Perhaps one of the more vague ones. Just picking up something that attracts them, like a magpie, and then holding on to it. They do sometimes wander into each other's rooms and they mostly don't lock their doors. But with the purse, well, that solution seems less likely. Because whoever took it would have had to actually open a drawer and I can't see any of them doing that."

Jeremy nodded.

"There haven't been any people working around the place lately? Any contractors or anything like that?"

Molly shook her head.

"No. I checked through the old invoices. The last contractors on site were the roofers and that was ages ago. Gordon the gardener does all our odd jobs and general maintenance. He does the security as well, locking up and so on. He's been at the Lodge since Mrs. Randall bought it I think."

Jeremy looked thoughtful.

"One of the care workers or cleaners then?"

"It could be, we've had a few new ones start over the last month. But they've all had DRB checks. It was one of the first things I saw to." She smiled. "I'm not sure if some of the older staff that have been with us for some time have had them, though. They should have but Thomas might not have gotten round to it."

"Well, DRB checks don't necessarily mean anything, anyway. A clear DRB could just mean that somebody hasn't been caught yet. Look at old Bob whatisname at Donoghue's. He was cleaning out the clients for years before anybody rumbled him."

Aubrey looked up, interested. He remembered old Bob whatisname. A round, jolly fellow with big red cheeks, he'd played golf with Jeremy a few times and had occasionally come back to the house for a drink. Turned out that he had a lot to be jolly about with all that client money stuffing his pockets. Not so jolly now, though. His wife had left him and he was doing two years at her majesty's pleasure.

Molly nodded.

"I guess so. The thing is, until we put a stop to it, everyone will constantly be under suspicion. We can't stop the residents talking about it among themselves and there's already an atmosphere starting to build up."

From under the table where he and Vincent were busy hoovering up the cat treats that they had stored after Molly dropped the packet earlier, Aubrey agreed. Their visit today hadn't been the usual pleasant experience. Everyone had been on edge and even Martha, who was the kindest of care workers, who always had a friendly word and a hand ready to stroke them, and the one that they always hoped was on duty, had barely spared them a second glance this morning. She had hurried past them, hands stuffed into her overall pockets and looking as though she might burst into tears at any minute. In fact, everybody had been going around with a sort of tight, watchful expression and, for the first time, both he and Vincent had been glad when Molly's shift ended and they could all go home.

"I've been thinking that really we should call the police, but Thomas doesn't want to," said Molly. She gave a great sigh. "In fact, he's pretty adamant that we shouldn't. He doesn't want them involved and I can't just go over his head."

"I don't understand. Why not let the police handle it? Surely that's the sensible thing to do? At the very least it would warn whoever's doing this that the Lodge are taking it seriously?"

"Thomas says it's about the reputation of the home. He wants to keep a lid on it all. Any kind of scandal and people get nervous and start leaving. You can't really blame them."

Jeremy nodded.

"I suppose so. Any clues as to the culprit?"

Molly shook her head.

"Not really. All the things that have been taken are portable, easily slipped into a pocket. And carers and residents are in and out of rooms all the time."

"What about putting cameras in?"

"I talked about that to Thomas, today. He's always been against installing them, but I'm beginning to think that cameras would be a good idea. Even if it's only to act as a deterrent."

"The modern ones, Moll, they're barely noticeable. And they're wireless, too. You don't have to have any major installations. I was thinking of putting up a couple here, just so we can see who's coming and going when we're out."

"If we put them in at Lilac Tree Lodge would we have to get the residents' agreement to install them?"

"Probably. But if you explain that it's in their own interest, particularly if they're taken ill in the night or anything like that, they probably won't mind. My guess is that after a while they won't even notice them. I mean, how often do you notice them in supermarkets or banks? Or on the street?"

Molly nodded.

"Yes, I suppose that's true."

"Lots of schools have got them now. The only reason we didn't have them at Sir Frank's is that the kids would have nicked them. That and the fact that we didn't really want to see what they were doing when we weren't there." He paused. "Is Carlos home yet?"

"He's working on an assignment in his room. Something to do with food safety. He was down here earlier, going through the cupboards and checking on sell-by dates." She smiled and then said, "Talking of food, the Lodge is short-handed in the kitchen at present. I need to start looking for someone to relieve Simon for some of the evening shifts. At the moment he's doing breakfasts and lunches and dinners as well, and since Ali left a couple of weeks ago, he's been doing weekends too. I've been using some agency staff, but it works out expensive and they're not always clued up to catering for the elderly. Simon doesn't complain, but it's too much for one person." She paused. "He's an odd bloke, Simon."

"In what way?"

"There's something about him that I can't quite work out. Maybe it's his voice."

"His voice?" Jeremy sounded amused. "What about his voice?"

"I don't know. I can't quite place him. He's got a sort of neutral accent, slightly educated if you know what I mean. And he never has a coffee or anything in the staff lounge. He just keeps himself to himself."

"Maybe he's just a private person," Jeremy suggested.

"Probably," Molly agreed. "Just out of curiosity, I checked his HR record. There's nothing on it except his name, national insurance number, address and date of birth."

"No references or anything?"

Molly shook her head.

"No." She sighed. "Something else that Thomas obviously didn't get round to. But I'm not complaining. He's always polite and he's good at his job. We never get any complaints from the residents about the food."

"So will you put in an ad for a replacement for Ali?"

"I thought that maybe Carlos could help out. He could do some of the evening shifts, as well as some weekends. Well, I say evenings, it's more like late afternoons really, just to prepare the residents evening meal and clear away afterwards. It shouldn't interfere with his college work and he'd be finished by about seven at the latest. It would be some extra pocket money for him, as well as good experience."

CHAPTER SEVEN

UPSTAIRS, AUBREY AND Vincent watched from the windowsill as Carlos tapped away at his laptop. Tucked into a corner of the screen sat a picture of a small pretty girl with a heart-shaped face and green and blue strands in her hair. He turned to face them; his expression serious.

"Thing is, I need to get at least a Merit on this. Or a Distinction." He turned back to the screen; his brow furrowed. "A Distinction. Because one day I'm going to have my own restaurant. A real one," he added. "Not just, like, burgers and stuff."

Vincent turned to face Aubrey.

"I quite like burgers."

Aubrey nodded. He did too. He'd acquired quite a taste for them when he'd lived on the streets. There was always an abundance of them lying around in their Styrofoam boxes in the early hours. Although, to be honest, there weren't many foods that he didn't like, now he thought about it. Apart from toast. He didn't like toast. All those crumbs got in his fur. Carlos lifted his hands from the keyboard and leaned back, stretching his arms above his head and making his T-shirt ride up and reveal his flat white stomach. He reached into the open bag of crisps by his side and pulled out a handful. It was a matter of complete astonishment to both Aubrey and Vincent that Carlos could eat huge amounts, and frequently did, and yet remained as slender as a sapling. While poor old Jeremy, although a fairly healthy weight, had to struggle to maintain it. It's the beer, he'd said mournfully to Aubrey one morning as he stepped back from the scales. And the wine, thought Aubrey from the edge of the bath where he'd been watching him.

"Nearly done." Carlos screwed up the empty crisp bag and threw it across the room towards the bin, missing it completely. He stood up and retrieved it and then looked across at the two cats, their fur lit by the late afternoon sunshine streaming through the window. He smiled at them. "College is really good, it's not how I expected it to be. I mean, when Jeremy first suggested it, I thought, yeah, right, more school." He rolled his eyes. "Like I'd want that. And I didn't think I'd get in, anyway. Or if I did, it'd be, like, on some course for rejects. But I couldn't believe it when I got my results."

He suddenly bounded across the room and stared at the piece of paper pinned to the cork noticeboard on the wall.

"I couldn't get my head round it to start with. To tell the truth," his voice dropped conspiratorially, although there was nobody to hear him except for the two cats. "I thought that they'd made a mistake. You know, like, got me mixed up with someone else, but Jeremy said that he'd check, and he did, and it was me. Me."

He stabbed himself in the chest with his forefinger and then spun round and jumped on to the bed in one great leap, causing the mattress to bounce and the frame to creak.

"On my first day I was really worried. Like, I didn't know anybody and that, but it was all right. It was, like, we were all in the same boat. And everybody works, sometimes you can't get a space in the library. At Sir Frank's, it was, like, nobody even knew where the library was. Well, except for the kids that went there to nick things. And if you did your homework and that, then you got your head kicked in if you didn't let the other kids copy it." He lay on his back and stared at the ceiling. "At college, when you don't have lessons, you can do what you want. Like go to the common room and that or walk into town. And the teachers don't nag you or anything. They say it's up to you to do the work. And you call them by their first name. Teddy's at college, too. Well, sort of. Her school's got a sixth form." He turned his head and looked across at the picture of the girl tucked into his computer screen. "She's doing A-levels. When I open my restaurant," he continued, "I'm going to call it Maria's and have a big opening night and Teddy's going to be the guest of honour, with Molly and Jeremy. And you two, of course."

Aubrey glanced at Vincent. Vincent hadn't known Teddy, but Aubrey had. Carlos had met her and her brother Casper when they were all living at Fallowfield. He looked back at Carlos, whose eyes were shining. He hoped that Teddy wouldn't forget Carlos. Apart from Molly and Jeremy, Teddy was the one good thing to come into Carlos's life since his mother was killed.

CHAPTER EIGHT

AUBREY AND VINCENT watched with interest as Carlos rapidly chopped a pile of carrots and onions and dropped them in the large stainless steel bowl. It was like magic. You could hardly see his hand moving, he worked so fast. He looked down at them and grinned.

"Come on then." Dropping the knife on to the work surface and wiping his hands on the cloth tucked into the pocket of his chef's whites, he crossed the kitchen to the fridge and pulled out a plate of cling-filmed cold meat. Pushing open the fire door, he dropped two slices on to the gravel outside. "Eat them quickly. I'll get in trouble if anyone catches you two hanging around."

He spun round, letting the fire door slam shut behind him as the kitchen door opened and a small woman with thin dark hair and over-plucked eyebrows strolled in. His happy mood evaporated. He hated it when she came in the kitchen, which she did all too often. Usually to avoid work. He picked up the knife and began chopping again, keeping his gaze fixed firmly on the workbench in front of him.

"Hi, Carlos. What's on the menu tonight?"

"Shepherd's pie. And a vegetarian version."

The woman propped herself up on a stool, hooking her ankles around the legs, and took out a packet of cigarettes from her overall pocket.

"I don't know why you bother; they can't tell the difference. You might as well give them dog meat for all they'd know."

"Maxine, you know that you can't." He pointed towards the packet of cigarettes with the blade of the knife he was holding.

"All right, keep your wig on."

She slipped off the stool and strolled across to the fire exit. Leaning over, she propped the door open with the fire extinguisher and then stood with her back against the doorjamb. She lit a cigarette and watched for a moment as the smoke circled upwards and wreathed around her head.

"What do you think about these thefts that are going on?"

Carlos shrugged.

"Don't know. Nothing."

The woman's eyes narrowed.

"What does Molly think?"

Carlos shrugged again.

"I don't know."

He turned back to the chopping board. He did know, very well, but Molly had given him strict instructions not to discuss it with anybody at the Lodge. Molly, he knew, didn't buy Thomas's theory that it was a forgetful resident. Molly thought that it was a member of staff.

Maxine took another drag on her cigarette and exhaled it through her thin nostrils.

"I reckon it's Carla." She considered for a moment. "She's always volunteering for extra shifts. She obviously needs the money. Either that, or she likes hanging out with geriatrics." The malice in her voice dripped through her pursed lips. "And all those kids she's got. What I want to know is, who's looking after them when she's at work?" She adopted a virtuous tone and opened her small eyes wider. "Left on their own all the time. I mean, it's not right. Someone ought to contact Social Services about it. Don't you think?"

Carlos remained silent. His own mother had worked all hours, because she had to. In the country as illegal immigrants, trying to make a better life for them, she had taken all the cash in hand jobs she could get to keep them afloat, and that meant working evenings and early mornings, and sometimes nights too. But he hadn't been neglected. True, they hadn't had much, but he had never actually gone without. There was always warmth and some sort of food in the flat, and she had always tried to get him the things that the other kids had, even if those things were a bit crap sometimes. Like the knock-off designer jeans she bought down the market that never fitted him properly so that he had to keep hoiking them up, and the cheap trainers that made him walk funny and that the other kids had laughed at. But she did her best. Everything that she had done, she had done for him. Unbidden, the sound of her voice suddenly crashed into his head, swirling around and filling his mind.

'One day, Carlos, all will be better. We will live in big house. Nice house. It is definite. We will have big telly, huge telly, and every day for our tea we will have cakes with the cream in. And jam. Always we will have jam. And if your big fat bum-face of a father is knocking at our door, we will laugh and we will not open it."

He dipped his head, forcing back the tears that suddenly welled. Who was Maxine to judge? She was nothing special. Living with her horrible, big-bellied husband in one of those houses on the new estate, what did she know about anything? He'd seen them in town, strolling around like they owned the place. Where did they get all their money, anyway? Her old man seemed to be permanently unemployed, but they always had a new car. Anyway, he liked Carla, and he hated it when Maxine was spiteful about her. Carla was everything that Maxine was not. She was soft and warm and all the residents liked her. Maxine was hard and cold, and nobody liked her.

He swallowed and gripped the chopping knife harder as Maxine continued.

"Thomas doesn't seem too bothered, anyway." said Maxine, taking another drag on her cigarette. She watched him for a moment, as though considering. Carlos realised suddenly why she was always dropping into the kitchen. She liked causing trouble, and she told him things, hoping he would tell Molly. And, he thought guiltily, sometimes he did. As if to prove his suspicion she said, "I saw something on his computer the other day."

Carlos stopped chopping and looked across at her.

"What?"

Maxine smirked.

"He's got a habit."

Carlos felt his heart sink and a small wave of weariness ripple through him. He hoped to God that Thomas wasn't a perv. They were everywhere, and they came in all shapes and sizes, as he'd learned from the other boys at school. Just because a bloke was kind and friendly, it didn't mean that he wasn't one. In fact, according to Darren Winter, the kinder and nicer they were, the more likely they were to be a perv. And Darren should know. His mother's last boyfriend had been one. But not Thomas. Surely not Thomas. He was a good bloke. He was clever and kind and he cared about the residents. All right, he was obviously about a hundred years old and his hair always looked as if someone had hacked at it with nail scissors and he did wear those stupid cardigans, but he was what Jeremy would call decent. Thomas took time out to watch cartoons on the telly and drink tea with the residents and he always joined in when that singing bloke came round to do songs from the war or something, although some of the residents wished that he wouldn't. Thomas liked Aubrey and Vincent, too. He'd seen him talking to them the other day when he'd come into work. And any mate of Aubrey and Vincent's was a mate of his.

"What sort of habit?"

Even to his own ears, his voice sounded small. Maxine sucked in her teeth and smirked.

"Gambling. Online."

"How do you know?"

"I was in his office the other day." She paused for a moment before continuing. "I needed to check on something. He'd left his computer on."

"He might just have been playing a free game."

Maxine shook her head.

"No. He's got an account. I saw it on the screen."

"That doesn't mean anything. Anyone can have an account. It doesn't make it a habit."

"It does when that amount of money is involved. Anyway," she pinched the end of her half-smoked cigarette and put it in her pocket. "Must go. I've got someone to see."

Carlos watched her as she left the room. There was something about her that always left him with a bad taste in his mouth. It was, he realised, that she never had anything good to say about anybody. She was the sort of person that would sneer at a saint. He wished she wouldn't come into the kitchen, but he didn't see how he could stop her. It wasn't like he had any authority round here. He just worked here, like she did. He crossed the room and peered out of the fire door. Aubrey and Vincent were gone.

CHAPTER NINE

IN THE STAFF lounge, Aubrey and Vincent settled themselves on the lumpy sofa to wait for Molly to finish her shift. They had discovered early on that the door to the staff lounge was always propped slightly open so that staff could hear if any of the residents suddenly called out, and it had become their place to wait for Molly. Outside it was cold and grey, with a threat of rain in the air. It was the kind of autumn afternoon that made a cat want to be at home tucked up under a radiator. Or better still, ensconced among the clean washing in the airing cupboard.

"Fancy the bins again later if the weather clears up?" asked Aubrey.

Vincent nodded, his gold neck tag glittering slightly in the strong overhead artificial light. They didn't need to ferret around the bins on the Happy Camper camp site, but the attraction was strong. Also, they were both only too well aware that while life might be sweet at present, everything could change in the blink of an eye. Having secondary feeding sources made good sense, as well as being good fun, and it was as well to make regular checks on them.

They looked up as the door opened wider and Maxine came in, followed by the man they had seen in George's room the other day. They slipped noiselessly over the arm of the sofa and wedged themselves beneath the small coffee table next to the fridge. They would need to stay very still in case Maxine spotted them. Unlike most of the other care workers, who generally stroked and made a fuss of them, Maxine made it clear that as far as she was concerned, visiting pets, and in particular, Aubrey and Vincent, had no place in Lilac Tree Lodge. Lately she seemed to have taken their mere presence as a personal affront. Last week she had shut a cupboard door on Vincent's tail when he was exploring, and in Aubrey's opinion, she had done it deliberately.

Maxine turned to the man and tilted her mouth in a slight smile, deepening the feathery lines caused by years of smoking and exacerbated by the slick of dark red lipstick she wore that bled into them. She gestured towards the now empty sofa. The man sat down and leaned forward; his hands clasped between his knees.

"So, Mr. Carson..."

Toby was about to say, call me Toby, please, but stopped himself just in time. She wasn't his friend. This was a business transaction and once it was over, he never wanted to see or hear from her again.

"You wanted to talk about your brother?" she continued. "What was it that you wanted to know? Is it something in particular?"

Toby looked at her, his expression appraising. It would be so much better if he could get two of the care workers on board. Just in case anybody took an interest. After all, what would be more likely than George asking staff at the place he was living? He bit lightly on his bottom lip. He was taking a chance here, he knew, but he didn't think that he was wrong. He'd come across too many like Maxine in the past. Could he be subtle? He doubted it. He gave her one of his best 'no interest to pay for four years' smiles and opened his eyes slightly wider.

"Oh, no, nothing specific. Not really. I just wanted a chat about how he's doing and so on."

"Well, if you want my opinion, I'd say that he's not been too good lately. Lost some of his spark. He seems to have gone downhill at quite a rate, although you'd have to ask his doctor for details."

"You mean…"

Maxine nodded and waited for him to continue; her hands with their chunky gold rings rammed over her thin fingers, stuffed in her overall pockets. Toby hesitated for a second and then plunged on.

"The other thing is, I need to sort out some of his paperwork." He pulled his mouth down. "Because of course, I'm all he's got now."

"He never married? No kids?"

Toby shook his head.

"No."

Maxine smiled again, a nasty snarky twitch of the lips. Not a nice smile, thought Aubrey. More a smirk than a smile. Why, he wondered, did George not having a wife and kids give her that pleased look? It was like she'd suddenly found out something really important. Maxine, he suspected, was one of those people that liked knowing things about those around her. A collector of other people's secrets. Just in case they came in handy. She kept them, thought Aubrey, like little sharpened sticks. Ready to poke people with. Toby continued talking, his voice low.

"So I was checking through some of his documents. Making sure that everything is in order. His will, and so on," he added.

Maxine reached behind her and nudged away the door wedge with her foot. The door swung to and closed with a quiet click.

"What about his will?"

"Well, the thing is, silly old fool, he's only gone and forgotten to get it witnessed." He chuckled, a conspiratorial chuckle, his eyes twinkling but never leaving the woman's face. "And of course, I don't want to bother him with it, not now."

The silence hung between them for a moment. Toby continued.

"So I was wondering…"

Maxine interrupted.

"Wills need two witnesses."

"Yes, that's right," Toby agreed. And waited.

"I've got a friend… she does some shifts here sometimes."

Toby spoke so softly so that Aubrey and Vincent had to crane forward to hear him.

"Of course, I wouldn't expect you to go to all that trouble for nothing."

CHAPTER TEN

AT THE CAMPSITE, the damp early morning air was still, the only sound that of the distant hum of a generator as it vibrated gently into the atmosphere. On one corner stood two men and a woman, hoods pulled low over their faces and their heads bent closely together. As Aubrey and Vincent watched, they suddenly separated and walked off in different directions.

"How are we going to persuade it to come out?"

Vincent turned to face him, the expression on his dark handsome face worried.

"I don't know. But it can't stay there. It's too dangerous."

Aubrey nodded. The tiny puppy that they had discovered last night when they had been hunting through the dark odorous cavern of the refuse area was wedged beneath a large recycling bin, his small face peering out into the darkness. They had almost missed the glowing eyes that followed their movements around. It was only when Aubrey heard a slight rustling sound that they had seen it. They had stared back at it, the thoughts of both of them immediately running in the same direction. Animals on their own, especially small animals, all too often met with an unfortunate end. And at this time of year, the Happy Camper campsite wasn't exactly exuding the milk of human kindness. With one or two exceptions, most of the pets that lived on the campsite were half-starved cats, and dogs that were shut out all day, the latter sometimes being tied to a post. Aubrey and Vincent had witnessed the poor creatures straining against the tatty lengths of rope that tethered them, and almost throttling themselves in the process. As Vincent had observed to Aubrey, it was tough sometimes, being a cat. But it was often tougher being a dog. Apart from anything else, people had fewer expectations of cats. And were disproportionately thrilled when those expectations were met, never mind exceeded. And as Vincent had also observed, they only knew the half of it. Just think how they'd react if they only knew what we could really do.

They approached the bins silently, creeping forward with such precision that only a creature with the hearing of a bat might have been aware of them. They had tried the previous evening to coax the puppy out, but they had succeeded only in frightening the little creature so that it had retreated even further back. In the end they had retired, defeated. But it had been on both their minds for most of the night and this morning they had headed back to the site just after day break.

"How do you think it got there?"

Vincent shrugged.

"Who knows? Abandoned?"

Aubrey nodded.

"Probably."

Both cats paused and instinctively raised their heads and studied the landscape for a moment, their eyes scanning for any movement. They preferred to come here in darkness and it had unnerved both of them to see people around this early. They crept forward towards the huge plastic containers that loomed in front of them. Aubrey shuddered. Each bin had an uncompromising lid clamped on the top. The residents of the camp site weren't always too careful about closing the bins. Woe betides any creature that accidentally fell in to one when it was open. It would never get out once that lid was shut. It would stay there, slowly suffocating among the debris until it was emptied into the municipal dust cart, to be churned up along with the rest of the rubbish.

Aubrey watched as Vincent, the leaner of the two, lowered himself to the ground and crawled forward on his stomach, inching towards the underside of the recycling bin in which they'd spotted the puppy last night.

"Any sign, Vin?"

Vincent backed out again and straightened himself, shaking his head.

"Can't see anything. Hope the little fellow's all right."

They both turned, suddenly aware of a presence behind them. Sitting on the grass verge sat a tiny golden puppy.

"IT'S NO GOOD looking at me like that, Carlos. We can't keep it." Molly turned as she spoke and looked at the small puppy that was sitting between Aubrey and Vincent on the kitchen floor. She looked at the gash on its leg, which was sore and weeping, and sighed. "God knows where they got it from. I thought that cats were supposed to bring home mice. And how on earth did they get it here?"

More easily than she might suppose, thought Aubrey. After several seconds of solemn contemplation, the puppy had simply got up and followed them. Getting him through the cat flap had been slightly trickier, but in the end, after some futile pushing and shoving, it had been managed by them demonstrating how to use it. The puppy had watched, his head on one side, and then squeezed himself through after them.

As Molly spoke, the puppy sank down and rested its head on its paws, his eyes never leaving her face. She looked away, trying to hide the smile on her face.

"It probably belongs to someone," she continued. "In fact, it almost certainly does. There's probably someone out there now looking for it."

"It hasn't got a collar," pointed out Carlos.

"I expect it's micro-chipped. Look, Carlos, I know how much you'd like it, but you know very well that we can't keep a dog. It's just not practical. We're all out all day. It wouldn't be fair. And Jeremy will say the same, I know."

Even as she spoke, she knew the lie of the words and so did Carlos, Aubrey, and Vincent. All three of them were permanent residents in the Goodman household because of Jeremy's complete inability to abandon a creature in distress.

"Can we give it a name? Just till we find its owner?" pleaded Carlos.

"Carlos, you know that will only make it worse when we have to give it back. It's better not to get too attached to it."

Carlos thought for a moment.

"Can't it be a visiting pet? You know, like Aubrey and Vincent? The residents would like it," he added.

"Well, yes, I expect that they would, but it would still have to come home with me in the evening. And who's going to take it for walks? And there's holidays and weekends to think of, too. You can't ask a neighbour to pop in and feed a dog. It's not like a cat."

All of them, including the puppy, looked round as the door opened and Jeremy came in. As if on cue, the puppy limped over to him and began wagging his tail. Aubrey and Vincent grinned at each other. Game over.

CHAPTER ELEVEN

ON THE END of George's bed, Aubrey and Vincent stretched out, one on either side of him with the tips of their paws tucked neatly beneath them. Buster had been removed by Molly earlier, having knocked over a jug of water while leaping up to catch a fly. Aubrey and Vincent had watched the removal of the small bundle of indignant golden fur with a tinge of sadness. Buster as a visiting pet wasn't really working out. Adorable though he was, he was incapable of sitting still for more than three seconds and several times this week he had almost knocked residents over in his enthusiasm to greet them. They could hear him outside now chasing rabbits, his joyous bark shattering the peace of the garden.

Inside the bed, as insubstantial as a ghost, George's thin body shifted slightly, his mouth working, and then he lay still, his hand resting on the quilt cover. Aubrey watched him for a moment, his face sad, and then turned to Vincent.

"What do you think, Vin?"

"He doesn't look great."

Aubrey nodded. The thing that the nurse had put in his arm seemed to settle him, although it had taken her ages to do it. When they had come today, poor George had been restless and fretful. Unable to find the strength to leave his bed, his exhausted eyes had constantly roved the room, the expression in them slightly puzzled, as though he was checking where he was. It was only when the nurse had come in with the little box that he had seemed to find some peace. By common consent, Aubrey and Vincent hadn't visited any other residents since they'd arrived with Molly, but had parked themselves in George's room and had remained there.

They looked up as the door opened and Martha came in, her round kindly face concerned. She crossed the room to the bed and leaned over them.

"Now, what are you naughty lot doing in here? Come on now, George needs his rest."

She made a move as though to sweep them away, but George stopped her, one thin hand moving protectively towards the animals. Martha smiled and reached across to stroke Vincent.

"Okay. But ring the buzzer if they start annoying you. Now, is there anything that I can get you, George? Are you comfortable?" She adjusted his pillow slightly as she spoke and smoothed down the quilt cover with her small capable hands. "Do you have everything that you need?"

George nodded and then, as if an afterthought, he lifted a hand and pointed a finger that trembled slightly towards the wardrobe in the corner of the room.

"Do you want something from the wardrobe?"

With what was clearly an effort, George nodded. He watched as Martha pulled open the wardrobe door and regarded the neatly hung shirts and trousers. She turned back, a puzzled expression on her face. George nodded again and waved his hand upwards. Standing on tiptoe, Martha reached up and groped along the shelf. Her hand closed around a photograph in a small silver frame. She passed it to him and waited. Taking the photograph from her, George studied it, his face screwing up with the effort, and then held it to his chest. He closed his eyes.

IN THE KITCHEN, Carlos finished cleaning down the work bench and switched on the dishwasher. Once he'd finished setting out the resident's mugs for one of the carers to come in and make their night time drinks later, his shift was done. He looked around him with satisfaction. The meal had gone down well this evening, nearly all the residents had eaten it. There had barely been any left overs. Simon had warned him when he'd started that they could be a fussy lot. That he mustn't take it to heart if they left food on their plates, but it hadn't been his experience. Not so far, anyway. The secret was, said Simon, to make it look nice and not pile too much on the plate. And he was right. The residents liked their food, they just didn't like too much of it. Not all at once, anyway.

He thought for a moment about Simon. A tall, lean man in his early forties, Simon was all right, really. He didn't talk much, but he was friendly enough and he was really good in the kitchen. He wasn't scary like some of the chefs he'd heard about. One of the lads at college told him that he actually had a knife thrown at him by one chef at the pub where he worked weekends. It was only him flinging himself out of the way so quickly that had stopped him being pinned to the wall by his shirt sleeve. But Simon wasn't like that, although to be fair, he didn't see that much of him. Simon did breakfasts and lunches and prepared the evening meals on the shifts that he didn't work. He did all the ordering and meal planning, too, and once a week would come back in to go through the week's menus and make sure that Carlos was comfortable with them. Other than that, the only time that their paths crossed was when Simon stayed on to make a special birthday tea for one of the residents, the highlight being the cake that he would make with the resident's name iced across the top.

Carlos gave the work surface a final wipe and wondered how the Lodge would manage when it came to exam time. At the moment, he was doing five of the seven evening shifts, but he wouldn't be able to do so many shifts once he started revising, although he supposed that he could always prepare food for the freezer at a push. But whatever happened, the exams had to come first. They were going to be difficult, though, he knew. When he was at school he hadn't really revised. He'd just sort of known the answers. But he'd have to revise for his catering exams, no doubt about it. Trouble was, he didn't really know how. He could always ask Molly or Jeremy, he supposed, but they probably took their exams, like, about fifty years ago, and it was all different now. He felt a sudden wash of relief. Teddy would know. He would ask Teddy. He caught his breath at the thought of her. Only a bit longer to go and she would be here. Tomorrow morning, he could hardly wait.

He opened the fire exit door and smiled at the scene in front of him. At the far end of the garden, Buster, his leg now healed, was leaping in the air and spinning round, watched by Gordon. Laying down the spade he'd been wielding in the vegetable patch, making the most of the last of the light evenings, Gordon reached towards the puppy and fondled his ears. Thank goodness nobody had claimed Buster yet, although he'd done as Molly had asked him and put notices in the newsagent's window and the vet's. Jeremy was glad, too, he could tell, although he was holding the party line with Molly. But the first thing Jeremy asked on returning home every evening, was whether there had been anyone coming forward to claim him, and it was difficult to miss the note of anxiety in his voice.

Noticing Carlos framed in the doorway, Buster twisted away from Gordon and bounded towards him, ears flying. Carlos leaned over and buried his face in the wriggling ball of golden fur.

"Come on, home time. Let's go and find Molly. See if we can round up Aubrey and Vincent on the way."

ON THE FIRST floor, the doors of the second lift—the one at the end of the corridor that was for the use of staff only—quietly opened, and two men in dark suits emerged. From the shadows on the landing where Aubrey and Vincent had been sitting, they watched as the men entered George's room. They waited silently until the men emerged again, carrying between them a large covered object and headed back towards the lift.

CHAPTER TWELVE

THE ROOM WAS completely silent, the atmosphere chilly. The bed that George had slept in was stripped and the windows thrown open. Aubrey slipped through from the balcony and padded around. Jumping up to the bedside cabinet, he studied the photograph that George had been so anxious to see the previous day. He tipped his head on one side and regarded the young man with the tanned skin and strong healthy limbs. Bare-chested and handsome, standing on the deck of a boat, the white sails behind him, glass in hand, he was smiling into the sun. At his feet sat a large black and white cat staring proudly into the camera.

He jumped down again to meet Vincent, who had just slipped on to the balcony from the room next door.

"All right, Vin?"

Vincent nodded and stared in at the empty bed.

"I'm going to miss old George."

"He was one of the good ones."

They were both silent for a moment and then Aubrey said,

"I thought he might be around for a bit longer."

"Me too."

"Wonder who we'll get in there next?"

"Let's hope it's another George."

They stepped back from the window as the door opened and Molly came in, followed by Toby Carson. She walked across to the bed and stared down at it for a moment. When she spoke, her voice was low and solemn. Not the usual cheerful tone that Aubrey and Vincent were accustomed to.

"Poor George. He was always positive, he always had something pleasant to say, but he always seemed to me to be slightly lonely. We tried to get him involved, but he never really mixed with the other residents. He came down to the dining room for most of his meals, but that was about it. He didn't sit in the lounges with the other residents or join any of the clubs. Nobody came to visit him except you." She sighed, a small gust of sadness. "He wasn't the only one lacking visitors, though. Some of our residents don't get any at all, at least he had you."

Toby walked across to the bedside cabinet and stared for a moment at the photograph that Aubrey had been looking at seconds earlier. He picked it up and, flicking it over, inspected the back of the silver frame before looking up again and smiling at Molly, a winsome smile that gave a slight twist to his mouth and crinkled his eyes.

"Yes, it's so sad. Dreadful to be old and alone." He sighed, a heavy theatrical sound, and pulled the corners of his mouth down. "But George was a very reserved man, you know. He didn't socialise much so I'm not surprised that he didn't have visitors. Of course, George and I were always close, even though he was so much older than me. He's left me everything in his will, you know?" He paused and heaved another great sigh. "I suppose, as his next of kin, I ought to be thinking about the funeral."

"Yes," said Molly. "I'm sure that some of the carers would like to attend. He'd pre-paid everything, of course. Thomas has the documentation when you're ready."

The cats watched as an unmistakable expression of relief flooded across Toby's face. He re-arranged it quickly into one of sorrow. When he spoke, his voice was low.

"Thomas has been very kind". He smiled a small sad smile, swallowed, and fell silent for a moment, as though attempting to compose himself and contain his grief. Molly remained respectfully silent.

"George was such a reserved man," he continued. "He very rarely spoke about his private life. I think that I'll need to go through his things and find any contacts and so on. There may be an address book or something. I'm sure that there must be someone who'd like to say farewell to the old chap."

There was a slight catch in his voice and Molly patted his arm.

"Yes, of course. And," she hesitated, "I don't want to seem insensitive, but there are his things to remove." She nodded towards the wardrobe. "Of course, I know that money isn't an issue, but as long as they remain here, I'm afraid that Lilac Tree Lodge will charge for the room."

MOLLY COLLECTED THE plates together and began stacking them in the dishwasher. Jeremy drained the last from his glass and rested his elbows on the table. He glanced across at Carlos, who was scrolling through his phone.

"Molly, I…"

Molly turned to look at him.

"Jeremy, I know what you're going to say, but it's just not sensible."

Jeremy sighed.

"No, I guess not."

"I love him. Everybody loves him, but he's causing chaos at the Lodge. This morning he jammed the entrance by jumping in and out of it and making the automatic doors open and close."

Aubrey looked up from beneath the radiator where he'd squashed himself in. He'd been rather impressed with Buster's tricks this morning. So had Vincent. It had taken real talent to work out how to land with sufficient force on just the right spot in order to trigger the door's mechanism.

Molly slammed the dishwasher door shut and deliberately avoided looking at Buster, who was sitting quietly for once in the cat dome and silently chewing on Jeremy's slipper, which he had dragged in there with him. She sat down again at the table.

"And he's incapable of keeping still. He no sooner gets settled on a resident's lap then he's off running up and down the corridors. He knocked a tea tray out of Martha's hands this morning," she continued. "But I have thought of a possible solution."

Carlos dropped his phone and stared up at her hopefully. He had been, Aubrey could tell, listening while pretending not to.

"I was thinking that maybe Gordon might take him," said Molly. "The gardener and handyman."

"Do you think that he will?"

"He might. I haven't said anything to him yet, but it could be the perfect solution. Gordon lives on his own but could easily bring Buster into work, he lives in the cottage in the grounds of the Lodge. And then there's all that space in the gardens for him to run around in."

"Who? Gordon?" said Jeremy.

Molly pulled a face at him.

"Does that mean I could still see Buster?" asked Carlos.

"I should think so," said Molly. "We probably all could."

Including me and Vincent, thought Aubrey. Like everyone who came into contact with Buster, they were already very fond of the little chap.

Jeremy nodded.

"It sounds like a sensible solution, if Gordon agrees. I know it's not practical really for us to keep him. Not while we're both working full-time. And when you're on nights, I guess it would be impossible. We could never get him to be quiet during the day while you're trying to sleep. It's hard enough settling him down at night as it is." He reached across and poured himself another glass of wine.

"I think it's worth asking, anyway. If Gordon is keen, then we'll need Thomas to ask Mrs. Randall to agree to it because the cottage is owned by the Lodge, but I can't see why she wouldn't agree. As long as Buster is kept under control."

Good luck with that one, thought Aubrey. Buster might be little, but he had huge ambition, which Aubrey and Vincent had every intention of encouraging. He shifted on to his other side and wondered where Vincent was. Sleeping on one of the beds, probably. He flicked his ears as Molly started speaking again.

"It's strange. Even when you know that you're going to lose a resident, it still comes as a shock. We knew when he came in that George's condition was terminal, but I still wasn't prepared for it. I don't know, I'm no expert in these matters, but somehow it seemed a bit sudden. I thought that he might have had a bit longer." She reached across the table for the wine bottle and poured herself a glass. She stared down at it for a moment. "That brother of his was in today. To see to his things and so on." She paused. "There's something about him that I don't really like. I don't know why. He sort of makes me feel uneasy. And I'm sure that I've seen his face somewhere before. It looks familiar. For some reason sofas come into my mind."

CHAPTER THIRTEEN

AUBREY CLIMBED THE last of the stairs and, turning left, strolled down the corridor. He'd left Vincent in the residents' lounge sprawled on the lap of Elizabeth, dutifully listening to her tales of when she flew missions with Bomber Command in the war, which were inter-spliced with the story of how she had escaped from the Titanic in a rowing boat even though she had a broken arm. Neither Aubrey nor Vincent knew what Bomber Command or the Titanic was, but it didn't matter. They had certain duties, and one of them was to sit with the residents. As they frequently told each other, they couldn't be larking about all the time. Also, Elizabeth was very free with the digestive biscuits, which Vincent particularly liked.

Jumping on to the windowsill, he sat upright and wrapped his tail around himself. Outside, Buster ran straight through the flower beds with a ball in his mouth which he dropped at Gordon's feet with every expectation of an instant response. Now virtually banished from the Lodge on the grounds of the constant chaos that he caused; Buster had adapted quickly to his new home. It had been a good idea of Molly's to re-home him with Gordon, even though they had all been sad to see the little chap go.

He turned as the familiar clunk of the lift sounded and George's brother emerged, carrying a roll of something under his arm. He watched as Toby headed towards George's room, his head bent as if he was determined to avoid eye contact, although there was nobody to see him except for the large tabby watching him from the windowsill. Aubrey thought about it for a moment and then headed towards Flora's room. Her door was nearly always ajar and so was her window, which meant that he could get out on to the balcony, as long as he could manage it without her seeing him. If she did, that would mean the next hour was gone while she sat him on her lap and brushed him. Normally, he would make time for Flora and he wasn't averse to a bit of grooming. He did scrub up rather nicely, even if he did say so himself, but today he had an urge to see what Toby was up to. Whatever it was, he was clearly anxious not to make contact with anybody else. There had been something distinctly furtive about the way he'd exited the lift.

With one eye on the gently snoring Flora, he crept silently across her room and then leapt gracefully across the low barriers that separated the balconies. He drew to a halt outside George's room. The window was open just a crack, with the curtain half pulled over, but he could see Toby clearly enough as he tugged open George's wardrobe door. Pulling a black plastic sack from the roll he'd been carrying; Toby began pulling garments from the hangers and throwing them into it. Slamming the wardrobe door shut again, he crossed to the bedside cabinet and grasped the framed photograph. He stared down at the image and then tugged it out from the frame. Tearing it in two, he threw that into the plastic sack, too. Aubrey felt a flash of anger. George had liked that photograph. He watched as Toby considered the small silver frame for a moment and then pushed it into his pocket.

Toby moved quickly around the room, sweeping the small row of paperbacks from the shelf and emptying the toiletries from the bathroom. He paused in front of the family photographs and stared at them, his mouth tight and his eyes hard. Pulling them one by one from the wall, he stared down at each one, his lips pressed firmly together and the frown lines across his forehead deepening, before he ripped the images from the frames and tore them into tiny shreds. Aubrey watched as they fluttered down into the open bin bag. Finally, he knelt down and opened the door of the bedside cabinet. Removing the leather document wallet, he flicked it open and began checking the contents. He jumped up as the door opened and Maxine came in.

"They said that you were here." She looked around her. "Sorting his things, are you?"

Toby opened his mouth and looked for a moment, Aubrey thought, as though he were about to make a sharp response, but then thought better of it. Instead, he sat down on the bed, one hand still grasping the leather wallet.

Maxine continued, her sharp eyes taking everything in.

"I heard that the funeral's tomorrow. That's a bit quick, isn't it?"

Toby shrugged.

"There's no point hanging around. The funeral directors could fit it in, so I thought I might as well get it over with. I mean," he added hurriedly, pulling the corners of his mouth down, "I've got to face up to it at some point. My brother's gone."

The pair regarded each other silently for a moment and then Maxine said, "About George's will…"

"I thought that maybe we might meet somewhere. You and your friend."

CHAPTER FOURTEEN

MOLLY WALKED INTO the kitchen and shrugged off her black jacket. Unwinding her scarf, she draped it along with the jacket across the back of the chair. Jeremy looked up from the table, where he was reading a report.

"Sorry, Moll. I'll clear this lot away." He began shuffling papers together and clipped the top back on the highlighter pen. "So, how did it go?"

"As well as these things usually do, I guess. It was a bit joyless. Which," she added, "I suppose is the point. Funerals aren't meant to be jolly. It's just that this one had, I don't know, a particularly sort of grim flavour to it. It was," she thought for a moment. "Sort of perfunctory, as though it was just going through the motions."

"Many there?"

Molly shook her head.

"No, just me and Thomas. His brother Toby. And Martha. That was it. I think that Carla wanted to come but one of her children was ill. Afterwards we all stood about for a bit and then we just sort of fizzled away. There was nothing laid on. Not much point, I suppose, with so few of us."

Jeremy nodded.

"I guess so. Although it wouldn't have killed the brother to put on a few sandwiches and a glass of wine, as a mark of respect as much as anything else. What was the service like?"

"There wasn't one, not really. Not as such. It wasn't religious. No hymns or vicar or anything. The celebrant, or whatever they're called, did as good a job as she could. She read out some stuff about George. Apparently, he was the managing director of some big engineering company. Then they played some music, sort of light classical stuff. It didn't sound like anyone had put much thought into it. It was the kind of music that businesses play when they put you on hold. I half expected an announcement that my call was important to them. And that was it." She thought for a moment. "I know that crematoriums aren't exactly meant to be cheerful, but that one was particularly depressing. Very modern. Lots of exposed brick and pipe work. And no heating. I suppose that it was even more depressing because there were so few of us there."

Jeremy grinned suddenly.

"Not like grandad's funeral then."

Molly laughed.

"No, not like grandad's funeral."

From the cat dome that he and Vincent had agreed that, as a concession to Molly, they would use occasionally instead of just lying across the top, Aubrey grinned. He'd heard all about grandad's funeral when Jeremy had telephoned his cousin in Australia to tell him about it. According to Jeremy, the majority of mourners were a gang of old reprobates, most of whom the family had never heard of, and nearly all of whom had become incapacitated by alcohol at the wake which was held in the local pub. There had been much loud singing and breaking of wind, the latter necessitating the windows being opened. The exotic fish in the ornamental tank hadn't looked too well, either. Within an hour, a number of the mourners had been stretchered off. The last of them had been bundled into a taxi after being found trying to remove his trousers to much applause in the public bar. It was only his complete inability to co-ordinate hand and eye that had prevented him in succeeding.

"Did Teddy and Casper turn up okay?" asked Jeremy, tucking his papers back into his briefcase. "Was their train on time?"

"Just Teddy. Casper is apparently confined to barracks; his mother phoned this morning. Carlos brought Teddy back here to leave her things in her room and then they went out."

"Where did they go?"

"The beach, I think."

Aubrey looked up. So that was where they'd gone. He might mosey on down there and join them. He wasn't doing anything else. Could catch up on a rock pool or two.

Jeremy frowned.

"Isn't he supposed to be in college?"

"It's study week. No lectures." She smiled. "It was the first thing I checked."

AUBREY LIFTED HIS paw from the rock pool and stared at the glittering droplets falling from it before dipping it back in and stirring the water again. He watched, fascinated, as the tiny creatures scurried around in alarm. He raised his head again and glanced across at Carlos and Teddy. They were sitting on one of the huge boulders that were scattered along the beach, each with their knees drawn up under their chin and their hands clasped around their shins as they stared out to sea. Carlos's hands looked big and raw compared to the soft pinkness of Teddy's small fingers, although they could be as gentle as silk as Aubrey knew very well. That time he'd been chased by a mad bloke, just because he'd had the temerity to stretch out on the roof of his car, it had been Carlos who had scooped him out of harm's way and held him until his breathing had steadied.

The beach was almost empty this afternoon—the small fun fair on the promenade, usually thronging with small children in the summer months, was silent and still and the little kiosks selling ice cream and drinks were draped with great padlocks. The beach huts, painted in their candy colours, were deserted. In the distance a lone dog walker drifted along the tide line. Her large depressed looking dog trailed along behind her, nose and tail to the ground.

Teddy turned her head to face Carlos.

"Why don't you just say something to Molly about it? She'd understand."

"I know. But it sort of feels like I ought to deal with it by myself. I mean, it would be like telling tales, like running to mum if I went to Molly about her. Well, not like mum exactly," he added hurriedly. If Maria had still been alive and he'd told her that Maxine was upsetting him, she'd have torn Maxine limb from limb. He'd learned early on not to tell his mother if somebody was bothering him. The fall out was just too awful to contemplate. There were teenaged boys even now who instinctively legged it in the other direction at the sight of a pair of sparkly flipflops marching towards them.

Teddy thought about it for a moment.

"I guess so. But you shouldn't just let her keep strolling in and out when you're working, not if it upsets you. I mean, just because she's older than you, it doesn't mean like she's your boss or anything. You should at least say something."

"What should I say?"

"I don't know," admitted Teddy. "Maybe just, like, you're busy or something?"

"That won't stop her. She just walks in whenever she feels like it. I mean, she can see I'm working and that. Then she kicks the fire door open and starts smoking. If Thomas smells smoke in there, he'll think it's me. And she's always got something nasty to say. The other day she was blaming one of the other care workers for the thefts and sort of trying to get me to agree with her."

Teddy looked interested.

"What thefts?"

"At the Lodge. Somebody's nicking the resident's stuff."

"What, like properly stealing?"

Carlos nodded.

"It was just small stuff to start with but now it's getting serious. Molly's really worried about it. They've installed cameras. One lady had her purse stolen, and last week one of the blokes said that fifty quid had gone missing from his jacket pocket. It's really horrible because it's like everyone feels under suspicion and that Maxine's making it worse. She keeps pointing the finger at people."

"Maybe it's her?" suggested Teddy.

"Could be," agreed Carlos. "But I don't think so."

"Why not? In detective stories it's always the one who goes round blaming other people who turns out to be the culprit. Well, not always," she conceded. "But often. Anyway, won't these camera things catch her skiving in the kitchen?"

"I don't think the system's running yet. But even when it is, Maxine will know a way round it."

He unclasped his hands and leaned forward. Fiddling with the lace on his trainer and keeping his head down, he said,

"It's really nice to see you again. I've been looking forward to it for ages."

Teddy smiled.

"I've been looking forward to it, too. Casper's sulking because mum and dad wouldn't let him come with me. He got expelled from school again," she added.

"What for?"

"He was supposed to be doing cross-country running but he and another boy took a detour to the boy's house and got drunk on vodka and lemonade. It wouldn't have been that bad, but Casper took a wood chopper from the boy's shed and went back into school with it. He started running around the quad with his blazer over his head pretending to be the mad axe man. Some of the younger boys started crying. Dad was furious. He had to go and collect him."

Carlos thought for a moment.

"Doesn't sound that serious to me. At Sir Frank's I only ever knew one boy get expelled and that was for organising a roof top protest."

"What was he protesting about?" asked Teddy.

"I don't know. I don't think he knew either. He just got on the roof with some other boys and started throwing stuff down on everybody. Bottles and that. I suppose," he added, "that they must have taken the bottles up there with them. Anyway, they let him back after two weeks."

Teddy sighed.

"With Casper, it was just the last straw. It always is with him. He sends his love, anyway."

Carlos glanced down at his phone.

"I've got to go and get ready for my shift in a minute. You can come with me if you like. I mean," he added hurriedly, "only if you want to, only if you wouldn't get bored and that."

CHAPTER FIFTEEN

TOBY GLANCED DOWN at his phone. They were due any minute. He had considered getting them to come to the caravan, but, on reflection, this was better. More anonymous. The less they knew about him, the more he liked it. Anyway, there was only the bed to sit on in the caravan and there was something particularly revolting about the thought of sitting on it with Maxine and her friend. Also, he'd noticed a peculiar smell coming from the mattress earlier and while he didn't much care what they thought of him, he did have some pride.

He thought again about Maxine. There was something about her vulpine features, with those over-plucked eyebrows and foul red lipstick, that just reeked of corruption. She was the sort that always had an eye for the main chance. Which, he supposed, was exactly why he'd been drawn to her in the first place. It had been like a heat-seeking missile. If you put Maxine in a line-up of dodgy people, she'd get picked, no question. He was surprised that Thomas had employed her. Although, on reflection, not that surprised. Thomas was the sort of pain in the arse that saw the good in everyone. He'd not had much contact with him, but he seemed to have the patience of a saint. That time he'd witnessed one of the residents throw a glass of orange squash all over him had astonished him. Thomas had barely batted an eyelid. Just wiped himself down and carried on smiling.

He sat back and sipped at his pint. Once this was all done and dusted, he need never see Maxine or Thomas or anybody from Lilac sodding Tree Lodge ever again. Thank goodness. The effort of playing the part of the loving brother was beginning to wear him down. There were only so many ways he could present the fraternal smile. Not that George would ever have blown his cover. To have told the carers how much he hated Toby, he might have risked them finding out why, and that would have involved disloyalty to the old bag, aka his mother, and that was something that George could never allow to happen. In George's fantasy world, his parents had the perfect marriage until his mother came along with her pretty face and short skirts and ruined it for everyone. The fact that George's mother was about as interesting and attractive as a tin of dried milk past its sell by date and her main topic of conversation was herself was, apparently, neither here nor there. It didn't matter now, anyway. George had very conveniently dropped off his perch.

No, now that the funeral was over and done with, he had no intention of seeing any of them ever again. He had been very careful to make sure that the Lodge wouldn't be able to contact him either, even in the unlikely event that they wanted to. He had made sure that the staff at the Lodge only had his mobile number. They didn't know where he lived, and he had every intention of getting rid of his current phone as soon as all this was over. He was going to get as far away as possible, just in case, on the remotest off-chance, Beth turned up and started asking questions. It wasn't very likely—George and Beth hadn't spoken for years, but they'd had the same mother and father which made her closer than him as George's next of kin and he wasn't taking any chances. In the words of the sofa ads he'd once starred in, this was a once in a lifetime opportunity. He sipped at his lager again. It tasted faintly warm and slightly sweet, the kind of drink that he would have liked when he was a teenager. Frankly, right now he could have done with a couple of large vodkas instead of this fizzy water, but that would have to wait. Get the business over with first. Time enough to celebrate later.

He laid the palm of his hand flat on the brown envelope in front of him and glanced around. This was a good choice of venue. The pub was a modern anonymous looking building on the main road out of town, the sort that had a standard menu which never changed, in contrast to the staff who were constantly changing. They were, he guessed, mostly those prepared to work for less than the minimum wage, at least for a short time, if it was cash in hand. In any event, it suited his purposes. This was a pub that attracted drinkers who would mind their own business rather than anyone else's, the exact opposite to the town centre pubs which attracted regulars who might remember a group of strangers in their midst.

He had made sure that he arrived early so that he could choose a table that wasn't overlooked, and he'd been lucky. Tucked away in the far corner, nobody would notice them. On the off-chance that anybody might be interested, the little group would just look like three friends having a drink. He half-smiled to himself. Less likely friends than Maxine and this friend of hers he couldn't imagine. But, he remembered soberly, he wasn't exactly flush with friends himself at the moment. It was all that stupid woman's fault. When he'd sent her those texts, it was just a joke. A joke. She had completely overreacted. Some women had no sense of humour. He didn't even fancy her that much. Not really. In fact, now he thought about it, she should have been grateful that he'd even noticed her. Well, he'd see how many friends he had when he copped for this lot. They wouldn't all be so suddenly unavailable then.

He thought about the contents of the brown envelope again and its counterpart, which was tucked under his mattress at the caravan. Had he been foolish to keep it? Should he have destroyed it? It would probably have been the sensible thing to do, but some small part of him was reluctant. As long as it still existed, he could draw back at any point. He'd sailed close to the wind before, God knew, but never quite this close. Mind, the reward had never been so great. Thank goodness he'd had the foresight to check out the details, though. He could easily have made the mistake of witnessing the will himself and that would have been him blown clean out of the water. He could be the executor though; he'd checked very carefully on that. He felt a thrill of tension run through him. He would be rich. Loaded.

He looked up as the pub door swung open and Maxine and another woman walked in. He half-rose to greet them and then sat down again. They'd spotted him. The two women made their way to the table and sat down. Both small, with thin dark hair, both with the faintest suggestion of a widow's peak, both with the same sharp eyes and narrow lips—they could have been related. God, he wouldn't want to come across these two on a dark night. They looked like a pair of Victorian poisoners. He smiled. Not his best beaming nothing to pay for six months smile, but a small reserved tilting of the mouth. Just enough to be welcoming, but not so much as to encourage them to think that they were all friends or anything. Luckily, he'd been able to get his hands on some cash, so at least he could buy them a drink to oil the wheels.

"May I get you ladies a drink?"

They nodded, and he could feel their cold eyes on his back as he made his way towards the bar. He felt a sudden twinge of doubt. He didn't know the first thing about them. What if they reneged on the deal or tried to blackmail him? But no, they wouldn't be here if they didn't intend to go through with it. And once they signed, they were as complicit as he was. It would be too late then for them to say that they'd changed their minds. And he'd told Maxine that there would be no payment until probate came through. He had been very firm about that.

Once he'd finished here, he'd tuck the brown envelope safely back into the caravan and then he'd go over to the Lodge and see what that old fool Thomas wanted to talk to him about. He hadn't been very specific when he'd rung him earlier. It was probably some outstanding fees still owing on George's room or something. Well, he would pay anything that was owing. That was, after all, the honourable thing to do, and he was an honourable man. At least, he was when circumstances allowed him to be. More to the point, though, the last thing he wanted was some debt collection agency chasing him. They were horribly good at finding people, as he'd discovered to his cost in the past. But he would tell Thomas the same as he had told Maxine and her cousin. Nothing doing, until probate came through.

CHAPTER SIXTEEN

ON THE WASTELAND at the back of Lilac Tree Lodge, Aubrey and Vincent rustled through the undergrowth. Above their heads, the spikes of tall weeds wavered in the faint breeze. The threat of rain earlier had cleared and now the blue sky above them showed clean and bright. They had only recently found this patch of land, with the remains of the old house looming above it, having followed Simon when he walked over there on his breaks. Tucked behind the care home and next to the new estate, with all the food opportunities from the people living there, they were seriously considering adding it to their list of additional resources along with the Happy Camper caravan site.

Vincent stopped and raised his sleek, dark head. Looking about him, he sniffed the air.

"This place reminds me a bit of home."

Aubrey looked at him, surprised. Vincent never mentioned their old neighbourhood and neither did he. It was an unspoken agreement between them. For Vincent, the memories of his former owners were too painful. He waited for him to continue.

"Remember The Laurels?"

Aubrey nodded. He was hardly likely to forget. A day centre for the elderly, The Laurels would be forever imprinted on his memory. It was where Carlos had been held prisoner by the psychopath that had murdered his mother and where he and Vincent had perched on the roof and witnessed the dreadful events unfolding below. He could see what Vincent meant about this place, though. The grounds of the Laurels were very much like those surrounding them here. Although the grounds surrounding the Laurels had been maintained, it had been to only a minimum standard so that the same air of faded glory and neglect hung over everything.

He looked around him at the broken fencing and crumbling stone walls which ran along the border with the housing estate. The building that had once occupied this space had long since fallen into disrepair and stood, broken, empty and dilapidated, surrounded by weeds and scrub which served as a convenient depository for old mattresses and broken freezers. The latter generally being deposited by the type of person who regarded a no entry sign as a challenge rather than an instruction.

The two cats moved further forward, enjoying the challenge of new exploration, and feeling the fresh autumn breeze ruffle their fur. It was on days like this that Aubrey felt just glad to be alive and made him almost long for the freedom of the road that he had once had. Almost, but not quite. Romance of the great outdoors aside, he knew when he was well off, and so did Vincent. No amount of bright autumn days and unexplored territory would compensate for the days of endless scavenging and still failing to find anything half-decent to eat, or the fear of being hit by a car and left by the side of the road with nobody to even notice that he was missing, never mind bothering to look for him. Jeremy, Molly and Carlos were royalty among owners and hardly a day went by when he didn't give thanks for it.

He turned to speak to Vincent, and then stopped and stared down at the ground. Something felt different. The springiness of the grass and weed around them had given way to a flattened stretch which felt different under foot. It looked as though something had been dragged across it. In the air a strange metallic tang, like a wisp of invisible smoke, drifted across his nostrils. Aubrey felt himself tense. Suddenly the beauty of the day had darkened and carried with it an unidentified threat.

"What do you think, Vin?" asked Aubrey. "Something big?"

Vincent nodded and narrowed his bright green eyes.

They moved forward slowly, lifting each paw as if in slow motion, all their senses on high alert. The smell was becoming stronger. They stopped and turned at the sound of van doors slamming and men's voices carrying across the open space. Pushing through the biggest gap in the fencing, two men moved towards them, pulling an old stained mattress behind them. Creeping behind an abandoned fridge, they watched as the men halted and then lifted the mattress slightly and heaved it into the long grass. Putting a hand on the small of his back, the older of the men doubled over and then straightened up again, glancing around him.

"When we was teenagers, we used to hang about over here, after they closed the old asylum down."

The other man nodded and lit a cigarette.

"Wonder who it belongs to now?"

The first man shrugged and scratched at his stomach, which was threatening to erupt from his shirt.

"Some developers. It used to be the local manor house or something, till the family went broke and then some posh doctor bought it and turned it into the asylum. When he died, the developers bought the whole lot. There's talk of turning the house into flats but they've still got to get planning permission or something."

He wiped his hands down the front of his jeans.

"Ready?"

Without waiting for an answer, he turned to go and then stopped. Peering to his right, he pointed to where a dark object lay caught among the weeds.

"What's that?"

"What?"

"That, over there."

The other man looked in the direction in which he was pointing.

"Looks like a leather jacket. Someone's dropped it."

He moved eagerly towards it, hands outstretched, and then stumbled backwards, his hand over his mouth.

CHAPTER SEVENTEEN

CARLOS LEANED OVER and adjusted the temperature of the big industrial oven. It was better than the ones they had at college. More state-of-the-art. He straightened up again and looked around. It was a good job that he'd decided on a quick supper tonight, it mostly being dishes that he'd frozen earlier. This mess in here wasn't going to clear itself up, so it was down to him. Nobody else was going to do it. He sighed. What a state. Dishes and pans piled up everywhere, the remnants of food congealed and stuck to their surfaces and cutlery just thrown in the sink. They could have at least stacked the dishwasher. He began lifting the plates and scraping them into the bin and then looked up at the sound of the kitchen door opening. That was quick. After having her offer of helping him to get things straight while he got the supper on refused, Teddy had said that she was going exploring but she hadn't been gone for long.

"Sorry about the mess." Maxine smirked at him, her thin red lips twitching unpleasantly. She didn't look very sorry. "I got called in for an extra shift this morning, to help get the lunches out, so of course I came in."

She smiled the smile of the virtuous. Carlos remained silent.

"But I had a doctor's appointment after so I couldn't stay on any longer." She looked around her and pursed her lips, tightening the feathery lines that ran around them. "I would have thought that one of the others might have cleared up, though. Not just left it all here for you to sort out."

Carlos turned his back and began stacking the dishwasher. She didn't, he noticed, offer to start helping him now. She reached into her overall pocket for her packet of cigarettes.

"I knew that this would happen sooner or later. This is just the beginning, believe me. I've seen it all before. It starts with the odd day and then before you know it they're on the sick for months on end. If you ask me, that Simon's more trouble than he's worth. I've always thought so. And he never joins in on anything. When we asked him if he wanted to come for a drink with us last Christmas, he looked as if we'd just invited him to an orgy. Probably thinks he's too good for the likes of us."

That's because he is, thought Carlos. For you, anyway. He tried not to listen as her thin nasal voice dripped vitriol.

"I don't know what he's got to be so high and mighty about, anyway. He's only a cook. And he always looks a bit shifty, something around the eyes. Do you know what I mean? Like he's hiding something. I mean, he never talks about his home or family or anything. I don't even know if he's married."

Carlos turned back from the dishwasher to face her, deliberately keeping his face blank. Who cared whether Simon was married or not? Anyway, what did it have to do with her? Simon could have ten partners, for all the business it was of hers. She hadn't, he noticed, expressed any concern at the fact that Simon appeared to have gone walkabout. For all they knew, he could have had an accident. He might be lying injured somewhere. Or worse.

"Has anyone checked if he's all right? I mean, has anybody heard from him?"

He knew that Simon hadn't turned up for his shift that morning. It was Molly's rest day, and she wasn't due in, but Thomas had rung and asked her if she could go in to help him sort things out. The carers had put the residents' breakfasts together, being mainly toast and cereal, but lunches were another matter. He had offered to come in and do it, but he'd been secretly relieved when Molly had said that they'd manage, that she'd ring round and get a couple of the carers in to do an extra shift. After all these weeks of waiting, he had been counting down the minutes until he could meet Teddy off her train. He'd had the clothes he was going to wear ready and waiting for over a week. He'd also cleaned his best trainers and sprayed them with some of the cologne that Molly had bought Jeremy for Christmas.

Maxine shook her head. Strolling over to the fire exit, she kicked it open and lit a cigarette.

"Not a word. And he's not answering his phone, either."

Carlos didn't bother to ask her how she knew. Maxine always knew. He drew in his breath and squared his shoulders slightly. Now was the time to face up to her and tell her to leave the kitchen. He opened his mouth to speak, and then stopped. From the passage way outside came the sound of feet running and Teddy burst in, her small heart-shaped face white and her hair flying back from her face.

"It's the police. The police are here. They're all over the place. They've found a body. Over at the back. A dead body," she added.

CHAPTER EIGHTEEN

MOLLY PUT HER key in the door as Jeremy came out into the hall to meet her. He pulled her to him and held her for a moment. Drawing back but keeping his hands on her shoulders, he looked down into her face.

"Okay?"

Molly nodded and dropped her bag on the hall table.

"I'm fine. Honestly. Fine."

Jeremy brushed a stray lock of hair from her forehead and smoothed it down.

"Sure?"

She smiled, a weak smile that did nothing to wipe the weariness stamped across her face.

"I'm sure. You've obviously heard about what's happened. How did you find out?"

"It was on the local news. It's odd, I wouldn't normally have the TV on so early but I'd just finished a report and I didn't feel like starting anything else, so I made a cup of tea and switched it on. It was the first news item that came up. I tried ringing you but it kept going to voice mail. I was just thinking whether to come over and collect you when I heard the front gate go." He hesitated for a second. "Was it awful?"

"It was pretty dreadful." She thought for a moment. "It's odd. It felt like there were loads of police officers swarming all over the place, but there probably weren't. It's just that they seemed so big compared to the residents, who suddenly looked really little. It's funny how people shrink when they get older." Her voice cracked slightly, and she swallowed. "But it reminded me of, well, you know… Fallowfield and everything."

Jeremy nodded and remained silent. Molly drew in her breath and continued.

"And then, on top of everything else, one of the residents broke his leg, and another one had a massive panic attack and started screaming. I'm not surprised. The Lodge is usually an oasis of calm at that time of day. Honestly, most afternoons you can practically hear a pin drop. It's one of Thomas's rules that all televisions and radios must be off in the sitting rooms downstairs for at least an hour after lunch. He says that it helps the residents' mental well-being to be quiet and calm for a period. So, it was all just as usual. Some of them had gone to their rooms, a few were reading, some were dozing in their chairs. Then, suddenly, out of the blue, there were all these burly men in uniform who were shouting. I kept trying to tell them that not all old people are hard of hearing and even those that are have hearing aids. There was no need to raise their voices. But it fell on, well, deaf ears." She smiled wryly. "Anyway, it was total chaos."

She sank down on the bottom stair and put her head in her hands.

"God, what a day. Simon not turning up this morning was the least of it."

Jeremy leaned over and pulled her gently to her feet.

"Come on, let's go and sit down. You look completely done in."

Jeremy sat down in the armchair while Molly walked over to the window and stared out. He watched as her shoulders gradually relaxed.

"When I was a child, the sea side was a real treat. We looked forward to it all year. Not just me and my brother, my parents too. Dad used to pin a chart on the kitchen wall and we'd take it in turns to cross off the days. Once my mum made a little sort of summer advent calendar. Behind every door was a picture of something to do with the seaside. I think I've still got it somewhere." She breathed a small sigh of contentment. "I don't think I'll ever get used to being able to see the sea from our own front room." She turned and smiled. "Well, a bit of it anyway. On a clear day. What was it that the estate agent called it?"

"Sea peeps, I think. Or sea glimpses. Something like that. As opposed to sea views, which would have put another hundred grand on the house." Jeremy paused, and then said, "There used to be a song that they sang in the music halls, something about 'with a ladder and some glasses yer can see the Hackney Marshes, if it wasn't for the 'ouses in between'. At least we haven't got too many 'ouses in between."

Molly smiled and sat down on the sofa. Jeremy studied her for a moment before speaking.

"Do you want to talk about it?"

"There's not a lot to tell, really." She fell silent for a moment while she ran the events of the day over in her mind. "Just a normal day. Up until the point when two men found a body over on the waste land at the back and called the police. And because the land is overlooked by the Lodge, they came and questioned everybody." She laughed suddenly, a light cheerful note that helped to wipe the weariness from her face. "Lucy took one look at them and starting singing the auntie Mary song."

Jeremy looked appalled.

"Not the one about the canary up the leg of her drawers?"

"The very same. I expect that the police have heard worse. Although possibly not," she conceded, "from a retired headmistress."

Jeremy grinned.

"And then," Molly continued, "some of the others started humming it, you know, in that kind of low insistent tone. Honestly, they're like school kids some times."

"What did the police officers do?"

"What any sensible teacher would do. Divide and rule. They took them out and questioned them individually in the dining room. Well, not questioned in that sense. Just asking them if they'd seen anything suspicious or noticed anything unusual. I sat in with them in case they got upset or confused. One or two of the answers they got may have been rather surprising. Elizabeth told them that the body was that of a German fighter pilot that she'd shot down from her window." She paused and then continued; her tone thoughtful now. "To be honest, I think it was the most excitement that the residents have had in years, but I don't think that they were able to tell the police much. They won't have seen anything worth reporting, I shouldn't think. At this time of year they're either in the residents sitting rooms or in their bedrooms. They don't go out much once the autumn sets in. Not even in the garden."

"Did the police question the staff?"

"Yes, all of us. They did us first. And I had to give them a list of those staff that weren't on duty today as well, so I guess that they'll be contacting them too."

"What did they ask you?"

"The usual sort of thing. The same as they asked the residents. Whether we'd noticed anything unusual, anybody hanging about the place or behaving suspiciously. Fortunately, everybody who visits the Lodge has to sign in so I was able to show them the visitors' book. And of course, they'll have to question everyone on the housing estate, too."

"How long do they think that the body had been there?"

Molly shrugged.

"They didn't actually say but not long. At least, I don't think so. They were asking whether we'd noticed anything in the last few days so it must have happened quite recently."

"What did happen? Did they tell you?"

"No. They just said that a body had been found, and that it was a man. I guess that it must have been a suspicious death or they wouldn't have been questioning us all."

"Have they identified him yet?"

"If they know who he is, they didn't say although I suppose we'll all know soon enough. What did it say on the news?"

"Not a lot really. Just that a man's body had been found on the waste land where the old manor house had been. They had a reporter over there and there were lots of shots of the Lodge."

"Thomas won't be very pleased about that. He seems to live in fear that Mrs. Randall will be displeased about something or other. Let's hope that he doesn't see it. As far as he's concerned, the more low profile the Lodge, the better. Anyway, then, on top of everything else, in the middle of it all Jack fell over and broke his leg. God knows how he managed it; he was only going to the bathroom. To be honest," she added, the slight note of guilt evident in her voice, "it was probably our fault really. Normally a carer would have helped him, he's not very steady on his feet, but we were all so distracted... Anyway, obviously we had to call an ambulance and then Flora went off into melt down." She shuddered slightly at the recollection. "All we needed was for the fire brigade to turn up and we'd have had a complete set."

"Was Thomas on duty?"

"Yes, thank goodness. He was great. He got Flora calmed down, and put some soft music on and it worked like magic. He's not great at admin and paperwork but he's actually very good with the residents. He has a real sense of how to handle them. He used to be a mental health nurse at the old asylum, so when it comes to strange behaviour, I guess nothing much fazes him. In fact, I think if Thomas hadn't been there we would have had a hell of a job to restore any kind of order at all. At one point they were all talking at once—nobody was listening to anybody else. I thought my head would burst. But Thomas just took it in his stride and got the sherry out." Molly thought for a moment. "He's been very distracted lately. Like he's got something on his mind. He seems to be permanently on edge. We used to have a coffee together in the staff room most days, but lately he hasn't been in there. He's spending much more time in his office, although what he's doing in there, I have no idea. He's not catching up with the paperwork, that's for sure. I asked him the other day if he was all right and he barely seemed to hear me."

"You don't think that he's ill or anything?"

"No, he looks well enough. Apart from a permanently worried expression, that is. Perhaps he's got some problems at home or something. I expect he'll tell me if he wants to." She glanced down at her watch. "Carlos and Teddy should be back soon. Carlos was just finishing off when I left."

"How was he when the police questioned him?"

"He was fine. He knows that the police have to talk to everybody. I went to the kitchen to sit with him. Teddy was there as well. He seemed to take it pretty much in his stride. Like the rest of us, he had nothing to tell them."

CHAPTER NINETEEN

TEDDY TWISTED HER head up and stared at the small black object on the wall.

"What's that? Is it a fan or something?"

Carlos shook his head.

"No. It's one of those camera things I was telling you about. They're in most of the rooms now."

Teddy looked appalled.

"What, even the bathrooms?"

Carlos laughed.

"No, not the bathrooms. At least, I don't think so. Most of the other rooms, though."

Teddy thought for a moment.

"So who gets to look at what's on them? I mean, can anyone?"

"Just Thomas and Molly, I guess."

"Don't you mind? You know, like being watched all the time? Doesn't it feel like you're being spied on?"

Carlos shrugged.

"Not really. I expect Thomas and Molly only look at stuff when they need to. Like if something's happened or something. And when you think about it, there's cameras everywhere, anyway. You can't walk down the high street without being caught on camera at some point. Lots of schools have got them now, too. And hospitals and car parks and that."

Teddy thought for a moment.

"I suppose so. It just seems a bit, oh I don't know. Sort of Big Brother."

Carlos smiled and nodded. Teddy sometimes mentioned books and films that he'd never heard of, but he knew about Big Brother. *Nineteen Eighty-Four* was one of the books that Jeremy had read them in English at Sir Frank's. He'd enjoyed it so much that he'd read *Keep The Aspidistra Flying* too.

"I don't think they're connected up yet, anyway. Gordon only started putting them in a couple of days ago."

Teddy watched in silence as Carlos checked all the controls on the oven and then scribbled some notes on a sheet of paper which he pinned to the notice board. She walked over and read it, frowning.

"Do you have to do this every day?"

"I don't have to do it; I just prefer it. It means when I come on shift I know exactly what I'm doing, like what I'm cooking and whether I need to ask Simon to order anything and that. It just makes it easier. They taught us that at college."

"Does the other chef, Simon, do it too?"

Carlos shook his head.

"To be honest, he doesn't really need to. He's a lot more experienced than me. He told me once that he used to work in a really massive kitchen with, like, loads of people to feed. He didn't say where though."

"What will happen if he doesn't turn up again tomorrow? I mean, will he get fired?"

"I don't know. He isn't answering his phone and Molly was talking about going round to see if he's okay, to check that he's not ill or anything, but Jeremy said that she shouldn't go on her own. He said that it was up to Thomas." He thought for a moment. "I suppose I could go. You know, like just turn up and say, like, are you all right, mate?"

"Do you know where he lives?"

"Somewhere on the other side of town, I think. It'll be in Molly's office though; she looks after all that stuff. We can go and check when I've finished here."

"Are you allowed in her office?"

Carlos smiled and held up the small plastic card attached to the lanyard around his neck.

"It opens all the office doors. Anyway, Molly won't mind. I mean, it's not like we're doing anything wrong."

Teddy nodded.

"I'll come to Simon's with you if you like. Anyway, it'd be better if there were two of us. Just in case."

THEY STARED AT the rotting wooden window panes and the blistered, peeling paint of the surrounding houses. The bins, overflowing with an unpleasant cabbagy stench hanging over them, were pushed together in the small front gardens, looking for all the world like rows of rotting teeth jostling together in a decayed mouth. As they stood there, a large brown rat stopped in its tracks as it scuttled across the dividing wall and looked directly at them with bold, beady eyes. Teddy glanced at its long muscular tail and then looked away with a shudder. She pulled her parka more tightly around her and pushed her hands deep into her pockets.

"Are you sure this is the right street?"

Carlos looked down again at the piece of paper in his hand and nodded. Since they'd moved here, he'd only really been as far as college and the town centre. This was an area with which he was completely unfamiliar, and they'd had trouble finding it. Tucked near to the railway station and in what was once a desirable district, these big Victorian houses had been built originally to accommodate the affluent and professional classes. They had been the habitat of the local solicitors and doctors, the owners of small businesses and bank managers, each house with a name as well as a number, each with a maid and a cook. But those occupants had long since moved out and now the majority of the properties were very clearly in multiple occupation.

Closer inspection showed faint indications that some properties had moved back into family use. Gentrification was slowly tapping the edges with delicate fingers. Here and there individual houses had the front doors painted in tasteful muted shades and plants in tubs were arranged up the steps. Brass door furniture had been restored to a muted gleam, and the windows held curtains in expensive linens that matched. But for the most part, the once grand houses looked dilapidated and depressing. Their conversion to flats and bed sits in the latter half of the previous century, with an endless succession of tenants and landlords had clearly taken its toll. Like many of the caravans off-season on the Happy Camper caravan site, a number of these properties were now occupied by those whom the local authority found difficult to place elsewhere.

Carlos walked through the narrow space where a gate had once been and looked up at the house. This one looked like somebody had started to make it respectable again. The front door was painted a neat dark green and all the windows had curtains. Teddy followed nervously behind him. He glanced down at the piece of paper again.

"It just says the number, not which flat. It could be any of them."

Teddy looked up at the windows and then down again at the wall where a bank of door bells were fixed.

"We could try all of them," she suggested.

Carlos nodded.

"You can give it a go. I bet they don't work."

Experience of living in the flat at the Meadows had taught him that where there was an element of communal living, standards inevitably dropped to those of the occupant that cared the least. At the Meadows nothing had worked, and in the end, the local authority had given up sending out repair men. He watched as Teddy jabbed a small finger against the bottom bell. Amazingly, it worked, although there was no response from the other side. He pulled his phone out of his pocket and began running his fingers over the keypad.

"I'll just text Molly and let her know that we're here," he said. "They'll have been expecting us back by now."

Teddy nodded and stubbornly continued to press each bell in turn, and then started again at the bottom, a look of fierce concentration on her pretty face. Carlos stuffed his phone back into his pocket and smiled suddenly.

"I was thinking the other day, like in the old days, what did people do when they wanted to meet someone or something?"

Teddy stopped mid-jab and turned to face him.

"What do you mean?"

"Well, like, if you didn't have a mobile, how did you know where to go or what time?"

Teddy thought for a moment.

"Well, people did have phones. But not proper ones," she added. "My mum told me that when she was young, there was only one phone and it was in the hall. And you couldn't walk about with it or anything like that."

Carlos looked puzzled.

"Why not?"

"I think they were attached to the wall or something, you know, like with one of those curly wires. So you had to stand next to it. Mum said that they had what she called a telephone table, like a special table just for the phone, and she used to sit on the bottom stair when she wanted to talk to her friends. And her parents had to pay for it so she wasn't allowed to use it for long. You didn't get any free minutes or anything. She said that her dad used to time her."

Carlos opened his mouth to reply and then stopped. Above them a window had opened, and a man was leaning out, looking down at them. Carlos nudged Teddy in the ribs.

"It's him," he whispered. "It's Simon."

CHAPTER TWENTY

TILTING HIS HEAD back and raising his voice, Carlos called up to the man above them.

"Simon, you all right, mate?"

The man hesitated for a moment.

"Wait there."

He slammed the window shut again. Teddy and Carlos waited until the front door slowly opened and, without speaking, Simon beckoned them upstairs.

Carlos looked about him, his eye running across the tiny kitchen leading off from the sitting room and back again. The furniture, bulky and covered in faded flowery cotton, looked as though it had belonged to the previous generation. Not old enough to be antique and not interesting enough to be retro. There was no television that he could see. The only point of any interest in the room was a big stack of books piled up on the floor. The room was clean but felt cold.

Next to him, he felt Teddy's small hand creep into his. His heart swelled slightly as he gave her hand a reassuring squeeze. She was, he knew, afraid. But he wasn't. He might not know the names of classical composers or how to read a menu in French, but in this environment he was supreme. Teddy and Casper had spent their whole lives in bright, comfortable, secure homes in which the furniture had been bought new or inherited, the windows were clean, and the neighbours were people whose names you knew. This world that he had just brought Teddy into was a completely alien one to her, the kind that she had only encountered on film or television. Whereas he, living with Maria in the heat of the back streets of Sao Paulo and then in the cramped little flat in the Meadows, was only too familiar with this style of living. If living it could be called. Existing might be a better word. Although, in truth, Simon's place wasn't so bad. In fact, compared to some of the places that they'd rented in Sao Paulo this was quite luxurious. At least Simon had his own bathroom and kitchen, albeit very small ones.

His mind drifted back to the last place in Sao Paulo, where he'd lived with Maria after his father had left them and before they had come to England. Even working as many hours as she humanly could, his mother had struggled to find enough work to get the money to keep a roof over their head and save for their passage to England.

In the end. they had been reduced to one rented room in a shared house. There had been nine of them to share the bathroom on the first floor, and Maria had been the only one who ever cleaned it. The lock on their door had been broken and, with a landlord that was long on promises and short on action, every night they had gone through the same routine of dragging the table across it before huddling up in the little camp beds under the window, frightened of waking to hear the splintering noise as somebody kicked their door in. They'd learned from bitter experience that having almost nothing didn't stop someone else from trying to take it. In that neighbourhood, hard though it was to believe, there were people even worse off than themselves.

He pulled himself back to the present and took a deep breath. Simon looked like absolute shit.

"So, Simon. You all right, mate? Just thought I'd call round and see how you're doing. This is Teddy. She's my," he hesitated and glanced quickly down at her. "My friend."

Simon nodded; his lean unshaven face unsmiling, his deep brown eyes sunk back in his head, the depth of their colour emphasised by the pallor of his complexion. He looked at them intently, his gaze completely focused, and then looked away again, blinking and shaking his head slightly as though he had inadvertently looked into direct sunlight. The sweat shirt that he was wearing, although clean, hung on his body and his knuckles looked raw and red, as though he had been scrubbing them.

"Only," Carlos paused, feeling carefully for the right words. Much as he liked the feeling of Teddy holding his hand, he was starting to think that coming here wasn't such a good idea. Simon was never one for the social chit chat, but this was something else. There was clearly something wrong with him, something that was beyond the experience of either himself or Teddy to deal with. Jeremy was right when he said that it was up to Thomas to check on him. After all, Thomas was the boss. This was grown up stuff and he and Teddy would have done better to keep out of it. He fought the urge to turn on his heel and lead Teddy out of there. He should at least check if Simon needed anything first. He pressed on, trying to keep the anxiety out of his voice. "Only, I was a bit worried about you, mate. Like when you didn't turn up to work and that."

Simon drew in his breath and stared at him for a moment before answering. The words, when they came, were unexpectedly mundane.

"Did they get the breakfasts and lunches all right?"

Carlos nodded, a trickle of relief washing through him. Maybe Simon wasn't as out of it as he'd thought.

"Molly sorted it out. She got a couple of staff in to do an extra shift." The silence fell between them again and he searched hurriedly for something else to say. "They left the kitchen in a right mess. I cleared it up all right though."

He smiled as he said it. Simon took kitchen hygiene very seriously, even more seriously than his lecturers at college. The smallest spill was wiped up immediately, and he was insistent on separate preparation areas for different foods. When Carlos had first started at the Lodge, Simon had written up his rules for the kitchen and pinned them to the noticeboard. Carlos was scrupulous in obeying them.

Simon nodded and looked at the floor, his brow creasing and his eye wandering the once rich but now faded rug that curled in frayed edges into the corners of the room.

"So, mate, are you coming in tomorrow?"

Next to him, he felt Teddy give him an almost imperceptible nudge in the ribs. Following her gaze, he saw the large plastic tub of pills on the small gate-legged table. His heart dropped, and he swallowed nervously. The last time he'd seen a tub of pills like that, it had been scattered up the communal stairs of the block of flats in the Meadows, with an unconscious man lying on his back next to it.

"So the thing is, mate, if you need any help and that… like with any shopping and that?"

He bit his bottom lip. Why had he said that? If they went out to get Simon some shopping, they would obviously have to go back with it. And right now, all he wanted was to go home and take Teddy with him.

"The thing is, I've got a lot on my mind…" Simon paused, as if he'd already forgotten what he was going to say. He stared helplessly at them; his dark eyes confused.

"Yes?" asked Carlos helpfully, trying not to look at the door.

"Things have got a bit, a bit…" he paused. "Difficult."

Carlos nodded and waited for him to continue.

Suddenly, Simon dropped his head in his hands, his big bony fingers splayed across his face, and began to cry. Great splashing sobs that heaved up from his chest and spilled down his unshaven cheeks. Carlos felt Teddy stir. Unhooking her hand from his, she sped across the room and knelt next to him. Reaching up, she gently stroked his uncombed hair.

"It's all right, Simon. Everyone gets sad sometimes. Don't they Carlos?"

Carlos nodded, unable to speak.

"MOLL, IT'S ON AGAIN."

Molly came through from the kitchen and sat next to him on the sofa. On the screen in front of them, the facade of the Lodge, with its familiar logo of a lilac tree, showed briefly before the camera panned back towards the waste ground. The reporter spoke in low, solemn tones.

"The police have confirmed that the body discovered earlier today has been identified as that of a local resident, Toby Carson. The police are appealing for anybody with any information to contact them. Any information given will be held in the strictest confidence."

Jeremy started forward, staring at the screen and almost jolting Aubrey from his lap. Aubrey righted himself and stared along with him.

"Toby Carson? That's a familiar name. Isn't that…"

Molly's brow furrowed.

"Yes, it's George's…" she stopped as the light melodic ring of her mobile sounded from the kitchen. "I'll just go and see who that is."

Jeremy and Aubrey continued staring at the screen. The reporter continued.

"The body of Toby Carson was discovered by two men who were out walking today in the grounds of the old county asylum…"

They both looked up as Molly came back into the room, her mobile still in her hand. She looked different, thought Aubrey. Sort of frozen.

"It was Thomas," she said.

Jeremy nodded and turned back to the screen. The reporter continued talking.

"The victim was identified from documents found on the body. However, they are anxious to trace any next of kin .."

"Jeremy."

Molly's voice sounded harsh and shrill. Nothing like her usual soft tones.

Jeremy and Aubrey turned back to face her.

She dropped the mobile onto the coffee table and stared at them.

"What? What's happened?"

"The police have just been talking to Thomas."

"Is there more news?"

She nodded; her face ashen and sank down on to the sofa next to them.

"They were asking him about Simon." She paused. "You remember me telling you that Thomas hadn't completed all the DRB checks?"

"And?"

"The police have just told Thomas that Simon has spent time inside. He's got a conviction for murder."

CHAPTER TWENTY-ONE

AUBREY MOVED OVER to make room for Vincent on the big squishy floor cushion. He didn't ask him where he'd been. Vincent often disappeared for a few hours; it was almost like a show of independence. Aubrey didn't mind. He enjoyed having his mate living with them and if he wanted to go off on his own sometimes, that was fine by him. They weren't joined at the tail. Sometimes he liked to be on his own, too. And as much as he enjoyed the company of Carlos, it wasn't like they could go ratting together or anything. Apart from anything else, the rats would see them coming.

He pushed his paws deeper into the soft velvety fabric and gave a small, contented sigh. He liked the conservatory. They didn't have one at their other house and, at first, he'd been wary. He'd never seen anything like this room with its glass walls and soft lighting, and he'd been reluctant to go in there to start with, even with Molly and Jeremy. But now, he'd discovered, it was great, especially when it was raining. You could be sort of outdoors, but indoors.

Also, when next door's dog Beryl got into their garden, he could drive her to distraction by running up and down the length of the glass wall, knowing that Beryl couldn't get to him. Sometimes he jumped in the air too, copying the star jumps that he'd seen Carlos doing in the garden, flinging his paws out and twirling his tail, to mix it up a bit.

He glanced across at Carlos and Teddy, who were standing with their backs to him. He hadn't realised before how little Teddy was compared to Carlos. Her head barely came up to his shoulders.

"Casp will be furious that he's missed all this," said Teddy. "I'll text him later."

Carlos nodded and sank down onto the rattan chair behind him, his long legs stretching out across the tiled floor, and his arms flopped behind him. A faint scent of Jeremy's cologne drifted up from his feet. Teddy perched on the edge of the small sofa and picked up her needlework. Carlos watched as her small fingers flew in and out of the fabric. There was something very soothing about it. She was making him, she told him, a book mark with his initials. The mere thought of her making him something, something that he could keep forever, made his heart swell with pride. Nobody had ever made him anything before, not even Maria. She was always too busy working. He wasn't going to waste it on books, though, in case it wore out or something. He was going to keep it in the drawer in his bedroom where he kept all his precious things, including Maria's handbag containing her purse, comb and rosary, the scarf that his grandfather had given him woven in the blue and gold colours of the Brazilian national football team and the small black china cat that he had given his mother for her birthday the year before she died.

His expression sobered at the thought of the china cat. At school they'd been asked to write a short piece about what they'd done at the weekend. He'd written that he had been fishing with his uncle, which was of course untrue. He didn't even have a fishing rod, let alone an uncle. What he'd actually done was get caught shop-lifting from the local gift shop. A small china cat as a birthday present for his mother. The owner had caught him, not surprisingly. His clumsy attempt to stuff it into his jeans pocket would have alerted the most visually impaired. When he'd burst into tears and told her what it was for and that he didn't have any money, she'd given him the cat, and a card to go with it.

Teddy snipped the end of the thread and selected another colour, holding it up to the light and then threading it carefully through the tiny needle.

"Do you think that Jeremy's calmed down now?" she asked. Carlos nodded.

"I expect so, but it's all right, he wasn't cross with us. He was just worried. He shouts sometimes when he's worried."

Aubrey and Vincent looked at each other. Shouting was an understatement. They'd never seen Jeremy move so quickly, or shout so loudly. When the news about Simon had come through, he had been out of the house and in the car before you could say cat treat. When he'd returned with Carlos and Teddy in tow, he had begun shouting again and was obviously still worked up. It had taken Molly two glasses of his favourite whisky to bring his shoulders down to a normal level.

"My dad shouts when he's worried sometimes, too. And my mum. It's usually about Casper," she added.

Carlos felt a gentle warming glow seep through him. She'd called Jeremy his dad. Well, not quite, but that's what she meant. He had never admitted it, not even to himself really, but he secretly liked it when other people thought that Molly and Jeremy were his parents. He never contradicted them, even though he obviously didn't look anything like either of them. Once, after seeing the three of them together, somebody had said that she expected that he looked like his grandparents. And he'd agreed. He did look like his grandparents. Well, his grandfather anyway. It was only later that he realised that she meant Molly and Jeremy's parents and he had felt beyond thrilled. Not that he was being disloyal to his real mother, he thought hurriedly. Nobody would ever replace Maria. But it was just nice to feel entitled to be somewhere. To think that you belonged. And to think that other people thought that you belonged.

"But I still don't really get what he was worried about." Teddy looked up from her sewing and frowned. "I mean, you texted Molly, so it's not like we didn't tell them where we were."

Carlos shrugged.

"I don't know. Maybe he had a bad day or something." But he didn't really think so. Jeremy never took things out on other people. Even that time when he'd had to break up the annual ritual end-of-year fight between Sir Frank's and St Oswald's, the neighbouring grammar school, and he'd come home shattered with his hair all sticking up and his shirt hanging out, he'd just sat in the garden, had a drink, and then lit the barbecue. As he'd said to Molly, most kids celebrate the end of exams by going out with their mates and trying to get served in the local pubs. The kids at Sir Frank's and St Oswald's try to kill each other.

It took an awful lot to rile Jeremy, he reflected. Not like his real father, who thought nothing of lashing out both physically and verbally if he couldn't so much as find a bottle opener. That last time, when he had failed to appear after another drinking session with those horrible greasy blokes that he called his mates, it had been three days before they had made any enquiries and such enquiries as they had made had been distinctly lacking in enthusiasm. By the second day they were all aware that the atmosphere in the small hot flat had lightened considerably and they had all, he knew, been secretly praying that he'd disappeared for good. And their prayers had been answered. Neither he, his mother or his grandfather who lived with them had seen him from that day to this. What a difference to Jeremy. If Jeremy went missing, he'd be out on the streets day and night looking for him and so would Molly and Aubrey, he knew.

But whatever had upset Jeremy today, it was obviously something serious. After standing outside Simon's flat and shouting at them to come out, he had been silent and tight-faced all the way home, his eyes staring straight ahead and his fingers gripping the steering wheel as though he was struggling to control it. He and Teddy had sat quietly in the back, only glancing nervously at each other when Jeremy had screeched up to a halt at a red light and swore under his breath. It wasn't the worst word that either of them had heard, but it wasn't one that they'd ever heard Jeremy use.

"Maybe they don't like us being out when there's been this murder," he said. "I mean, I know it's, like, nothing to do with us but…" he trailed off. The ways of the grown-ups were still a mystery to him. He wondered sometimes how you learnt the rules. Maybe you just woke up one day knowing them.

"Perhaps," conceded Teddy. "Do you think that Simon's all right?" she continued. "I felt really bad just leaving him there like that."

"I expect he'll be okay. But he did look like shit," he added. "Like he'd been up all night."

Teddy thought for a moment.

"What do you think is wrong with him?"

Carlos shrugged.

"I'm not sure. Something mental, I think. I mean," he stopped, suddenly confused. Were they allowed to say mental anymore? They all said it at Sir Frank's. It was used as part of the everyday language, usually as an insult and often accompanied by the eff word. But, somehow, he got the feeling that Teddy wouldn't like it. He searched for the right word. "I mean, like depressed or something."

Aubrey thought for a moment. He knew about depression. His first owner, Raj, had suffered from it. Which wasn't really surprising, given Raj's circumstances. Struggling to make even a small profit from the newsagents and grocers which he was forced to keep open at all hours, frequently harassed by racist neighbours who wouldn't have crossed the road to help him if he'd collapsed in the street, but were only too keen to be his friend when they wanted credit from him, and abandoned by his wife and children, there had been little for him not to be depressed about it. In truth there had been almost no light in his life and even the little that there was had been snuffed out early when the shop had been broken into and he'd been stabbed to death.

When the depression had struck Raj, it had dropped over his head and muffled him like a thick black cloak. Aubrey had always been able to sense it immediately, usually before even Raj himself was aware. He sometimes thought that he could smell it and he had always hurried to at least be near him. He couldn't do anything, but at least it might help Raj to know that he wasn't entirely alone. The worst times had been late at night when Raj had hit the whisky, mumbling to himself and absent-mindedly tapping the ash from his cigarette down on to Aubrey's head while they watched recorded episodes of EastEnders and the Morecambe and Wise Christmas Specials. In the mornings following, Raj had struggled to drag himself out of bed, the shroud of depression made worse by a hangover, but he had battled through. Not once did he fail to open the shop on time, and he was never less than courteous to his customers. Even when they staggered up to the counter, high on drink or drugs and called him names, he had simply smiled politely. As he'd said to Aubrey, 'thing is Cat, if no shop, then what else have I?' To which the truthful answer had to be, 'not much'. In fact, rock all. At least Raj had been able to take some comfort from the fact that some mate of his, Winston Churchill, suffered from it too. Aubrey had wondered sometimes why Raj and this Winston bloke didn't get together and sort of help each other out a bit.

Next to him he felt Vincent shift and mumble, his big warm shape curling in on itself. He regarded his sleeping friend with affection and then looked up as the door opened and Molly came in. She crossed the room and sat down next to Teddy on the sofa.

"That's pretty," she said, glancing down at the bookmark. She sounded, thought Aubrey, distracted. Perhaps Jeremy was still cross. Jeremy being cross was such a rare thing that it invaded the whole house like a gathering storm.

"Thank you," said Teddy, holding the small scrap of fabric up to show her. "It's for Carlos."

Molly smiled and nodded. She looked across at Carlos and then back again at Teddy. When she spoke, the words came out slowly, almost ponderously, as though she wanted to emphasise their importance.

"When you saw Simon today," Molly paused for several seconds and then continued. "I know that you were being kind. Very kind," she added. "Thoughtful. But I, we, would prefer it if you didn't go there again. Not for the moment, anyway."

"Molly," asked Teddy, laying aside her needlework and looking directly at her. "Has Simon done something? I mean, Jeremy didn't really say very much. He just said that we had to get in the car and not to argue, so we did, but he seemed really angry."

"Tell them, Moll."

CHAPTER TWENTY-TWO

JEREMY OPENED THE door quietly and stood next to Carlos, who shifted slightly and tucked his feet under the chair. He hoped that the scent of cologne on his trainers wasn't wafting in Jeremy's direction.

Molly drew in her breath and held it for a moment before answering.

"Simon has got a prison record."

"Is that all?"

Carlos was astonished. When he'd been at Sir Frank's, half the kids there had been done for something and it was nothing for some of the parents to be what was euphemistically referred to as having a little holiday. And those that had a clean record only had it because they hadn't been caught. Teddy looked from Molly to Jeremy and creased her forehead.

"But he's out now, so doesn't that mean, well, that he's paid his debt to society? I mean, he's being a good citizen, and he's got a job, and he's paying taxes and everything."

Jeremy tried, and nearly succeeded, in hiding a smile.

"Well, yes," he said. "In theory. But it's not really quite as straightforward as that."

"Why not?"

"Because some crimes are more serious than others."

"What's he done?"

"According to the police, Simon was in prison for murder."

Carlos and Teddy stared at Jeremy as they digested this information. It was Carlos who spoke first, his tone carrying a faint suggestion of aggression. He felt, Aubrey could see, wrong-footed. Perhaps it was because he'd taken Teddy there, and now he was feeling guilty.

"How come he's out then? I thought that murderers were supposed to get life?"

"That's the sentence that the judge passes," said Jeremy. "But most of them don't actually serve a whole life sentence. Once they've served a minimum term, if they've behaved in prison then they're let out on what's called licence. That means that they can be called back if they do anything wrong. Criminally wrong," he added.

"But Simon hasn't done anything wrong," protested Teddy. "I mean, I know he didn't turn up to work today, but that's not a crime." She paused, suddenly confused. "Is it?"

Jeremy shook his head.

"No. But with things as they are at present, we would prefer it if you didn't go round there again."

"Did Thomas know about Simon?" Carlos demanded.

Jeremy shook his head.

"No, he didn't do the proper checks."

Carlos nodded. He was, Aubrey could see, not surprised. And neither was he. Thomas much preferred spending time with the residents to dealing with admin. He thought about him now, the kindly pale face and the quick ready smile. But he seemed distracted of late. Something was up with him, and whatever it was, it wasn't something trivial. Several times he had looked around his office door to see him sitting at his desk, surrounded by files, with his head in his hands. And he hadn't been spending as much time with the residents lately, either.

"Does that mean that the police will think that he's done this other murder?" asked Teddy.

"I guess it will make him a person of interest," said Jeremy. "If you think about it," his voice was gentle now, "it's bound to, isn't it?"

Teddy opened her mouth to speak and then closed it again and nodded, her expression glum. She looked, thought Aubrey, exactly like some of the kittens had at Sunny Bank rescue centre when they were separated from their brothers and sisters. That same defeated air of resigned sadness. Jeremy continued.

"But, in any event, for the time being, as Molly said, we would prefer it if you didn't go there again. Which reminds me, how did you know where he lived?"

Ignoring the question, Teddy nodded.

"All right, we won't go there again. We promise." She paused. "Who did he kill?"

Teddy's voice sounded small, almost thought Aubrey, as though she didn't want to know the answer. Jeremy glanced quickly across at Molly and then back to Teddy.

"I'm not sure of the details."

DOWNSTAIRS, THE KITCHEN was dark and quiet. From upstairs the gentle sound of Jeremy snoring fluttered through the house, competing with the low humming of the big chest freezer in the utility room. Aubrey and Vincent slipped silently through the cat flap. With a bit of luck, the utility door had been left ajar and they'd be able to get into the washing basket. Failing that, they could always slip round the outside of the house and tap on Carlos's window. They'd had a great time at Gordon's visiting Buster, but now they were tired. Buster was good fun, but he had boundless energy—more than two cats could keep up with. And from the look of exhaustion on Gordon's face, more than he could keep up with either. When they left, Buster had been engaged in his favourite game of suddenly discovering his own tail and then chasing it. They had left, accompanied by the sound of smashing china.

They halted as the kitchen door creaked on its hinges, an irritating squealing sound that Jeremy kept promising to fix, but which Aubrey and Vincent were rather appreciative of. It meant that they always had advance warning when somebody entered the room, which was particularly useful when they raided the cat treat box which Vincent had worked out how to prise open. They watched from the shadows of the back door as Teddy and Carlos tiptoed in. Carlos paused and wrapped his dressing gown, an old one of Jeremy's that he had taken a liking to after his mother had died, more tightly around him. He sat down at the kitchen table and flipped his iPad open. Quietly drawing out the chair next to him, Teddy sat down and tucked her long cotton nightdress beneath her. She gave a sudden laugh and then stifled it.

"Weird," she whispered. "Texting someone in the same house to meet."

"I know. But Molly said that we mustn't go in each other's bedrooms. If we did, then she might think, she might think…"

Aubrey watched with interest as Carlos stopped and flushed a rich deep red, a crimson tide that swept up through his neck and hit the roots of his hair.

"It's okay. I know. Anyway, this is sort of fun. When Casper and me were boarding at Arcadia Academy at Fallowfield, we used to play this game he invented called Ghost Trek where we used to creep about at night looking for ghosts. I never really understood the rules. Actually, I don't think that there were any.

I think he used to make it up as we went along. We never saw any ghosts, anyway."

Aubrey smiled to himself. If only she had known. Maudie had visited the Academy regularly, and she had often accompanied him and his mate Trevor on their adventures. He still missed her now. Not only because she was good fun, but she also had the enviable ability to drift in and out of buildings without being seen. Maudie didn't need to rely on an unlocked cat flap. She could, literally, melt through walls.

Teddy leaned over and watched as Carlos flexed his fingers and began to tap rapidly on the keyboard. "Do you think we'll find him?"

Carlos nodded.

"Bound to. Everybody turns up on Google some time or another. Even Jeremy."

They both fell silent as Carlos continued searching. On Jeremy's insistence, there had been no further discussion of Simon or the murder of Toby Carson that evening. There was, he had said, no mileage in speculating until they knew more, although Aubrey had overheard him telling Molly before dinner that he didn't want Carlos and Teddy to start working themselves up, especially given everything that had happened at Fallowfield. Also, he was seriously considering sending Teddy back home. As he'd said to Molly, the murder had almost certainly made the national news, and they had a duty to her parents to consider. But he'd said it reluctantly. None of them had ever seen Carlos smile so much since Teddy had arrived and, several times, they had actually heard him singing in the bathroom. He had a surprisingly melodious voice.

"Stop. That's him," gasped Teddy. "It is. Look."

She pointed a small finger at the grainy portrait of a younger Simon. With longer hair and wearing a shirt with the kind of collar that was no longer fashionable, it was definitely him. The headline read 'Post Office Killers Jailed For Life'.

CHAPTER TWENTY-THREE

MOLLY TOOK ANOTHER sip of her coffee and leaned her head back against the wall. She closed her eyes and gave a small, almost imperceptible sigh. Peeling potatoes by the sink, Carlos watched her from the corner of his eye. Was she all right? It was unlike her to come into the kitchen. Normally she was too busy. He felt a flutter of anxiety. Perhaps she wasn't feeling well. She was definitely looking a bit pale, not her usual cheerful self. And with Thomas being off sick today, she probably hadn't even had a break yet. Normally she would have gone home between shifts, but today she had worked straight through. She opened her eyes again and laced her fingers around her coffee mug.

"Carlos," she paused for a moment and put her mug down on the work surface. She groped around in her pocket and pulled out a hair clasp. Pulling her hair back from her face, she gathered it together and pinned it up behind her head. She looked, he thought, suddenly very young. "It's funny when things change, isn't it?" she continued. "Don't you think? I mean, it's like everything is going on as normal and then gradually, almost without you realising it, you see that things are different. Nothing is quite the way that you thought it was."

He looked up in alarm. What did she mean, not the way that you thought it was? What was she talking about? He felt a sudden wave of panic and his stomach lurched forward like it had that time on the big fairground ride he'd been talked into going on when they had the school trip. He had struggled not to vomit, and he was getting exactly the same feeling now. He swallowed and gripped the potato peeler harder. Please don't let her tell him that she and Jeremy were separating, that they were getting divorced. One of the lads at college that he'd got friendly with, Ben Miles, had told him about when his parents got divorced. Apparently, Milo had guessed that something was up when they kept buying him things, like really expensive presents when it wasn't even his birthday, and taking him out and letting him eat loads of burgers and chips and stuff. It was, said Milo, like they were having a competition with each other over who could be the nicest. And then one morning they'd sat him down with his little sister after breakfast and broken the news. According to Milo, they had said that although they wouldn't live together any more, they would always be a family because they still loved each other very much. Milo said that he had seriously doubted that, especially after he saw his father on the station platform snogging the face off some woman, and then heard his mother on the telephone to one of her friends calling his father a complete prick.

Carlos pushed back the wave of nausea that was threatening to overwhelm him. He just couldn't imagine Jeremy snogging the face off some strange woman, or, if he was honest, any woman, and Molly probably didn't even know the word prick. And what would happen to him if they separated? He was only fostered by them. They weren't his real parents, no matter how often he pretended to himself that they were. They could just give him back. But give him back to who? He felt a sudden rush of despair and then checked himself. If Molly and Jeremy were getting divorced, then he should be supporting them, trying to help them, not thinking about himself. But it was difficult not to. The thoughts flew around his head like tiny creatures on a zip wire, flying so fast that they had barely formed before the next one came along. Where would he go? What would he do? Would they sell the house? They would have to. Milo said that was what all divorced people did. They sold the house and chucked the pets away, and then they started arguing about money and the children. But he wasn't their child. In fact, he wasn't really a child at all. Not now that he'd left school. If they split up and sold the house, he'd have to go and find some bed-sit, if he could even afford that.

He did some quick calculations in his head. Although Thomas had insisted that he be paid above the minimum wage, what he earned from the Lodge wouldn't take him very far. If he wasn't careful, he might end up as a sad old loner, doing washing-up shifts in cheap restaurants to make ends meet. And then there was college. He probably wouldn't be able to carry on with his catering course. Catering wasn't like other courses, there were extra costs involved. He would have to leave; his life would be practically over, and he wasn't even eighteen yet. And there was Aubrey and Vincent to worry about, too. He couldn't let them be chucked away, he would have to take them with him, and how would he be able to afford to feed them if he couldn't even feed himself? And were you even allowed to keep cats in a bed-sit, anyway? Like, where would the cat flap go?

He put the potato peeler down and looked directly at her.

"Molly," he paused, his mouth suddenly dry. Of all the questions that he didn't want to ask, this one was about top of the list. But he had to. He needed to know, and not asking wouldn't make it go away. "Are you and Jeremy getting, you know, like, divorced?"

"What?" She opened her eyes wide and stared at him. "Divorced? Whatever makes you think that?"

"Well, you know, like, saying things aren't the same and that."

111

To his horror, he felt his eyes fill and his bottom lip start to wobble.

"Carlos, of course we're not getting divorced. I mean, think about it. Who else would have Jeremy?"

She smiled the smile that always brought her dimples out and made her look like the school girl she had once been, and he felt his shoulders relax. He smiled back at her and cuffed his nose with his sleeve. He dropped his arm quickly. He'd get slaughtered if his lecturers at college saw him doing that in the kitchen.

Molly leaned back against the work surface and picked up her coffee again.

"No, when I said not the same, I didn't mean at home. I meant here. At the Lodge."

Carlos considered for a moment. Now he thought about it, it did seem different although it was hard to put his finger on exactly what it was that had caused the change. There was something in the atmosphere, almost a kind of expectant air. Of course, the murder had unsettled everybody. Molly and Thomas, he knew, feared that some of the residents' relatives might take them away and it could have what Molly had described to Jeremy as a domino effect. If a couple of residents left, then others might leave too. If numbers dropped too low, there was a real danger that Lilac Tree Lodge would have to close. And the thefts hadn't helped either, especially as the thief still hadn't been identified. The faint air of suspicion was still hanging around, although it was fair to say that nothing further had gone missing for the last few days.

"I mean," Molly continued, "When I first came to work here, I was struck by what a lovely atmosphere this place had. It was friendly and welcoming. I mean, I know that some of our residents are a bit challenging…"

You can say that again, thought Carlos. Only last week Flora had somehow got hold of a skate board and had to be physically restrained from skateboarding round the car park in her vest and knickers, cheered on from the sidelines by Pattie and Ron. She was pretty good though, he had to admit. She'd taken the speed bumps like a pro.

"And our carers are lovely," continued Molly. "They do such a difficult job but they're always cheerful. I don't think that we could get a better bunch. They work so hard and they've always got something positive to say."

Except for Maxine, thought Carlos. Maxine never had anything positive to say. Molly and Thomas never saw that side of her, though. When any of the managers were around, Maxine was all sweetness and light. Nothing was too much trouble for Maxine then. It was a different matter when she thought that she was unobserved. Only last week, when he'd gone to find Molly after his shift, he'd seen her walk straight past a resident who was asking for a drink of water, although he knew that she'd heard. He'd fetched the water for the resident himself.

"What do you think is different now then?" He picked up the potato peeler again. "Don't you like working here anymore?"

Molly considered for a moment. Carlos suddenly felt flattered. She was talking to him like he was a real grown-up. He stood a little taller and assumed what he hoped was an intelligent expression.

"I still like working here, of course I do. And I've become very fond of the residents. A lot of them have had such interesting lives. It's hard work, true, but in some ways, it's the best job I've ever had. I suppose I just feel a bit unsettled lately, what with everything that's happened recently. The thefts and then this murder." She paused, clearly thinking something over.

"Carlos, if I tell you something, can you promise not to tell anyone else?"

He nodded eagerly.

"I mean," she continued, "I expect that everyone will know soon enough anyway, these things always get around, but we shouldn't say anything just yet because it might have a bearing on other matters."

Carlos felt his eager anticipation drop away from him. Was this about Thomas and his habit that Maxine had told him about? He'd tried not to think about it since Maxine had told him, and he'd kept his mouth shut, although Maxine had obviously hoped that he would tell Molly. He had resisted the urge. Gambling wasn't so terrible; there were far worse things that Thomas could be doing and how he spent his money was up to him. But he shouldn't, he knew, be doing it at work. He felt suddenly depressed. Thomas had always been kind to him and he didn't want him getting into any trouble. Was he going to get sacked or something?

"Is it about Thomas?"

"Thomas?" Molly looked confused. "No. Why do you think it's about Thomas? It's about the thefts. We've found out who it is."

Carlos caught his breath. Let it be Maxine. Please let it be Maxine. He waited for Molly to continue.

"To be honest, I was starting to think that maybe it was Simon. Only because," she added hurriedly, "there haven't been any thefts since he's been away from work. But it's not Simon."

She hesitated and looked towards the window. From outside, the sound of Gordon attempting to call Buster to heel floated across the garden.

"It was George's brother, Toby Carson."

Carlos dropped the potato peeler on the work surface and stared at her.

"Toby Carson? The bloke who got murdered?"

Molly nodded.

"One of the police officers came in to return some of the stolen goods. Apparently, Toby Carson was living in a caravan at the Happy Camper caravan site. They found the things when they went to search it. They were tucked away in one of the little cupboards. Obviously, he'd spent the money, but Clara's purse and some other things were still there. In fact, the purse had a card with the Lodge address in it, that's how the police knew where to return it."

Carlos thought for a moment. Why hadn't it occurred to them before that the thief might be a visitor? They had all immediately assumed that it was either a resident or a member of staff. But visitors came and went at all times—they didn't have to book in or anything and there were no set visiting hours. Most visitors had the pass codes to the external doors. Once in the building, it wasn't difficult to just walk into the residents' rooms. Anybody could do it. He'd done it himself when he'd found Peter's library card dropped in the garden. And once a visitor was known to the staff, nobody ever asked them what they were doing or questioned them about anything. This Toby must have just gone into rooms and helped himself when there was nobody around. It was easily done, especially at meal times when most residents ate in the dining room.

"It's a bit tight," said Carlos. "I mean, nicking off old people."

Molly laughed and rinsed her mug under the tap.

"It's a bit tight nicking off of anybody but, yes, somehow it does seem worse when it's the elderly. Which reminds me, I must speak to Gordon about the cameras and make sure that they're switched on permanently from now on. They seem to be on some sort of timer. If they'd been up and running when the things were taken, we might have known much sooner."

"Why did he take the stuff? Did he need the money?"

"According to the police, he was broke. They tracked down his ex-girlfriend and she told them that he'd been out of work for months. That's why he was living on the caravan site."

"Why didn't George help him out? I mean, like give him some money and stuff? He was his brother."

He looked thoughtful as he said it. If he'd had a brother, he would have helped him, no doubt about it. He'd always wanted a brother. Or a sister. His mother had often said, given the nature of his father's weaknesses, he probably had loads, but it was, he knew, unlikely that he'd ever meet any of them. And if they were anything like his father, he wouldn't want to. But, he thought, his essentially cheerful nature bubbling up to the fore again, he did have Aubrey and Vincent. All right, they weren't exactly his brothers, but they were the next best thing. They were his mates, and he could tell them anything. And in fact, he often did. And he had Teddy and Casper. Especially Teddy. His stomach lurched again, but this time in a good way.

Molly shrugged.

"I don't know. Perhaps he didn't tell him."

They both turned as the kitchen door swung open and Maxine came in. Without pausing, she strolled over to the fire door and kicked it open while flicking open a packet of cigarettes. Lighting one, she tipped her head back and regarded the blue of the autumn sky.

"That rancid old bitch Flora's at it again. All that shouting. She needs teaching a lesson. She ought to be strapped down and something tied over her mouth to shut her up. That'd put a stop to her. And as for Michael. Jesus." She paused and blew a long column of smoke upwards. "He hardly even knows what day of the week it is. And all that money his family are paying. Better to have him put him down, if you ask me."

Molly stepped forward.

"You were saying, Maxine?"

CHAPTER TWENTY-FOUR

JEREMY LAID ASIDE his book and looked across at Molly. He had always envied the ability she had to be perfectly still, to be absorbed in the moment. It was a real gift, and he wished that he had it. He had always been restless, even as a child. He was the kid who, in spotting even the shallowest of hills, had to run up it so that he could wave his arms and shout from the top. It had stood him in good stead, though, when he had first started teaching and an older and wiser colleague had advised him not to stand still for too long in the classroom. 'Moving target, son,' he'd said, tapping the side of his nose and giving a sly wink. 'Moving target.' Later Jeremy had come to realise that it wasn't quite the joke that he thought it had been.

Sensing his gaze, Molly looked over the top of the newspaper she was reading.

"What?"

Jeremy smiled.

"Nothing."

"What are you reading?"

Jeremy flipped the book over and held it up.

"Agatha Christie."

Molly regarded him affectionately for a moment.

"You must have read that half a dozen times."

Jeremy closed the book and laid it down on the coffee table.

"I know. At least half a dozen. It's not even as if I don't know who did it. That's probably why I keep going back to them.

There's something about the certainty of it. The upper classes always have names like Dolly and Johnny. Whereas the lower orders are usually called Gladys or Edna, and they work as maids. Unless they're a bloke, in which case they're called Alf or Bert." He smiled. "When the lower orders make an appearance, they've generally got problems with their adenoids and sniff a lot. When they're not listening at doors, that is. They're also devoid of any natural feeling so that when half of their ten children are murdered, they're queasily willing to sell their story to anybody offering to pay for it."

"Sounds very unattractive," remarked Molly dryly. "Not exactly recommended reading for Year Tens."

"You'd be surprised," said Jeremy. "Lots of people start with the blessed Agatha at about the age of twelve or thirteen. Even at Sir Frank's, when I suggested buying some Agatha Christies for the library, they were nicked almost straight away."

"Why did they steal them? They were library books. Why didn't they just borrow them?"

"Because," said Jeremy, "borrowing is an alien concept to most of them. It carries with it the notion that the object in question has to be returned. Rather than flogging it down the market or swapping it for a packet of fags."

Molly smiled.

"But why Agatha Christie, anyway? It doesn't exactly reflect their own experience. Wouldn't they have preferred to read about things that they could identify with?"

"What? Like step-dad Phil doing a ten year stretch for wounding with intent? Or uncle Michael being a bit too willing to help out at bath time? Mum hanging around the supermarket at closing time so that she can pick up the reduced food items, or lying about in bed all day with a hangover?" He paused. "Sorry, Moll. I didn't mean to lecture you, but for some kids a bit of escapism makes life a bit more bearable. It takes them somewhere else. You know, a few years ago one of my tutor group was nicked for shop-lifting in Tesco. Do you know what he was stealing? A green gingham school dress and a pack of socks for his little sister so she could start school turned out properly." He sighed. "I know that the kids at Sir Frank's are tough to work with and some of them are right little bastards, there's no denying that, but the truth is that a lot of them have really difficult home lives. So why would they want to read about it? The Agatha Christie books opened up a whole new world to them."

"I suppose so," said Molly thoughtfully. "But they're still about murder and so on, aren't they?"

"But not the kind of murder that they know about. It's never a random spur-of-the-moment knife attack or shooting. Or a strangling in a deserted alley by the local pyscho out on day release. An Agatha Christie murder is always," he thought for a moment, searching for the right word, "crafted. Thought through. There's always a reason for it, it's never some crack head out of control."

For a moment they sat quietly and he stared down at the cover of the book he'd laid down on the table. A nineteen sixties paperback edition. It wasn't rare, but it wasn't one that had been particularly easy to come across. Like much of his collection of twentieth century crime novels, he'd picked it up at a boot fair. In lurid early nineteen sixties colours, the cover portrayed a corpse laid out on the floor with a glamorous looking woman nearby, standing with her beautifully manicured hands up to her face in a show of distress.

"It's strange when you think about it, isn't it?" he said. "So many of us enjoy reading about murders and watching detective shows on television, but most of those stories couldn't be further from the truth. The reality of the majority of murders is just revoltingly, disgustingly, sordid. Some squalid little drug deal gone wrong, gang warfare, a drunken fight that gets out of hand. Then somebody loses their life and some poor family gets the death knock."

"I know. For some people it's just an ordinary day, until…" Molly faltered and laid aside her newspaper.

"It's worse if it's just an innocent bystander. Somebody who's got nothing to do with any of it but who just happens to be in the wrong place at the wrong time. Maybe even doing something completely every day, like travelling to work."

"Do you think that's what happened to Toby Carson? That he was in the wrong place at the wrong time?"

Jeremy shook his head.

"No. Somehow, I don't think so. When you think about it, he wasn't a typical victim. I mean, he was a healthy male and capable of putting up a fight. And the place where he was found, there was no reason for him to be there. It's not exactly a local beauty spot. Somebody put him there and obviously went to the trouble of trying to conceal his body. I think that whoever did it intended it. He was definitely the target. But it's all just so squalid. Imagine being killed and then dumped on some waste ground like a bag of rubbish."

"I know." Molly stood up and looked out of the window, her face serious. "It's horrible. What if those men hadn't found him when they did… children play over there sometimes, you know? They're not supposed to, but they do. They get in through the gaps in the fencing. You can hear them sometimes from the Lodge."

Jeremy nodded.

"Talking of children, Moll, I'm getting a bit worried about the effect all this might have on Carlos. And Teddy, too, of course. I mean, I know that they're not exactly children, but they're not adults yet either. They've got far too much imagination, the pair of them. They get ideas in their head and rush headlong into things without thinking about the consequences."

"Like going round to Simon's flat," said Molly.

"Exactly. They romanticise everything. In fact, they remind me a bit of those kids in that film. It was on last Sunday. Whistling something."

"Whistle Down the Wind?" suggested Molly.

"That's the one," said Jeremy. "Although, I don't suppose they think that Simon is Jesus."

"Let's hope not." Molly wasn't smiling as she spoke. She hesitated for a moment. "Do you trust them?"

Jeremy looked grave.

"I want to say yes. But, to be fair, I remember what it was like at that age. There were no shades of grey. Everything was black or white and the words risk and danger never crossed my mind. I thought I was invincible. Well, I would have done if I'd known what invincible meant." He thought for a moment. "Near where we lived, when I was about twelve, there were new houses being built. Me and my mates regularly used to break into the building site and wander about the half-built houses. We even lit fires sometimes and sat around drinking cider and smoking roll ups while we talked a load of bollocks. It never occurred to any of us that we might hurt ourselves. And then there was the time I took on the school bully."

Molly looked surprised.

"You never told me about that."

Jeremy gave a rueful smile.

"It's one of the things I prefer not to remember."

"What happened?"

"There was a kid in our school, Stuart something. A bit overweight, rubbish at games. He had asthma, if I recall correctly. The school bully was a great big brick outhouse house of a kid. I swear he practically had a full beard by the time he was fourteen. Anyway, on this particular day the bully strolled up to Stuart in the playground and just kicked him straight in the stomach and followed it through with a punch to the head. Everything went quiet. All the kids stopped what they were doing and just stared."

"So what happened?"

"Before I could stop myself I went up to him and said something like, don't do that again or else." He smiled. "This kid was bigger than some of the teachers."

"What did he say?"

"He said, or else what? And I said, or else you'll be sorry. And the bastard just laughed. So I hit him."

"Oh God, did you get hurt?"

"Only totally. He beat the shit out of me. But the funny thing was," he mused, "most of the other kids stopped talking to him after that. And he didn't pick on Stuart again."

"Did you tell your parents?"

"Well, they could hardly fail to notice that my face had been re-arranged. I just said I'd got in a rough tackle during games."

"Did they believe you?"

"I shouldn't think so. But they could see that I didn't want to make a fuss."

They sat quietly for a moment and then Molly said,

"So, what do you think that we should do about Carlos and Teddy?"

"I don't know. I just don't want them being mixed up with any of this." Jeremy rubbed his temple with his forefinger.

"God, Teddy's parents must think that every time she comes into contact with us somebody gets murdered."

Moll turned back to face him.

"I know. It does seem a bit, well, unfortunate."

"Unfortunate is about right. Have the police got any further, do you think?"

Molly shook her head.

"No, I've not heard anything, anyway. They're still searching over on the waste ground."

"Has anybody said yet how he was killed?"

"Some of the carers told me that he was struck on the back of the head with some kind of blunt instrument, although they can't work out what exactly. Something big and heavy, anyway. Apparently, the police are still looking for it. Although how the carers know all this, I have no idea."

"They'll be saying it was something else tomorrow."

"Probably," agreed Molly. "A police officer came to the Lodge to ask me about George today."

"Did he? What did he want to know?"

"It was a she. She asked me how long George had been living at the Lodge, how often his brother visited, that kind of thing. They asked whether I knew anything about his life before he came to the Lodge as well, whether he had any other relatives. I kind of got the impression that they might be thinking it has a bearing on his brother's death."

"What did you say?"

"I told them that in actual fact I knew very little about him. All the residents have a personal file but very often there's not much on it. When they come to us we know the basics, where they lived before, who their doctor is, that kind of thing, and we do ask relatives to give us a bit of background if they can. Their likes and dislikes and so on. But other than that, we only know what they choose to tell us and apart from the fact that George was rather reserved, he wasn't with us for very long."

Jeremy nodded.

"It's strange, isn't it? When people go into care, other people seem to see them like some sort of inmates, rather than residents who pay for the privilege of being there. As if they'd got a record or something. Talking of inmates, what's the news on Simon?"

"The police told us that he's not at his flat and, according to one of the other tenants, he hasn't been there for a couple of days. Wherever he is, we still haven't had a word from him and he's still not answering his phone. I can't hold his job open much longer, even if the owner of the Lodge agrees to let him stay on which, frankly, I doubt. We're going to have to find a replacement soon. The goodwill of the carers working extra shifts is starting to wear thin."

"So the police haven't spoken to him yet?"

Molly shook her head.

"No. They can't find him. He seems to have vanished from the face of the earth. They've asked me to get in touch with them if and when he makes contact."

"He's being an idiot. He ought to come forward so that the police can wipe him off the list. The longer he's gone, the more they're going to be interested in him."

"I know. They're bound to be. But honestly Jeremy, what on earth reason could Simon have for killing Toby Carson? I doubt that he ever even spoke to him."

CHAPTER TWENTY-FIVE

FROM OUTSIDE THE conservatory, the rain lashed against the glass. Inside it was warm and cosy, the only light coming from the little electric stove with the fake coals that flickered and glowed red. Teddy and Carlos sat huddled together on the small sofa, listening to music. From his customary position on the floor cushion, Aubrey looked at the doleful expression on Carlos's face. He knew what the problem was. Teddy was due to go home in two days.

"We could always write letters," said Teddy.

"What?" Carlos sounded amazed. "Like posted letters? With stamps and that? Like in the olden days?"

"Yes. Instead of emails and texts. Or," she added, "as well as emails and texts. Letters, proper letters, are sort of romantic. All the famous authors and poets and people like that used to write them. And you can keep them. Forever. I mean, you can't accidentally delete a letter."

"All right."

From the anxious expression on his face, Aubrey could see that Carlos was already worried about how he was going to write a letter, never having attempted such a thing before. It was something else to add to his list of worries, along with his intermittent fear that the lovely home he lived in with Molly and Jeremy would be suddenly taken away for some reason beyond his control, and his permanent fear that Teddy would go off with one of the posh boys from her school and forget all about him. He'd told Aubrey and Vincent all about it when he was getting ready for bed last night. Apparently, the boys in her classes were all called Jasper or Julian and they spent all their spare time skiing in France and playing poker in the sixth form common room. Aubrey and Vincent had listened intently. Vincent had never heard the word posh before, but Aubrey had.

One of the cats that got killed at Fallowfield, Blue, was posh. His mate, Trevor, had told him. There had been a posh cat in their old neighbourhood too, Leonardo. He didn't go skiing in France or play poker in the sixth form common room, at least, not as far as Aubrey was aware. But he was valuable, so valuable that he only ever went outside with his owners and even then he was kept on a lead. Aubrey had managed to spring him one night when his owners had left a downstairs window open. They had spent the night ratting down by the canal, a pursuit at which Leonardo had been surprisingly successful. It had, Leonardo said, been the best night of his life.

Aubrey yawned and stretched. Where, he wondered, had Vincent got to? He'd been gone for ages and it was pouring with rain out there. He shouldn't be out in weather like this. Nobody should. He rolled on to his back and watched as Carlos got up and stood in front of the window. Cupping one hand over his brow, Carlos looked out across the garden to where the rain was beating the early autumn plants into a sodden mass and pushing the cracked guttering on the back of the garage to breaking point. He turned back to face Teddy and sank down on his haunches, his back against the glass and his expression grave.

"I wonder where he is?"

"He could be anywhere." Teddy tucked her legs beneath her and gnawed softly on the side of her thumb. "I just hope he's safe. I feel sort of guilty," she added.

"I do too. But what could we have done?"

"Nothing really," admitted Teddy. "I mean, we had to go with Jeremy, we didn't have a choice. But it seemed wrong to just leave him there. All on his own."

"We did give him our mobile numbers."

"We haven't got his, though," Teddy sounded doleful. "We should have got it when we got his address."

"It'll be in Molly's office."

"Will she give it to you?"

Teddy and Carlos looked at each other. They both knew that the answer was no. They both also knew that Carlos could access not only Molly's office but also her computer, which was how they had obtained Simon's address before. Molly, in spite of being told not to by both Jeremy and Carlos, used the same password for nearly everything, and it was a password that they both knew. Carlos hesitated and changed the subject.

"Did you believe it?" Carlos frowned. "That stuff about him in the newspaper reports and Google and that?"

"No." She didn't, thought Aubrey, sound very convinced. "Well, I mean, I suppose it is true that he killed somebody. They wouldn't have been allowed to print it otherwise. But I bet it wasn't like it said."

"What do you think it was like then?"

"Well," Teddy thought for a moment. "That person that got killed, I bet he wasn't a nice person. Or not as nice as they said. I mean, in those press reports it was all stuff like, he was a devoted family man and he loved gardening and his dog. They always say nice things about victims." She searched for something else to add. "Things like, he made fairy cakes for charity and was very popular in the local community. Or he crocheted blankets for animal rescue centres, that kind of thing."

Aubrey looked across at her. Nothing wrong with crocheting blankets for animal rescue centres. In his opinion, far more people ought to do it. He'd do it himself if he knew how.

"It's true," said Carlos. "When somebody gets murdered, they never say he was a right git and even his dog hated him."

"And what they said about it, what happened, I've been thinking that maybe it wasn't really like that?"

"What do you mean?"

"Well, they said that the man that got killed was shot at point blank range," she hesitated. "What does that mean?"

Carlos thought for a moment.

"I think it means close up. Like, right in front of him."

"But maybe it wasn't really like they said it was. It could have been more like an accident. You know, like the gun went off accidentally or something, and Simon didn't really mean it. Or maybe it was the other man. The paper said that there were two of them. Although," she paused and thought for a moment. "If it was the other man, then Simon wouldn't have gone to prison."

"I think he would. I think you can still go to prison even if you were just sort of there."

Teddy looked horrified.

"That can't be right. I mean, what if I was, I don't know, in a shop or a bank and there was a robbery? I'd be there, but they wouldn't send me to prison. Not just for being there."

"Well," Carlos considered for a moment. "I think you have to be sort of in on it or something. Like, not just literally standing there."

"What does that mean? In on it? What if you just knew about it?"

"I'm not sure," Carlos confessed. "I think it means that, like, you were in on the planning or kind of helped or something."

"Anyway, I just don't think that Simon is like that," said Teddy stoutly. "He's not that sort of person."

Carlos nodded.

"Maybe. But the bloke did die."

Teddy assumed the stubborn expression with which both Carlos and Aubrey were becoming familiar.

"Well, I think that it was all made worse because that man who got shot was a police man. That's why Simon spent such a long time in prison. It's always worse when the victim is a police officer or somebody like that," she added. "We learnt about it in sociology. Even if Simon did do it, he didn't mean it. He was probably scared, probably he panicked."

Aubrey thought about this for a moment. Teddy did have a point. Even cats did things that they regretted when they were scared. Like that time he'd really shouted at Moses because he'd crept up behind him for a joke. Poor little Moses hadn't stopped shaking for a full two minutes. But he wouldn't have shot him, even if he knew how to use a gun. And according to the press reports that Carlos and Teddy had dug up, Simon and this other man had been robbing a post office at the time. The irony was that the police officer who got shot had only stopped by to ask the manager to put up a notice about a missing person.

"They said in the papers that Simon was a heroin addict," said Carlos. "Maybe he was off his face when it happened."

He fell silent for a moment. When he had lived in the Meadows with Maria, a number of their fellow tenants had been addicts. Sunken eyed and hollow-cheeked, they had hung out in packs like stringy mongrel dogs, their heroin hunger swirling around them in a miasma of despair. He had seen the dealers too, men that came around at dusk, with their mean eyes and hands that moved so fast that you'd miss them if you blinked. They had slid in and out of the shadows like malevolent ghosts, leaving behind them a trail of discarded needles laying on the ground where the addicts hadn't even been able to wait to get somewhere private. Maria had warned him to stay away from them and he hadn't needed telling twice.

"So, in a way," said Teddy, "maybe it wasn't really his fault…" she faltered and leaned forward, putting her head in her hands. "Whatever happened, I just wish he'd come back. Just so that we'd know that he's all right."

AUBREY PAUSED UNDER the lamp post and looked to his left, towards the beach. He listened for a moment to the soft susurration of the tide as the moon dipped to meet it. He liked that noise—it was soothing. Now that the rain had stopped, it felt good to be outside. At home, with all the windows closed, it had started to feel stuffy and hot. Out here, the air smelled fresh and clean and the pavements were rinsed of the daytime dust. But he was starting to feel a bit worried about Vincent. He hadn't intended to come out and look for him—he didn't want Vincent to think that he was checking up on him or anything, but after Carlos and Teddy had gone to bed, he hadn't been able to settle. Although Vincent often went off on his own, he didn't usually stay out this long. What if something had happened to him?

He tried to quell his anxiety, his mouth suddenly dry, but there was no denying that the lives of cats were all too often cut short. Far too many didn't reach their natural life span. Vincent was a big, dark feline. Not easily missed in the daylight but all too easily missed once darkness fell, particularly as some of the street lights along this stretch were turned off after midnight, in spite of local protest. Right at this very moment, Vincent could be lying in the kerb, hit by a passing car, or stretched out, dead or dying, in a stranger's garden. When cats were hit and injured by cars, they frequently ran a few metres for cover before they died, an instinctive adrenalin rush that propelled them forward. They usually expired under a hedge or bush seconds later. Which was why their owners often spent heart-breaking hours searching and putting up notices on lampposts, but never found them.

Aubrey moved forward slowly, scanning the kerbs and listening for any sound in the dark shadows of the privet hedges of the gardens that he passed. If he found Vincent injured, he'd go home and wake Carlos up. Carlos would know that something was wrong. He paused as a small rustling sounded in the hedge next to him. He hesitated, his heart in his mouth, and then moved forward. Parting the lower leaves with his paw, he peered beneath them. A small hedgehog peered irritably back at him.

"Sorry, mate," he muttered, and moved on.

He reached the top of the road and looked towards the beach. Was it worth just having a quick look? He might as well—he was out now anyway. He stopped as a shape loomed up ahead of him and planted itself in the middle of the pavement.

"All right, Aubsie?"

"Vin, mate, I was getting a bit worried about you. You've been out for ages."

He felt the swell of relief in his chest as he hurried forward to meet him.

"Got something to show you."

Without waiting for a response, Vincent turned on his heel and ran swiftly down towards the beach. Aubrey followed him. Scrambling down the bank, they ran across the sand until they drew to a halt by the beach huts. Vincent turned and looked at Aubrey, his big green eyes gleaming.

"Hear anything?"

Aubrey tipped his head and listened.

"No. What am I supposed to be hearing?"

Vincent crept stealthily towards the hut at the end. A very faint light showed from inside.

"Listen."

From inside the hut came the sound of singing. A faint melodic noise that just caught on the night air before it was carried upwards towards the night sky.

"Who is it?"

"Come and look."

They crept silently on to the small wooden veranda and stared in through the half-open stable door. Inside, the candle flickered and showed Simon, his hair askew and his chest bare. Sitting on a padded bench and singing quietly to himself, he was absorbed in the untangling of a pile of netting. On the floor around him lay strewn the contents of the holdall that he had hurriedly packed before leaving his flat.

CHAPTER TWENTY-SIX

MOLLY INSERTED THE key in the lock and grasped the handle. She hesitated for a moment and then turned to Jeremy, a worried expression on her face.

"It still doesn't seem right. It feels like we're trespassing or something."

"Moll, nobody lives here now, and the owner has asked us to do it so we can hardly be accused of trespassing. So come on, we said that we would. The sooner we get on with it the sooner we can get out of here."

Molly nodded and climbed the step into the caravan, followed by Jeremy. They stood on the threshold and looked around them, taking in the pile of laundry thrown in the corner, a scruffy mess of socks and shirts, and the empty vodka bottle lying on the floor next to it. In the tiny kitchenette sat a small plastic bowl half full of grey, scummy water and dirty plates. The air smelled stale, with an unpleasantly warm tinge of something not quite definable.

Jeremy smiled grimly.

"When his ex-girlfriend said that he was broke, she wasn't kidding. Who would choose to live like this?"

"He could have tried tidying up occasionally." Molly stretched across and pushed open a window. A gust of fresh, sweet air swept through the little cabin. "Have you got the bin liners?"

She tore a bag from the roll that Jeremy handed to her and shook it open. Jeremy reached into his pocket and drew out a pack of disposable gloves. Pulling on a pair himself, he passed the pack to Molly.

"Here, put these on. Can't be too careful. God knows who's been in and out of here." He stared for a moment at the unmade bed with its rumpled, sweat-stained sheets and duvet cover and pulled a face. "It's horrible when you think about the reality of it all. If you die suddenly, or I suppose even if it's not sudden, there'll always be someone left staring at your dirty underwear and reading through your private letters. Although," he added, "I don't know why this Mike had to ask you to do it. Why couldn't he do it himself? I thought he was supposed to be his friend."

"He said that he didn't want to get involved. I got the impression that he was trying to distance himself, that he didn't want to have any contact with the police."

"But the police have finished here now."

"I know, but I think that there's been some trouble over here in the past. Anyway, he seems to want to keep a low profile." She shrugged. "It seemed like the least I could do for George. I mean, Toby was his brother after all and there doesn't seem to be anybody else. Although what we're supposed to do with his stuff, I have no idea. When Mike phoned, he just asked if I would clear his things out so he can let the caravan again."

"It'll need a bloody good clean first."

Molly smiled.

"Well, you'll be pleased to know that's something that I didn't agree to." She looked around her again. "So what shall we do with it all? We can't keep it at the Lodge and I'm certainly not taking it home with us."

"Take it to the tip, I suppose. I can't imagine any of the charity shops wanting any of it. Not even the starving poor would want this lot. Anyway, let's make a start. The sooner we get started, the sooner we'll finish."

He reached down and began shovelling articles from the laundry pile into the bin liner.

JEREMY LEANED BACK and stretched his arm across the back of Molly's chair. Reaching for his pint, he drank across the top in several long appreciative swallows. He placed his glass back down and wiped his top lip.

"Thank goodness that's done. It's the most depressing thing I've done in a long time, and that includes writing end of term reports for Year Nine."

Molly nodded and swirled the ice around in her gin and tonic. The gentle tinkling sound of the cubes against the glass matched the mellow lateness of the afternoon. The pub, situated conveniently at the top of their road, was generally quiet at this time. Too late for the lunch-time drinkers and too early for the evening ones, it was perfect for a pre-dinner drink.

"These things always take longer than you imagine, even in something as small as a caravan. Do you remember how long it took to clear your aunt's things? We were there for nearly three days and that was only a two-bedroomed bungalow." She took a sip from her glass and swirled the ice around again. "What do you think that we should do about that leather document case?"

"I guess that we'd better go through it at some point, just to check that there's nothing important in there, although what we're supposed to do with it if there is, I have no idea. I can't think why the police didn't find it though."

"Perhaps they didn't look."

Jeremy nodded and took another mouthful of beer, more slowly this time. "To be fair, we wouldn't have found it if we hadn't stripped the bed and turned the mattress over. Anyway, we'll have a quick flick through and then hand it to the authorities. Let them deal with it. I think we've done our bit."

He glanced up at the clock on the wall.

"What time do you think that Carlos will be back?"

"The usual time, I suppose. I can always text him and let him know that we're in here." She paused. "It's going to be tough for him when Teddy goes home. I've never seen him so cheerful as he's been these last few days, in spite of everything that's happened."

"Might mean that we get a chance in the main bathroom, though. I wouldn't mind so much if we could use the ensuite, but Teddy's got that. God knows what he's doing in there all that time. Did you know that he's actually setting the alarm on his phone so that he can get in there first?"

Molly laughed and felt herself relax for the first time that day.

"He does come out smelling nice though."

"Yes, funny you should say that. I've noticed that the level of my best cologne is suspiciously low. Anyway, Teddy can always visit again, the next time that they're off college. And there's nothing to stop him getting on a train to see her at weekends. Actually, I was half thinking about giving him some driving lessons."

"That's a nice idea. It would be good for him to have a bit of independence."

"Just a couple to get him started. And then I thought we might pay for some proper driving school lessons, for his birthday maybe."

"If he passes his test, he can drive to see Teddy. I wouldn't mind if he borrowed my car occasionally, he's pretty sensible."

She thought for a moment, wrinkling her brow slightly. "Do you think that they're behaving a bit oddly at the moment?"

Jeremy considered.

"Not really. About par for the course for teenagers. Why?"

"This morning, when I went into the conservatory, they looked distinctly shifty and they stopped talking. It was obvious that they didn't want me to hear what they were saying."

Jeremy laughed.

"They probably didn't. Would you have wanted your parents to hear what you were talking about when you were seventeen?"

CHAPTER TWENTY-SEVEN

FROM THE WINDOW sill where Aubrey and Vincent had parked themselves, they watched as Carlos touched the plastic card against the keypad and waited for the green light to flash. He pushed the door open and then hesitated. He turned and looked at Teddy.

"I feel a bit, like, bad."

"I know." Teddy nodded. "I do, too. But we only promised that we wouldn't go to Simon's flat again." An unmistakable note of virtue crept into her voice. "We didn't say that we wouldn't contact him. I mean, we're not breaking a promise or anything."

"It's not that, its…" Carlos waved his hand around the small neat office. A very faint suggestion of Molly's perfume hit his nostrils. If she walked in now, they'd have trouble explaining themselves.

"But we haven't really got a choice. I mean, how else are we going to find him? Carlos," she spoke softly, her head tilted slightly to one side. "What else are we supposed to do? We need to make sure that he's all right. We're probably the only people in the whole wide world who even care about him."

She lifted her shoulders slightly and, as though to add emphasis to her words, spread her hands palm upwards as she spoke. The rolled-up ends of the sleeves of the oversize sweater she wore fell back, emphasising her narrow wrists and small frame.

Aubrey gave a sigh. Teddy might be impulsive, willful even, but her heart was in the right place. And she was probably right. From what he had gathered, Simon didn't have anybody else. Not even a cat.

"And it's not like we're doing anything wrong," Teddy continued. "Not really. We're not, like, stealing or anything. We just want to know that Simon is all right, that's all. We just need to let him know that he's not all alone in the world. We need to let him know that he's got friends."

Jumping lightly down from the window sill, Aubrey and Vincent slipped into Molly's office behind them and watched from the shadows as the two teenagers stood and looked about them. In the gloom of the early evening, the office looked different. Normally bright, cheerful and busy, now the light from the ornamental lamppost in the garden threw a grey shadow across the desk and filing cabinets, making them look cold and dreary. Aubrey shivered slightly. It felt different in here without Molly. While he sort of agreed with Teddy with regard to Simon, what they were doing was surely wrong. And if they didn't think so too, why did they wait until Molly was away from the Lodge before going to her office?

He was starting to regret following Carlos to work this afternoon and regretting even more following him into Molly's office. This was something that he would have preferred not to know about. It was definitely one of those occasions when curiosity should not have got the better of the cat. He and Vincent could have just stayed at home and had a good kip on one of the beds. Or better still, spent a bit of time winding up Beryl next door. Vincent had discovered that by climbing to the highest point of the wall that divided their house from next door, they could make faces at Beryl without her being able to reach them. Yesterday had been particularly satisfying, when she got a bollocking from her owners for making a racket and then grabbed by the collar and marched ignominiously indoors. Poor old Beryl had practically burst with injured innocence. Vincent had laughed so much he had almost fallen off the wall. He wasn't laughing now, though.

"They shouldn't be doing this," he said, slipping further back into the shadow. "Not without Molly knowing. It's not right, and they know it."

Aubrey nodded. Of course Teddy and Carlos knew it was wrong. Otherwise, they wouldn't be creeping about like this. Both he and Vincent felt sorry for Simon, but this wasn't the right way to go about helping him. One way or another, Simon was going to have come out from that hut, and it would be better if Carlos and Teddy weren't involved. It was all right for Teddy—she was going home soon, but if there was any trouble it would be Carlos who would be left to face the music. But it was good to know that Vincent was starting to feel the same way about Molly and Jeremy as he did. Ever the cool cat, Vincent was only now really starting to settle in. Last night he had even sat on Molly's lap.

Carlos turned to Teddy and spoke in a whisper.

"We need to put a light on."

Teddy shook her head.

"No. Somebody might see it and wonder who's in here. Use your phone."

Carlos nodded and, without answering, pulled his phone from his pocket. Tiptoeing across to the computer, he switched it on and rapidly typed in the word Aubrey. Teddy leaned over his shoulder and watched as he scrolled across the files.

"There. Look." She prodded the screen with her finger. "Simon Turner."

Without answering, Carlos opened the file. Pulling her own phone from her pocket, Teddy leaned closer and quickly tapped in the mobile number next to Simon's address. For good measure, she took a shot of the screen and rapidly emailed it to herself.

"Anything else?"

Carlos shook his head. He was, Aubrey could see, itching to get out of there.

Stuffing her phone back in her pocket, Teddy nudged Carlos in the back.

"Right, let's go."

AUBREY WATCHED AS Teddy's small fingers deftly sliced the bread and cheese and packed it efficiently into the square plastic box. Glancing around, she pulled a packet of biscuits towards her and, removing three, wrapped them in clingfilm.

"He ought to have some fruit as well."

"Here." Pausing in his wiping down of the work surfaces, Carlos plucked an apple and two satsumas from the big fruit bowl and tossed them over to her.

Teddy tapped down the lid of the box and tucked it into her rucksack. She looked across at Carlos.

"Do you think that we should be doing this?" she asked, her tone doubtful. "I mean, in a way, it's stealing."

No 'in a way' about it, thought Aubrey. If stealing was taking something that didn't belong to you, then what they were doing fitted the bill. Although, he thought, slightly uncomfortably, his own moral compass hadn't always been quite so fixed when he lived on the street. But, to be fair, he had to eat and, after Raj died, he had to take what he could get. Which was, he supposed, what Carlos and Teddy were helping Simon to do.

"If we take it from home, Molly or Jeremy might notice," said Carlos. "Anyway, it's just a few bits and pieces. Simon works here, staff are allowed free meals if they have what the residents have." He thought for a moment. "And officially he still works here. I mean, he hasn't resigned or been sacked or anything. So," he repeated, "he's still a member of staff."

Not any more, thought Aubrey. Only that morning an email had come through from Mrs. Randall which had instructed Molly to start looking for a replacement and, truth to tell, Molly hadn't been completely reluctant. Whatever credit Simon had with the Lodge had well and truly expired. Molly herself had come in early to do the breakfasts this morning, and that was after working a late shift last night. Thomas was still off sick with no indication of when he might return, and Mrs. Randall had made Molly the temporary manager. Which, as she said to Jeremy, was all very well, but there was no talk of a temporary assistant manager which meant that she was doing Thomas's job as well as her own.

Teddy leaned back against the work surface; her expression thoughtful.

"Do you think that we'll be able to persuade him?"

"It's got to be worth a try." Carlos paused in his stacking of the dishwasher. "I mean, he can't stay hidden forever. He'll have to come out eventually, and like Molly says, the longer he stays away, the worse it's going to be for him. All the police want to do is talk to him, anyway. Like they did with all of us. Nobody's accused him of anything."

"Yes, but what if…" she hesitated. "What if he hasn't got, like, you know, an alibi? I mean, he lives on his own. He was probably just at home reading or something. He might not have anybody to say where he was when it happened."

143

"That's true. But it's still better to come out and face it. Because they'll find him anyway and then they'll say if he didn't have anything to hide, why did he leg it?"

He pulled open the fridge and took out a plate of cooked meat. Peeling two slices from the top, he took them over to the fire door and opened it.

"Come on, Aubrey. Have a bit of something to keep you going."

Aubrey strolled over to the open fire door and wolfed down the slices of meat. He wasn't hungry, but a little extra never went amiss. It made up for all the times on the street when to get anything at all, even a half-eaten egg sandwich, had been a result. In fact, now he thought about it, that half-eaten egg sandwich had been one of the best meals that he'd ever had, given that he hadn't eaten for eighteen hours. He sat back and gave his ears and head a quick wash. Carlos and Teddy hadn't exactly said what they were planning to do, but it was pretty obvious. They had barely sent the text this morning before Simon replied. He wasn't surprised. Simon must be starting to feel fairly hungry. Whatever food he had taken with him, if any, must have been eaten by now. And even if he had any money with him to buy more, that would mean him taking the risk of going out. But he couldn't stay there forever. Apart from anything else, once the cold weather really set in, it would be freezing in one of those huts. There was also the fact that the hut must belong to somebody. It was entirely possible that the owner would come to check on it. And Carlos was right. If Simon had nothing to hide, then the first question he would have to answer would be why he legged it.

He suppressed a sudden doubt. He'd been worrying about Simon, but he was in danger of forgetting about Carlos and Teddy. In some respects, for all their facade of maturity, they were innocents. They were dealing with a convicted murderer, and they were treating it like it was some kind of adventure. For all they knew, Simon might be mad, totally bonkers. True, he'd never displayed any evidence of it, but that didn't mean anything. In some ways that was worse, because it would be unexpected. He'd seen it in the cat world, and there was no reason to suppose that it was any different in the human world. He shuddered slightly. At their last house, the manor had been run by a pair of Siamese, the twins Rupert and Roger. Of the two, Rupert had clearly been insane and every cat who valued his whiskers took evasive action when he hove into view. But it was Roger, with his cool detached air and chilling blue eyes that could turn without a second's notice. What if Simon was like Roger?

He tried to comfort himself. It would be okay; he was sure of it. Simon was a good bloke. Of course he was. If being a good bloke meant that he always found something for him and Vincent to scoff and didn't throw them out of the kitchen as soon as they made an appearance. But what if he wasn't a good bloke? What if, in fact, he was a very bad bloke? Even cat lovers could do bad things, difficult though that was to imagine. He looked up as the kitchen door opened and Molly came in. She looked, he thought, close to exhaustion. The tiny tracery of lines around her eyes showed clearly today and her hair, usually tied back neatly, was escaping into wisps which floated around her face. When she spoke, her voice sounded weary.

"Hello, you two. I'm off in a minute. I've just come to see if you want a lift home?"

Teddy sprang forward, one foot nudging her rucksack behind her.

"Oh, that's really kind of you Molly, thank you. But I think we'll walk." She smiled, a sweet, innocent smile. Too innocent, thought Aubrey. He'd seen that look on Vincent's face, usually just before he indulged in a spot of cat burgling in neighbouring houses. It was amazing how many people left food lying around. "It's not far, and it's such a nice evening."

Aubrey looked up, surprised. Was it? Well, it wasn't raining, if that's what you called a nice evening.

Molly nodded.

"Okay. See you later but don't be too long. Teddy, have you got everything packed for the morning?"

"Yes, thank you Molly. I did it before we came to the Lodge."

"Good. We don't want to be late for your train."

Molly half-turned and then turned back.

"Aubrey, what are you doing in here? You shouldn't let him in here you know, Carlos. We'll have health and safety on our backs."

"He's outside, Molly. He's not in the kitchen."

Only technically, thought Aubrey, edging further away from the door towards the garden.

"Well, he can come home with me now."

Walking swiftly towards him, she reached down and scooped him up.

CHAPTER TWENTY-EIGHT

THE EARLY EVENING air smelled fresh and clean, the breeze blowing across from the sea swept their faces and fluttered their hair. Stopping to re-tie the lace on one of his trainers, Carlos looked up at Teddy.

"I wish that you didn't have to go home tomorrow."

"Me too. Casp is dying to hear everything, though. I'll have loads to tell him."

Carlos laughed.

"Loads," he agreed. He bit his bottom lip. "You will WhatsApp and Facetime, though, won't you?"

Teddy nodded eagerly.

"Of course I will, I'll…" she stopped abruptly and pointed. "Look, there he is."

Standing just outside the beach hut, Simon half-raised his hand and then let it drop. His eyes were dark and his face expressionless. Waving, they ran towards him. He turned and beckoned them into the hut.

MOLLY GLANCED DOWN at her watch.

"They're taking their time, it's getting late. They should be back by now. It's only a ten-minute walk."

"It's their last evening, Moll. They probably want a bit of time alone."

"I suppose so. But they mustn't be too late. Teddy has a train to catch in the morning."

"If they're not back soon, I'll go and look for them. Or better still, call them. They've probably just lost track of the time."

From Molly's lap, Aubrey glanced down at Vincent, who was draped across Jeremy's feet. They both knew where Carlos and Teddy were, and they were both starting to feel slightly uncomfortable about it. But, as Vincent had said to Aubrey, what could they do about it? They couldn't stop them. And anyway, Simon was all right. He'd just run off because he was a bit frightened, that was all. Carlos and Teddy would persuade him to come out and then the police would discover that he had nothing to do with the murder and everything would be fine again. But, thought Aubrey, he hadn't sounded totally convinced, and what if it wasn't all fine again? It was all very well Vincent saying that they couldn't do anything about it. It didn't stop him feeling guilty. He curled in tighter on himself, taking comfort from the warm softness of Molly. She reached down and stroked him, and then sat back again.

Jeremy regarded her for a moment, his eyes slightly narrowed.

"You're looking a bit tired. Are you feeling okay?"

"I'm fine," said Molly. She pushed a lock of hair back from her face and tucked it behind her ear. "God, I'm starting to look like a wild woman. I need a good hair cut but I just can't find the time at the moment. Or the energy. There's so much to do. I keep meaning to get on to the laundry but I just haven't got round to it. There were five bath towels missing again this week."

"I thought that the Lodge did its own laundry?"

"Only the residents' clothes. The big stuff, sheets and towels and so on, goes to a laundry service. They're not very good though, they keep losing things. I suggested to Thomas recently that we change them. He said that we couldn't because the company is owned by Mrs. Randall. They operate all over the south east. So, I guess that we're stuck with them."

Jeremy nodded sympathetically.

"Any sign of when Thomas will be back?"

Molly shook her head.

"He's suffering from stress, apparently. So, who knows? It could be weeks."

Aubrey listened with interest. He knew all about this stress stuff. At Sir Frank's, the teaching staff regularly got it and had to go and lie down or something. Although why Thomas had to go and lie down, he didn't know. It wasn't like he was attempting to teach a gang of fifteen-year-olds, who thought that he was some kind of clown sent to entertain them. As Jeremy had once said, when it came to Year Ten, all he needed was a pair of big shoes and a whirling bow tie that lit up, with him driving into the classroom in a comedy car from which all the doors fell off and the scene would be complete. But the residents at the Lodge weren't like that. They were at least polite. Well, he corrected himself, not always. But they couldn't help it. They didn't mean it. And Thomas had never seemed to mind, not even when Charles had accused him of being his dead wife's lover and called him a fat lying bastard while prodding him in the stomach with a biro which left a blue smudge on his shirt.

"Anyway," continued Molly. "At least it's given me a chance to get in his office and sort out some more of the paperwork. Some of it goes back months. Anyway, how's your inspection going?"

Jeremy leaned over and ran a hand over Vincent's soft, dark head. Vincent flexed his big velvety paws and rumbled a low purr in appreciation. Aubrey smiled to himself. When Vincent had first come to live with them, he had deliberately held himself in reserve, as though to purr would have been a show of weakness. Now, he did it automatically.

"Not sure. I still feel that there's something not quite right, but I don't know what." He thought for a moment. "But, to be fair, so far so good. All the teaching staff are properly qualified, and the teaching seems to be well up to standard. In fact, their results are pretty good. Which," he added, "they bloody well ought to be with an average class size of ten. Maybe it's just my prejudice. I think that all that money swilling around probably makes me uncomfortable. You should see the list of auction promises at the last fundraiser they held. Although why they need to raise funds at all is beyond me. Totally different to Sir Frank's. At Sir Frank's the only way to get money out of a parent was to pull a sawn-off shotgun on them. And I seriously thought about that once or twice."

Molly laughed.

"No, you didn't."

"No. I didn't. But it was tempting. Especially when the kids were sharing one text book between three. Not that it mattered, I suppose. They didn't read it, anyway. Well, one of them usually did, and then told the others what it was about." He glanced at his watch, and then reached over to the coffee table and picked up his phone. "You're right, it is getting late. I'll give Carlos a ring and see where they are."

He tapped the screen and put the phone to his ear.

"It's gone to voice mail." He frowned and looked across at Molly. "Now why am I starting to feel uncomfortable? Moll, if this is some stupid stunt so that Teddy doesn't have to go home tomorrow, he's in big trouble. They both are." He dropped the phone back down on the table and stood up. "Do you think that I ought to go out and look for them?"

"But they could be anywhere."

Jeremy sighed and ruffled the back of his head.

"I know. But if they're not answering their phones, I don't know what else to do."

Molly suddenly jumped up and grabbed Jeremy's phone.

"Moll, I told you, it's going straight to voice mail."

"No, Jeremy, remember? Find my phone?"

"What do you mean, find your phone? It won't make any difference if you ring him on your phone, it'll still go to voice mail."

"No." Molly shook her head impatiently. "Find my phone. The app. Don't you remember? Carlos put it on all our phones and that time you thought that you had lost yours, we found it. If we can track Carlos's phone we'll know where they are."

Aubrey smothered a grin. Ah yes, that time that Jeremy thought that he had lost his phone. He'd been out with his friend Harry playing golf in their fortnightly friendly, and, as it was Harry's birthday, the pair of them had become rather over-refreshed afterwards. Jeremy had fallen out of a taxi, barely able to stand and shouting, almost incoherently, that somebody had stolen his phone. Molly and Carlos had regarded him in patient silence before Carlos, trying to keep a straight face, had tapped the app on his phone and shown the current location of the stolen phone. Which was in Jeremy's inside jacket pocket.

Jeremy grinned.

"Of course."

CHAPTER TWENTY-NINE

CARLOS PROPPED HIS phone carefully on the pile of books, balancing the angle so that he was looking slightly upwards. Jack at college had told him that everybody looked better if they were photographed from below rather than above and Jack should know, he had studied photography. True, he'd failed, which was why he was now doing catering, but he had studied it. Carlos tilted the phone in another direction and lifted his chin slightly. He couldn't see the difference. He turned to Aubrey.

"What do you think, Aubrey? I can't see any difference."

Aubrey tilted his head to one side. He couldn't see any difference, either. But he didn't think it would matter to Teddy. This morning she had trundled down the stairs, small and forlorn, one strap of her denim dungarees slipping from her shoulder, bumping her packed case along behind her. Sitting in the kitchen with Carlos, Molly and Jeremy, she had looked as though she was trying not to cry. Carlos, sitting next to her, had looked, if possible, even more tragic.

"You do see, don't you, both of you, that we really had no choice?" Jeremy's voice had been unexpectedly gentle, his eyes soft and concerned as he poured them both coffee from the large jug on the table. "We know that you were trying to help but in the long term it probably would just have made things worse for him."

"We know." Teddy's voice was doleful. "But we had to do something. He's all alone in the world. He hasn't got anybody else."

"We don't actually know that, Teddy," said Molly. "But whether it's true or not, we had to ring the police last night. For his sake, as much as anything. You saw for yourselves the state that he was in." She laid a hand across Teddy's. "Whether or not he's got anything to do with the murder, he's clearly got problems and there are people better qualified than us to help him. The police will know the right people to contact."

From his place under the radiator, Aubrey had agreed. When Jeremy had arrived back at the house last night with Carlos, Teddy, and Simon in tow, Aubrey had been shocked at the change in Simon. When Simon had worked at the Lodge, he had always looked decent. His chef's whites, if not always ironed, had at least been washed, and his face was always clean-shaven. Last night, with his hair sticking out in greasy tufts and several days' stubble spread across his chin, his clothes looked like he'd slept in them, which he probably had. A faint odour of stale sweat had hung over him, adding to the impression of the sort of person who other people preferred not to sit next to on a train. Or anywhere else for that matter.

Jeremy had ushered him into the sitting room and he had shuffled silently to the far side of the room and stood with his back to the wall, his head hanging down as though he was afraid to look up. If he had been able to curl himself into a ball, Aubrey suspected that he would have done so. He looked just like the pair of tiny kittens that had been found abandoned by the slip road to the motorway and brought into Sunny Banks rescue centre. Frozen and half-starved, their eyes newly opened, they had clung on to each other in a tiny ball of fur and glued themselves to the corner of their pen. It had taken hours of patient wheedling on the part of the screws to tempt them to eat, leaving small bowls of food just within reach. In a similar show of instinctive understanding, Molly had made Simon a mug of hot chocolate and placed it with a plate of biscuits on the corner of the coffee table nearest to him.

The police had arrived ten minutes later, and Simon had followed them meekly out to the patrol car, his head still down.

"Aubrey, come and sit over here. Teddy will want to see you, too."

Obligingly, Aubrey rolled off the top of the chest of drawers and jumped on to the small desk. Tucking Aubrey in next to him, Carlos checked his appearance once more and then touched the screen of his phone. Within seconds, Teddy's small heart-shaped face appeared, her green and blue highlighted hair piled up around her head and held in place with what looked like a knitting needle. From the crook of Carlos's arm, Aubrey could feel the quickening of his heart beat.

"What's happening? Have you heard anything?"

Carlos nodded, his expression glum.

"They've charged him."

Teddy's gasp was audible. Her hand flew to her face, the tips of her bright green and blue nails pressing against her mouth.

"But they can't…"

"Well, they have. Molly told us. She heard it at the Lodge this morning. The police called to tell her. Well, to tell Thomas, but he's still off sick. She's really worried because she's going to have to tell the owner and there'll be loads of publicity and stuff and it'll be bad for the Lodge. Very bad," he added. "Like, they might have to close it or something."

"But what happened? Why did they charge him?"

"The policeman that spoke to Molly, he told her that Simon couldn't tell them where he was when the murder happened and then," he paused and cleared his throat. "And then he confessed."

"He did what?" Teddy leaned closer to the screen so that her blue-grey eyes, fringed with thick dark lashes, suddenly seemed huge, the pupils dilated.

"He confessed. He told them that he did it." Carlos spoke in a low tone, almost a whisper, as though to speak the words more loudly would give them the hard edge of reality.

"But that's not enough." Teddy's outrage sparked through the screen, her breath coming quickly. "They must need more than that. I bet loads of people go round saying that they did things when they didn't." She hesitated for a moment. "Well, not exactly, but Simon must have got confused. He's not well. Anybody can see that. They shouldn't have asked him questions when he's not well." She searched around for a word to express the vehemence of her feelings. "It's outrageous. It's oppressive"

Carlos nodded, clearly admiring Teddy's eloquence.

"I know. Outrageous," he repeated. "Oppressive."

Aubrey could see that Carlos obviously didn't know what oppressive meant. He had rolled the word around his mouth like it was a new and particularly delicious kind of sweet.

"The thing is, Carlos," she continued. "They can't just go around charging people for nothing. I mean, they have to have reasons and everything."

Carlos looked helpless.

"I suppose so. But if he said he did it…"

"But I bet there's no evidence. I bet Simon didn't even know that Toby Carson. I bet he didn't even know who he was."

"But he has killed someone before. He went to prison. He had a gun, and a man got shot."

Suddenly, the enormity of what he had just said hit him with the force of a lead weight. Unbidden, his mind flew back to that sweltering summer night in Sao Paulo and the memory that he thought he had suppressed. It had been too hot to sleep and he and his mother Maria had been sitting on the small balcony on the first-floor apartment that they shared with his grandfather before he died. His father, having spent twenty minutes vomiting down the lavatory, had been lying drunk and snoring on the bathroom floor. Around them the sounds of the city had reverberated through the hot night air, the tall spires of the neo-gothic cathedral looming on the skyline. The smell of street food, rich and spicy, had pushed against his nostrils. His mother had turned to him and covered his hand with hers. He had felt the small palm, roughened by years of cleaning and working in factories, press against his.

"One day, Carlos, when you are a doctor, we will live in a big house with a garden and we will eat ice cream. Yes, it is definite. And cakes. We will eat ice cream and cakes. And we will wear fine clothes and go to concerts where we will hear wonderful music."

He had smiled up at her. It was a game that they played. Imagining all the wonderful things that they would have at that uncertain time in the future when they left this place for good and started their new life. They always spoke in English, partly for practice for the longed-for day that they would go to England and partly because his father couldn't understand what they were saying. He opened his mouth to reply and then closed it again as from the alleyway opposite them a man burst out, chased by two more men. From a side street further down another man appeared and then the night air was rent with a volley of gun fire and the first man fell to the pavement. The two men that had chased him turned to the man that had appeared from the side street. For a moment there was silence and then the shots rang out again and the man fell to the ground, folding at the knees and clutching at his stomach. His mother grabbed his arm and pulled him to the floor just as the man who had been shooting looked up to the balcony, the small revolver still in his hand.

Carlos had felt his heart beating wildly as his mother gently held her hand across his mouth.

"Carlos, we do not see." Her voice came in a harsh whisper. "We do not hear."

How long they lay there, he didn't know. He felt the hard concrete of the balcony floor grate against his chest through his thin T-shirt. Eventually, stiff and frightened, they had crawled back into the apartment, fearing to raise their heads in case the gun man was still there. For days he had been afraid to go out, terrified that the gun man had seen him and would be able to identify him.

He looked at Teddy now. She had no idea of the reality; guns were something that she saw on television or in films. When he spoke, his tone was gentle.

"We can't just ignore it, Teddy. Simon does have a conviction."

"So, you think he did it?"

"No. I don't. I'm just saying."

"Well," said Teddy, slightly less vehement now. "All right. But remember that we've never heard Simon's side of it. We only know what they wrote in the newspapers. But anyway, that doesn't mean that he did this, does it? You're supposed to be innocent until proved guilty. Everybody knows that." She paused "What does charging mean, anyway? Does that mean that he's in prison?"

"Sort of. He's been put on remand. It's like being in prison, but it's sort of not."

"I don't understand. How can he be in a prison that's not a prison?"

"Well, it is a prison, but I think it's better than being, like, a normal prisoner. Not so strict and that. Anyway, he has to stay there till his trial."

Aubrey struggled to loosen himself. Carlos's grip had suddenly tightened. He was, he suspected, remembering his brief unhappy stay at Alderman Wenlock, the children's home in which he had been placed after his mother had died and before Molly and Jeremy had fostered him. Living in that last cramped room in Sao Paulo had been a walk in the park compared to that. At least in Sao Paulo, he had his mother with him. At Alderman Wenlock's he had been totally and absolutely alone, and at Alderman Wenlock there had been no lock on his door, broken or otherwise.

"Can he have visitors?"

"I think so. I don't know. I'll ask Jeremy."

"If he can, will you go and see him?"

Carlos nodded.

"Because," Teddy continued, "he has to know that we're on his side. Even when everyone else is against him."

Carlos stared at the small, pretty face, her large eyes blazing with all the passion of a condemned martyr. She was right. They had to be on Simon's side.

CHAPTER THIRTY

"SO HOW WAS HE?"

Molly looked back over her shoulder as she filled the kettle.

"Well, not like the Thomas that he usually is, that's for sure. Whatever's the matter with him, he's not himself. To be honest Jeremy, he looked like a changed man. I would hardly have recognised him."

"In what way?"

"Well, he looks ten years older for a start. And he's lost weight. But not in a good way, if you know what I mean. He's got this sort of gaunt look and he's got great big shadows around his eyes. He looks like he hasn't slept for a week."

"Was his wife there?"

"No, she was at work. She's seems very nice though. Thomas told her that I would be calling round and she left two slices of cake on a plate for us and a tea tray laid up ready."

Jeremy smiled.

"Doesn't sound like marital trouble then. What's their house like?"

"Three-bedroomed semi, modern estate. Very neat and tidy. Pretty much what I would have expected, really. You know, open lawn at the front, garage to the side. Easy to maintain." She smiled. "Which is just as well. Brilliant as he is with the residents, Thomas isn't exactly known for his practical skills on the domestic front. The last time he put a pan of soup on the hob at the Lodge for his lunch, he walked away and forgot about it. We were lucky that we didn't have a fire. I persuaded him to start using the microwave in the staff room instead."

"I suppose that there's no sign of when he's coming back?"

Molly dropped a tea bag into a mug and shook her head.

"No. I didn't like to ask. It seemed sort of insensitive, if you know what I mean, as if I was only there to push him into going back to work."

"What did you talk about?"

"Just stuff about the Lodge. I ended up doing most of the talking. I told him about the thefts being cleared up which he seemed relieved about. He asked if everything was all right, if we were all coping, but just in general terms, he didn't ask anything specific. And he didn't mention the residents at all, which was odd."

"Very," Jeremy agreed.

Molly continued.

"He seemed distracted, as if he wasn't really listening to anything that I was saying. It was almost as though he was just talking for the sake of it, like he had something else on his mind. A couple of times he looked as though he was about to say something and then stopped himself. All in all, I got the feeling that he was glad when I left," she paused. "Well, not glad exactly, more like relieved."

"Did he say anything about Simon?"

"No. But unless he's been deliberately avoiding the news, he must know about it, it's been in all the local papers as well as local television and radio."

Aubrey paused in his hoovering round of his food bowl. It certainly had been in all the local papers. Vincent had told him that he'd heard people talking about it outside the newsagents. Lacking any other local news of interest, both the Gazette and the Observer had carried a daily update. While conspicuously not naming the suspect, there had been more than enough detail to easily identify the man who had been charged. Described as of medium height, dark-haired, in his early forties and currently employed as a chef at a local care home, it didn't take too much of a leap of the imagination to identify Simon.

He thought back to this morning. The atmosphere at the Lodge had been charged, as though a bitter wind had blown through and unsettled everyone in its wake. Even Peter, the kindest and gentlest of men, had seemed grumpy and irritable, complaining that his morning coffee was cold and then saying that the air was stuffy and opening windows, much to the annoyance of some of the other residents who had immediately got up and closed them again. Aubrey had been glad when Molly had finished her shift and they had been able to go home. Even the Lodge garden had been unusually quiet. For once, there had been no sound of Buster barking.

Jeremy spread his hands in front of him and laid them palm down on the table. He stared down at them and then cleared his throat.

"Carlos came home early today. One of his lecturers is off sick. We had a bit of a chat."

"What about?"

"He and Teddy are worried about Simon. They think that he's not being treated fairly."

Molly blew lightly across her tea to cool it.

"What did you say?"

"Pretty much what we agreed. That Simon seems to have some problems and that we must leave it to the professionals. I said that it was better not to get too involved but I'm not sure that he was really listening." He paused and looked up. "He asked if it would be okay to visit him in prison."

Molly put her mug down on the work surface and regarded him for a moment.

"Do you think that's a good idea?"

Jeremy shook his head.

"No, not really. But to be honest, Moll. We're not really in a position to say no. He's a bit too old for us to be telling him who he can and can't see. And even if we did say no, short of locking him in, we couldn't stop him going."

Molly sighed.

"I expect you're right. And at least he did ask. I wouldn't want him doing anything behind our backs."

"I could offer to go with him. Just to sort of keep an eye on things."

CHAPTER THIRTY-ONE

JEREMY DROVE THE car into the last parking space and pulled up the handbrake. He glanced unenthusiastically up at the tall, forbidding building. Built in the nineteenth century, the prison reminded him of a toy fort that he'd had as a child. His grandparents had bought it for him, and he had rarely played with it. There had been something chillingly uncompromising about the grey wooden walls and the little turrets. He had much preferred his toy farm.

Next to him, Carlos sat fidgeting with the zip on his parka. He looked sideways at Jeremy, his complexion pale and his big dark eyes, so like those of his mother, sorrowful.

"Do you think that they're looking after him all right? You know, like giving him proper food and everything?"

"Of course they are. They don't feed prisoners on bread and water anymore. Anyway, he's not there for punishment."

"Why is he there, then? Why can't he stay at home till his trial? Why does he have to be locked up? Why can't he have that bail thing?"

"Because murder is a serious crime. I'm not sure but I don't think that you can have bail if you're charged with a serious crime. Not if the authorities think that you might still be a danger to other people. And," he added, "he has admitted that he did it."

"But why? Why did he confess?"

"I don't know, Carlos. Perhaps..." he trailed off. Perhaps because it was true, he thought.

"I mean," Carlos continued, his words tumbling out. "He didn't have to. It's up to them to prove that he's guilty, isn't it? He didn't have to say anything. You're allowed to just stay silent." He thought for a moment. "He could have pleaded the fifth amendment," he added triumphantly.

"Not in England, Carlos. We haven't got a fifth amendment. But you're right, he does have a right to silence."

Carlos looked mutinous. Teddy's words echoed around his head. They had to be on Simon's side. They had to stand his corner.

"Yeah, well, he should have just gone 'no comment'. The police must have forced it out of him. They must have been oppressing him."

Jeremy hid a quick smile. Carlos's vocabulary was increasing at a rate of knots since his daily WhatsApp's with Teddy.

"I don't think that they're allowed to do that. There's rules about it. And he did have a solicitor present."

Carlos threw him a baleful look.

"I bet they did, though. I bet they made him say it. I bet the solicitor bloke didn't even stick up for him. And Simon didn't even know that Toby Carson bloke. He didn't even have a motive," he added.

"Only as far as we know. Anyway, be that as it may, the police don't have to prove a motive. It's not like those cop shows on the television. I mean, it helps, obviously, if they can find a motive, or at least some connection, but they don't have to."

"Well, what do they have to find then?"

"Evidence, I suppose."

"Do they still have to find evidence if he just says that he did it?"

"Honestly, Carlos, I just don't know."

"You don't really think he did do it though, do you? I mean, not really."

Jeremy suppressed a sigh.

"I don't know," he repeated. "Probably not."

Carlos was already upset, there was no point in making him feel even worse. Something was distressing him that was about more than just visiting Simon. But whatever it was, he clearly wasn't up to any sort of reasoned discussion. Was it, he wondered, a mistake to bring him here? But if he hadn't, he would have come anyway. At least this way he could keep an eye on him and get him back home safely. Upset teenagers had a habit of going walkabout. Anyway, who knew what the future would bring? The way things had been going lately, anything could happen. Nothing would surprise him anymore. He took the keys from the ignition and opened the car door. "Ready?"

Carlos nodded and the two of them climbed out of the car and walked slowly towards the visitors' entrance. Carlos stopped suddenly and turned to face Jeremy.

"Does he know we're coming?"

"Yes. We're on his approved list."

"So we don't need, like, a permit or something?"

His expression was suddenly hopeful. Jeremy shook his head.

"No. He's on remand. He hasn't been convicted. Carlos," he hesitated for a moment. "You don't have to do this, you know. I can go in on my own if you prefer."

For a moment Carlos remained silent, and then he shook his head. He had told Teddy that he would visit Simon and visit Simon was what he would do, although in truth he would rather be anywhere else than here today. He hadn't thought that he would mind it but there was something about the building that just sweated grim despair and for some reason that he couldn't quite place, it reminded him of his father. From the far reaches of the back of his mind, a small fuzzy memory of an overcast day emerged. He had been standing outside a building similar to this and inside, he knew, was his father. He must have been small because in his memory he was holding his mother's hand, and she had been crying.

Inside, the building was no less depressing. Even the small floral display and set of countryside prints just inside the entrance did nothing to improve matters. If anything, they made things worse. The contrast between normal domesticity and the great bundle of joyless humanity that lay just beyond the electronic door was stark. Handing over their phones to the officer behind the screen, they waited while the second officer keyed in the door code and then followed him along the long corridor towards the visiting room.

"Some of these older prisons," Jeremy said to Carlos, in an attempt to engage him and lighten the mood, "have been sold and turned into apartments and hotels. They're quite popular, apparently."

Carlos smiled slightly.

"I wouldn't fancy it myself."

"Me neither," agreed Jeremy.

"I mean," continued Carlos, "people have been hanged and that in some of them. I mean, what like, if your bedroom was in the hanging place?"

What indeed, thought Jeremy. It was a horrible thought. Turning left, they were ushered into a brightly lit room set with chairs and tables at which remand prisoners and their visitors sat talking in low voices. In one corner, two children sat on the floor playing with toys. In the opposite corner a prison officer sat, legs stretched out, pen in hand, and his newspaper neatly folded down to the crossword.

"There he is," said Jeremy, as Simon rose to greet them. He was looking a lot better than the last time they'd seen him. Clean and tidy, with combed hair and freshly washed clothes, he'd lost that air of human wreckage that had clung to him when he'd been led out to the police car. Even after he had left the house, it had hung in the atmosphere like a sad ghost looking for a resting place. They had listened in silence to the sound of the police car doors slamming and then sat down and watched a comedy show on the television, but none of them had found it funny and they had all gone to bed soon after. Even the cats had stayed in all night, curling up together in the fake fur cat dome that they usually despised.

They walked quickly over to him and sat down. Simon stared at them both, his brow slightly furrowed, as though he couldn't quite remember who they were. His voice, when he spoke, had a faltering edge to it, as though he was struggling to find the right words to use.

"Thank you for coming."

Jeremy swallowed. He hadn't expected such a formal address, and he felt oddly touched by it. He thought rapidly for a suitable response.

"Have you had many other visitors?" he asked, and then immediately regretted it. What an insensitive thing to say. Of course Simon didn't have many other visitors. He would be surprised if he'd had any. Former convicted murderers tended to be a little light on the social front.

Simon shook his head.

"No."

"Teddy sends her love." Carlos spoke quickly, as though anxious to get some words out, any words. "She asked to be remembered to you. She said to tell you that she's going to write to you."

Simon smiled suddenly, a wintery flash that whipped across his strained face.

"It was good of you both to bring me that food. I appreciated it." He paused and then said, turning to Jeremy, "The beach hut. I didn't break into it."

"Oh." Jeremy felt suddenly nonplussed. Being accused of breaking into a beach hut was surely the least of Simon's problems. "Do you know the owner, then?" It sounded lame, but what else was he supposed to say?

"Sort of. It's mine."

"Yours?"

Jeremy was astonished. Simon lived on his own in a small flat which, from the description that Teddy and Carlos had given, contained furniture which was at least thirty years old and there had been little by way of creature comforts, not even a television. Beach huts were hard to come by. From what he'd heard, there was a waiting list, and they weren't cheap. How on earth did Simon afford it on the wages he was paid from the Lodge?

"It belonged to my parents. They died when I was…" he hesitated. "When I was away. I was an only child. They left it to me. And the house."

"The house?" Jeremy was aware that he was starting to sound like a parrot.

"The house that I live in. It belongs to me. All of it," he added. "That's why I came back. To get my house. And my beach hut."

"So, the flat that you live in…"

Simon nodded.

"It's mine. So are all the others. I converted the house. It gave me something to do before I got a job."

Carlos stared at him, his mouth hanging slightly open.

"So, like, your mum and dad were loaded?"

Simon looked back at him, his expression blank.

"Loaded," he agreed.

"So, your flat, why was it, I mean you could have had… I mean, why didn't you have…" he trailed off, suddenly unsure how to continue. Jeremy knew what he had been about to say. If Simon was indeed loaded, why was his flat so outdated? Why didn't he have some of the trappings of modern life? Simon looked at him, considering for a moment.

"It's just stuff," he said.

Carlos leaned forward, his elbows resting on the table between them. From across the room, the prison officer put his pen down and looked up. My God, thought Jeremy, they must have some kind of radar. He smiled across at him and nudged Carlos gently back in his chair.

"Simon," Carlos sounded hoarse, his face suddenly flushing scarlet. "Why did you say that you did it? Why didn't you just say, like, nothing?"

Jeremy laid a warning hand on Carlos's arm.

"Carlos, perhaps Simon doesn't want to talk about it."

Simon regarded them both in silence for a moment, his eyes solemn.

"It's tough out there," he said simply.

CHAPTER THIRTY-TWO

IN THE SITTING room, Jeremy and Carlos sat and stared at the little fire as the flames flickered up and cast a soft glow across the room. It was too early in the year really to have lit it, but Molly had prepared it ready for their return and they were grateful for the cosy atmosphere that greeted them. The visit to the prison had been a sobering experience, not helped by the ugly little incident that they had witnessed on the way out. Jeremy shuddered again at the thought of the poor soul who, although he had sat quietly and been well-behaved when his family were visiting, had suddenly started screaming and crying when they left. He had lashed out at the prison officer, who had quickly summoned assistance. It had taken three officers to wrestle him to the floor and subdue him, and his shouted obscenities had trailed along behind him as they wrestled him from the room, echoing along the corridor and growing fainter as they dragged him towards his cell. Jeremy and Carlos had barely spoken a word on the way home, each trying to banish the mental images that they had been left with.

"Jeremy," Carlos turned away from the fire where he had been kneeling and tickling the cats who had parked themselves there as soon as Molly had lit it. "Did you get it? I mean, did you get, like, what he was saying?"

"Sort of."

"Why? What was he saying?" asked Molly, entering the room with a tray of mugs. She placed the tray on the coffee table and sat back in the armchair next to the fire.

"Carlos asked him why he confessed," said Jeremy. "And Simon said that it was better inside than out. Well," he amended, "not exactly that, but that's what he meant."

Aubrey and Vincent both raised their heads and stared. Better inside than out? Simon obviously had even more problems than they'd thought. Nothing was better than being free. And nothing was worse than being locked up. Better to be outside and starving than in prison with a full stomach. They should know, they'd both been banged up in their time.

As if echoing their thoughts, Carlos said,

"I don't get it. How can being in prison be better that being outside. And free," he added.

"I think that's the problem, Carlos. If Simon was outside, he'd be free, that's true, but free to do what? All he had was his job at the Lodge and once the owner found out about his police record, he would almost certainly have lost even that."

Carlos thought for a moment, turning this over in his mind.

"Yeah, all right, but he didn't even need to work. I mean, like he's got all those flats and everything."

Molly frowned.

"What flats?"

Jeremy smiled.

"It appears that Simon is a man of means. He seems to have inherited a packet from his parents. He owns all the flats in the house that he lives in, plus a shedload or two of money. Oh, and the beach hut that he was sleeping in is also his."

"That's another thing," said Carlos, tickling Vincent's foot. "If he's got all that money, why hasn't he got, like, a big telly and... and computers and sound systems and that?"

"Like he said, Carlos. It's just stuff. Maybe he's not interested in those sorts of things."

Carlos looked doubtful.

"Anyway, why did he even work at the Lodge?" he repeated. "He's loaded. He could do anything he wanted to."

"Working isn't just about money," said Jeremy. "Try and imagine being Simon. If he wasn't working, what would he do with himself? He doesn't seem to have any friends. He lives alone in that little flat. He would be just staring at the same four walls all day. At least going to the Lodge every morning gave him something to do, gave him some structure to the day."

Carlos thought for a moment.

"He could have joined a club or something like that. He could have gone travelling."

"Probably not travelling," Molly pointed out. "At least, not to anywhere that requires a visa."

"Why not?"

"Some countries don't like people with prison records visiting their country."

Carlos thought for a moment. He and his mother hadn't had permission to live and work in England, but that hadn't stopped them. Although, he reflected, nothing much had ever stopped his mother once she decided on something.

"Well," he continued, "he could have got a girlfriend then. He could have done that on-line dating stuff. I mean, he's quite old and that but he's not ugly or anything."

"He'd still have to tell her at some point, though, wouldn't he?" said Jeremy.

Carlos nodded, his expression glum.

"I suspect," said Molly, her tone gentle, "that Simon doesn't find it very easy to make friends."

Jeremy nodded in agreement.

"I think that's probably true. At least when he's inside he's got people to talk to. And he doesn't have to keep explaining himself."

"What do you mean?" Carlos looked puzzled.

"Well, when you make new friends, they usually ask you something about yourself. Where you went to school or where you work, whether you have any friends in common, that kind of thing. I bet that you know all sorts of things about Teddy. And Casper."

Although, he thought privately, from the little that he knew about Casper, it was almost certainly more than enough. From his brief acquaintance with him when they had been living at Fallowfield, he was of the opinion that Casper was a boy who would go far. Possibly in politics. He continued.

"What could Simon say if someone started asking him questions? How could he explain where he'd been for the last however many years? If he lied, he might get found out, and if he told the truth, well..."

Carlos nodded; his expression thoughtful.

"I s'pose so."

Aubrey looked up at him. Carlos, of all people, would understand that. He never told people how his mother had died and she had been the victim rather than the perpetrator.

Jeremy continued.

"All the inmates are in there because they've been found guilty of committing a crime or they're on remand, like Simon, because they've been accused of committing a crime. It's the thing that they've all got in common. Maybe Simon just finds that easier."

"But that doesn't mean that he should be locked up for something that he didn't do."

Carlos folded his arms and sat back, looking, Jeremy thought, suddenly very much like his mother. She had that same belligerent air, the difference being that she had worn it for most of the time, it being her default demeanour and especially when it came to protecting Carlos.

"I agree." said Jeremy, his tone placatory. "Nobody should be locked up for something that they didn't do, but there'll be time before his trial to change his mind. It's best not to worry about it just yet."

Carlos stood up.

"I'm going to go and tell Teddy about it."

Molly and Jeremy watched as he left the room and listened as he raced up the stairs, his feet pounding on the treads, clearly taking them two at a time.

"Let's hope that she doesn't start winding him up about everything," said Molly. "I mean, I like her very much and in most respects she's been very good for Carlos. But she is a little…"

"Over-active in the imagination department?" suggested Jeremy.

"Over-active in the imagination department," agreed Molly. "So, how was your day?"

"Pretty much the same as usual. Still catching up on the paperwork and fire-fighting the odd crisis. Oh, and Buster has gone missing."

Aubrey and Vincent sat up, suddenly alert.

"Gordon was in my office today, almost in tears. Buster got out yesterday morning, and he hasn't been seen since."

CHAPTER THIRTY-THREE

AUBREY AND VINCENT jumped the low wall that divided the resident's rooms from the gardens and made their way across the lawn towards what had once been a small orchard but was now a patch of long grass with two remaining apple trees and an elderly pear tree that hung drunkenly to one side. They came to a halt and sat down.

"Any ideas?"

Aubrey shook his head.

"We've searched every inch of the Lodge and the grounds. And all the carers have checked the cupboards and everything." Well, not quite all the carers, he reflected. Maxine hadn't lifted a finger. "He seems to have just vanished into thin air."

"He must be somewhere. He can't have just disappeared. He might be lying injured somewhere."

"No, we would have heard him."

"Not if he was out cold."

"What about searching outside the grounds?"

"He's got a collar now. If he's gone outside, somebody would have spotted him running around. He's not exactly easy to miss."

They regarded each other in silence, neither being willing to put into words what they were both thinking. At last, shaking his head, Vincent said,

"He would never have gone quietly."

"They might have given him something to make him quiet."

An image of the manically energetic golden ball of energy that was Buster, innocently running towards a stranger and trustingly taking what was offered, sprang before him. He felt his heart squeeze and caught his breath.

Vincent raised his head and looked towards the wasteland beyond the orchard.

"We haven't been over there yet."

Aubrey followed his gaze and moved forwards.

"Come on, it's worth a try."

THE BLACKBERRIES FROM the brambles were over now, the small wizened remains clinging to the branches. The two cats moved slowly, picking their way through the undergrowth, eyes scanning to right and left, and ears pricked. In spite of the clear blue sky, the weather was growing colder, the chill of autumn ruffling the edges of their fur. From the housing estate the gently rhythmic shucking noise of a lawn mower filtered across to them as it made the last cut of the season.

"I don't really like it here now," Aubrey admitted to Vincent. "It feels sort of, I don't know… I just don't like it," he repeated.

Vincent nodded.

"Me neither. Not since they found the body. Tell you what, let's split up. You take that half and I'll take this. That way we'll get it done in half the time and then we can get out of here."

"What shall we do if we find him?"

"That depends," said Vincent gravely.

Aubrey looked at him without speaking and then veered off towards his left. Jumping across the old stained mattress that the two men who had discovered Toby Carson's body abandoned, he pushed his way through the tangle of undergrowth, finally coming to a halt in front of the ruined old house. It had clearly once been quite magnificent, but those days had long gone. Now there were jackdaws nesting in the chimneys and ivy pushing its long thin tendrils through the window frames and smothering any panes of glass that were left. Most of them had been broken by years of school children throwing stones at them. The great wide entrance, with its sweeping stone steps, was topped by a big oak door, the polish long since worn away and the brass door furniture removed by light-fingered locals. Next to it, the long heavy iron bell-pull hung uselessly. Thomas had worked here when he was younger, he knew. It was where they had looked after people or something. Where, he wondered, had all the people gone? Had they waited until the last one had died before finally closing the door for the final time?

Leaping on to a window sill, he stared inside into what had clearly been some kind of sitting room. The once gleaming parquet flooring was dull and scuffed and the chairs and sofas stood where they had been left, covered in torn and faded fabric, with stuffing bulging out of the backs and sides where mice had nibbled and nested in them. To the right, a smashed china cabinet lay on its back, empty, with its doors ripped off. Across every surface lay a thick layer of grime and dust.

He jumped down again and made his way round the side of the building. Towards the rear, a window hung drunkenly from its hinges, its bottom pane missing. He crept towards it and peered through. Inside, the walls were covered with flat cream and green coloured tiles and there was no furniture, only what looked like a long trestle which was placed in the centre of the room with a length of strip lighting positioned above it. He backed away. He didn't like that room. In fact, he didn't like the whole house. It wasn't just that it was empty. He'd explored lots of empty properties in his time, especially when he'd lived on the street and had been seeking safe places to sleep. But none of them had the unsettling, unhappy atmosphere of this place. He thought for a moment. If Buster had found his way in there, then surely he could have found his way back out. Unless he'd somehow injured himself. He tipped his head to one side. He really didn't want to go in there on his own. He'd go back and fetch Vincent.

He turned and began making his way back to where he had left him, his normally cheerful mood damped down by the seeping misery of the house that seemed to have got right into his fur and was sticking to him. Not even the freshness of the day could lighten it. Veering to his left, he began to skirt around a large bush, but then stopped. Now that he was closer, he could see that the bush was actually some kind of structure, something that stuck up in the air and was covered by ivy climbing across it. Intrigued, he walked up to it and peered more closely. The thing that was sticking up was some kind of brick structure choked with plants, with a small roof from which a rusted chain dangled loosely from the centre. He stared at it for a moment, confused, and then realised suddenly what he was looking at. At Fallowfield, one of the cottages had installed an ornamental well in the front garden. And that was what he was looking at now, although there was nothing ornamental about this one. The Fallowfield well had been painted red and white with flowers growing round it with a little bucket hanging from the central chain. This one was gloomy, with missing tiles on the roof, and those that remained were cracked and spattered with lichen. The bucket that should have hung from the chain was had long gone.

He moved towards it slowly, feeling his way carefully. The boards that had covered the well opening had rotted away years ago and it would be easy to fall down. Bracing himself against the side, paws planted firmly on the ground, he leaned over and peered down the brick lined walls. Looking back up at him, his little golden back wedged against a brick shelf, was Buster.

AUBREY AND VINCENT watched as Buster drank from his water bowl, his pink tongue flicking in and out and working at twice its normal speed. He was clearly dehydrated.

"Poor little lad," said Vincent.

Aubrey agreed. Poor little lad, indeed. Racing back to the Lodge, their hearts in their mouths, they had made straight for the kitchen, where Carlos was writing his notes for the next day. They had burst in through the open fire door, howling at the top of their voices. Vincent had jumped on to the work surface and tried to knock Carlos's pen away, while Aubrey had twisted himself up into a half-hoop to get Carlos's attention. Carlos had risen from the stool without a word and followed them across the gardens and out into the waste land at the back, pausing only to grab his mobile as he went.

Hauled out by the big burly firemen, Buster had looked bedraggled and pathetic, his golden fur matted and his normally bright eyes dulled. For once his little body had remained perfectly still as he was carried back to Gordon's cottage.

"Do you think he's injured?" asked Aubrey.

Vincent shook his head.

"He's eating all right. Anyway, Gordon's called the vet to give him the once over."

"I wonder how he came to be down there?"

"Exploring, I expect, and fell down."

"You don't think that anybody, well, you know…"

"No, I don't think so. He was probably chasing rabbits or something and just tumbled in."

They both looked up at the sound of the door knocker rattling. Ushering Molly and Carlos into the room, Gordon leaned over and ruffled Buster's head. Molly glanced at Aubrey and Vincent, her expression stern.

"What are you two doing in here?"

"They're okay. Just visiting." Gordon smiled. "They quite often call in. And if it wasn't for them…" he trailed off. "I'll stick the kettle on."

"Is he all right?" Carlos spoke quietly. "I mean, he's not really hurt or anything?"

Gordon shook his head.

"Not that I can see. Lucky that he landed on the shelf, though. It's a twelve-foot drop down there."

Carlos frowned.

"Why did it have a shelf?"

Gordon reached for the china teapot.

"Lots of them did. Shelves and a ladder. In case anyone fell down."

"Did you know that the well was there?" asked Molly.

Gordon nodded.

"I haven't seen it but I've heard about it. It should have been filled in years ago. They took away the ladder to stop anyone trying to climb down, but that was about all they did."

Molly reached out for the mug of tea he handed her and looped her fingers around it.

"There was something else down the well," said Gordon. "The fireman told me. When they got Buster out, he shone his torch around a bit, just to make sure that there was nothing else down there, and there it was. He brought it back up with him."

Carlos looked up from where he was stroking Buster.

"What was it?"

"A marble clock. I recognised it. It used to be in George's room. I saw it when I was fixing the camera in there."

Molly took a sip of her hot tea.

"I wonder how it got down the well?"

"Perhaps George threw it away?" Carlos suggested.

Molly shook her head.

"No, even when he came to us, he couldn't walk far. He would never have made it over to the back there. Anyway, what would be the point? If he'd wanted to get rid of it, he would have just asked a member of staff to take it away. But he liked that clock, it was still in his room after he died. When Toby Carson cleared his belongings, it was one of the things that he left. I thought that he'd forgotten it and I kept meaning to ring him about it, and then I forgot about it myself. Where is it now?"

"Over there." Gordon nodded towards the kitchen window sill where George's clock sat, squat and uncompromisingly heavy.

Molly sighed.

"I don't know what we're supposed to do with it. Take it to a charity shop, I suppose. But it looks as if it weighs a ton."

"If nobody else wants it," said Gordon, "I'll have it. I could do with a decent timekeeper."

CHAPTER THIRTY-FOUR

MOLLY SAT DOWN at her desk and ran a hand through her hair.

"God, I'm tired."

From the small sofa in the window where he lay stretched out, scrolling through his phone and his long legs hanging over the end, Carlos observed her for a moment.

"Why don't you take a few days off?"

"Carlos, how can I?" She pulled a face at him. "What with Thomas still being off and everything." She looked down at the papers on her desk and switched her computer on. "Shan't be long and then we can go home."

From the top of the big metal filing cabinet where he normally parked himself when he was in Molly's office, Aubrey rolled on to his back and stared up at the ceiling. He liked this time of day. There was something peaceful about him and Carlos wandering down to Molly's office to wait for her when she was working late. Vincent sometimes joined them and sometimes not. He wondered where he was now. Being fed digestive biscuits by one of the residents probably, or visiting Buster. He thought affectionately about the little dog. He had given them all a terrible fright, but being young and healthy, he had soon got over his ordeal and was bouncing around again with his usual frenetic energy. But Molly, he thought, looked less well. The continued strain of managing the Lodge on her own was beginning to tell and matters had taken a turn for the worse in the last few days with a number of the residents being struck down with some mystery virus which had doubled the work of the carers, two of whom had gone down with the virus themselves. He watched as she picked up a pen and began scribbling in a small notebook before laying it aside and turning back to her monitor. Carlos leaned more closely over his mobile and smiled. He looked up again and turned to Molly.

"Teddy sends her love."

Molly raised her head.

"That's nice. Send mine back to her. Tell her we're all looking forward to seeing her again." She looked back down again at her screen and frowned. "Carlos, do you know how to work this thing? I need to get to grips with it or there's no point having it." She clicked the mouse on the image in front of her. "It's saying that it's full but I don't know how to clear it. Do you think that it does it automatically?"

Carlos rolled on to his side and tipped himself off the sofa. Leaning over her shoulder, he looked down at the screen. From the top of the filing cabinet, Aubrey shifted on to his stomach and watched. Across the screen danced a set of images, each showing different areas of the Lodge. Carlos pointed to a small side bar.

"There, look. It tells you how much storage you've got and lets you set how often you want stuff deleted. It looks like it's set at thirty days. Do you want to keep stuff that long?"

Molly shook her head.

"No, I don't think so. How long do you think?"

Carlos thought for a moment.

"A week?"

"Okay, a week," Molly agreed. "Are all the cameras working now, then?"

Carlos swiped the images to the right and nodded.

"It looks like it. Do you want me to go through stuff to see if there's anything worth saving while you finish your paperwork? Then I can re-set it."

"Good idea. Do you want the mouse?"

Carlos shook his head and watched as Molly pulled the cable from her laptop and handed it to him. Settling himself back on the sofa, he hunched over and began scrolling through the images. For several minutes they worked quietly, and then Molly looked up.

"Anything?"

"Just shots of the residents in their rooms and the corridors and that." He grinned suddenly. "Oh, and one of Maxine smoking in Peter's room."

Molly flung her pen down irritably.

"We're going to have to do something about her." She sighed and picked her pen up again. "The trouble is finding someone to replace her Especially at the moment with this damned flu doing the rounds."

Opening one eye from where he had just been nodding off, Aubrey became aware of a sudden tension in the room. He sat up, alarmed.

"Molly," Carlos's voice was suddenly very quiet. "I think that you'd better look at this."

Jumping from the top of the filing cupboard, Aubrey joined Carlos as he dragged a chair across the room and placed the laptop back on Molly's desk. Wordlessly, Carlos touched the screen. Together, the three of them watched as the image slowly emerged. They held their breath as a door quietly opened and a man entered a dimly lit room that was empty of possessions other than a big marble clock that sat on a shelf.

Molly looked up at Carlos.

"But that's George's room."

With his back to the camera, the man crossed the room and sat down on the bed. Turning, Toby Carson looked about him, seemingly unaware of the camera fixed high up on the opposite wall. He leaned back and rested on his elbows, a bored expression on his face.

"What's he doing?" Molly sounded bewildered. "Why has he gone into George's room? It's all been cleared out."

She caught her breath as the door opened again and a second man entered. They watched silently as Thomas stood perfectly still on the threshold. Under his arm he carried a cardboard folder. She turned wordlessly to Carlos, who leaned forward and touched the screen. The sound of Toby Carson's voice suddenly surrounded them.

"What is it that you want? Don't think that I'm paying any more rent for this room, because I'm not. I'll pay up until the end of last week, but that's it. And you'll have to wait until the estate's settled."

Thomas remained where he was. His face looked grey and drawn and he licked his lips, a nervous flick that barely wet the skin. The cardigan with the football buttons that he habitually wore hung loose on him.

"I don't understand," said Molly. "If there's a problem with George's account, then we'd sort it in the usual way. What are they doing in that room?"

Thomas turned to one side and moved over to the far side of the room. He stared for a moment at the big marble clock and then turned to face the other man.

"It's not the fees," he said simply.

"Well, what is it then?"

Toby Carson sounded irritable; his voice sharp.

"It's George's will."

"What about George's will? What's it got to do with you, anyway?"

From beneath his arm, Thomas drew out the cardboard folder.

"George was a wealthy man. You told Molly that George left you everything."

"Yes, so what? What's it got to do with you?" he repeated.

"He didn't though, did he?"

As Molly, Carlos and Aubrey watched, Toby Carson's face visibly tightened and he sat up straighter.

"Didn't what?"

"Make a will leaving everything to you."

"Of course he did. I was his brother." His tone sounded slightly less strident now, a note of uncertainty creeping into his voice.

Thomas shook his head.

"No," he said, simply. "He didn't."

For several seconds neither man spoke. In the distance, the sound of Gordon calling Buster filtered into the room.

"I haven't got time for all this. What is it that you want?" Toby Carson half rose and then sat down again. He leaned forward, clasping his hands together. "What's this all about?"

Without speaking, Thomas flipped open the cardboard folder that he was carrying and withdrew the contents. Holding up a closely written document, he looked directly at the other man.

"This is George's will. All the residents place copies of their important documents with me, for safekeeping. According to this will, George Carson left the bulk of his estate to animal charities."

"He made a later will."

Aubrey watched with interest as Toby Carson's face reddened. He was, he thought, beginning to lose his nerve. Thomas shook his head.

"No," he said simply. "He didn't. If he had, he would have lodged a copy with me. This," he tapped the document, "is his last will and you are not mentioned in it at all. But, if you want to contest it, then obviously you're free to do so."

Toby Carson stood up. He was much taller than Thomas and Thomas instinctively took a step backwards, almost tripping over in his hurry to move away.

"I don't need to contest it," he snapped. "George's will is genuine. I am his heir."

"All right. Have it your own way. I will, of course, take this to the police."

Thomas shrugged and moved towards the door but was stopped by the other man barring his way.

"What is it that you want" he repeated.

"The thing is, Mr. Carson," Thomas spoke slowly. He sounded, thought Aubrey, as though he had rehearsed what he was going to say. He could hear the strain in his voice as he forced the words out. "I've got a bit of a problem at the moment." He looked suddenly even more diminished, a small shambling man, his eyes darting this way and that and his hand trembling slightly. He was not at all like the cheerful, bumbling, slightly over-weight Thomas that they were used to. "To be honest, it's a very big problem. One that you could help me with."

"What sort of problem?"

Toby Carson tipped his head on one side and considered the older man, his eyes narrowed. The charismatic bonhomie of the former star of sofa ads was nowhere to be seen.

"Money," said Thomas, his tone flat. "I owe money. A lot. I might lose my house. I'm desperate."

"Borrow it from the bank, like other people do."

"I already have," said Thomas simply.

"So what do you expect me to do about it?"

We could come to an… an arrangement."

"How much?"

Thomas ran his tongue over his lips.

"A hundred thousand?"

Toby Carson laughed suddenly, a horrible rasping noise that made Aubrey, Carlos, and Molly recoil instinctively from the screen.

"Why not? Your brother was rich. And you haven't even sold his house yet."

"You must be joking. You seriously think that I'm going to let a washed-out old bloke like you blackmail me? And what's to stop you coming back and asking for more? Anyway, I'm only taking what's rightfully mine."

Suddenly he lunged forward and grabbed the document from Thomas with one hand while gripping him round the throat with the other. Thomas choked and spluttered and tried to push him away, but the younger man was stronger. Toby Carson suddenly let go and pushed him with a snort of laughter. Thomas staggered backwards, arms flailing as he hit the wall and slid down. The other man looked at him with contempt.

"Don't bother trying that on me again. You're wasting your time. Don't think I'm scared of the likes of you; I've been frightened by experts. Get lost, you pathetic little excuse for a man. Go back to your cocoa and geriatrics."

He stuffed the document in his jacket pocket and turned to go. Thomas stood up slowly and rubbed the back of his head where he had hit the wall. And then, a loud wail of despair erupting from him, he turned and closed his hands on the clock. Moving swiftly forward behind the other man, he grasped the clock with both hands and brought it down with a sickening thud.

CHAPTER THIRTY-FIVE

MOLLY, CARLOS AND AUBREY watched in appalled silence as Toby Carson sank to the floor, knees folding as the blood slowly seeped from the back of his head, a sticky dark mass, just visible as it soaked into the deep blue carpet. For a moment, Thomas stood immobile, the clock still in his hands. Then, dropping the clock on the bed, he crossed the room and left it.

"What…"

The words had hardly left Molly's mouth before the door opened again and Thomas returned, this time pushing a wheelchair with what looked like a bucket filled with cleaning products stacked on top of it. Turning, he locked the door behind him. Throwing the cleaning products to the floor, he felt in the dead man's pockets and retrieved the will. Then, standing behind him, he clasped his hands around his chest. Slowly, clearly with effort, he began to drag him towards the wheelchair. Pausing to gather his breath, he hauled him up and into the seat, tucking in his arms before pulling the thin coverlet from the bed and draping it across him. He stared down at him for a moment, his face expressionless, before reaching for the clock and placing it in the dead man's lap. Sitting down in the small armchair, he regarded the wheelchair and its contents before dropping his head in his hands. The sound of his crying filled Molly's office, harsh brittle sobs that were painful to hear.

Instinctively, Molly began stroking Aubrey's head as if seeking comfort. He could feel the faint tremble in her fingers.

She looked at Carlos, her eyes dark. He looked back at her, his face blank. Neither of them spoke. In the room, Thomas stood up and blew his nose on a large white handkerchief. Stuffing the handkerchief back in his pocket, he picked up the bucket and crossed to the small bathroom. As they watched, he re-emerged and then knelt and began to scrub the carpet, pausing occasionally to raise his head and look about him as though he were afraid that he was being watched. Straightening up, he grasped the handles of the wheelchair and wheeled it towards the door. Locking the door behind him again, he left the room.

"Where's he going?" Even to his own ears, Carlos's voice sounded small and frightened. He cleared his throat. "He can't have wheeled him through the building, somebody would see him. One of the residents or carers."

Molly leaned forward and touched the screen. Flickering into view came Thomas, wheeling his dreadful cargo towards the end of the corridor, shoulders hunched with the effort. At the end, he stopped and pushed the button for the staff lift.

"Of course," she said. "The staff lift. It runs straight down to the back entrance that leads on to the gardens. It's how, well, when a resident dies, they're taken out of the building. Rather than upsetting the other residents by wheeling them all through the Lodge and out of the main entrance, we take them down privately. There's a small parking space there right by the exit. It's where the private ambulance takes them away," she added.

"What are we doing to do?"

Carlos looked at Molly, his face white with shock.

Molly put her elbows on her desk and rested her forehead in her hands for a moment. She looked up again and tried to smile, an unconvincing stretch of the mouth that did little to reassure either Carlos or Aubrey. The room felt cold and cheerless, the companionable atmosphere of earlier had evaporated to be replaced with a sense of dread and foreboding.

"Well, obviously we're going to have to tell the police…" she faltered and cleared her throat. "But I think that we should go home first and ring them from there."

What she really meant, thought Aubrey, was that they all wanted to get away from the Lodge.

"Jeremy will want to know, too," she added.

At the mention of Jeremy's name, a comforting sense of normality began to seep back into the room. While they were watching the camera footage, time and reality had been suspended and they had all three of them been caught in a frozen surreal nightmare in which they had watched a man being killed. With the prospect of home and Jeremy, the world slowly tipped the right way up again. Carlos's shoulders visibly relaxed.

"We'll have to take my laptop home with us. We'll need to keep it secure." Molly stood up and looked down at Carlos and this time her smile looked more natural.

JEREMY CAME BACK from showing the police officers out. He stood for a moment with his hands in his pockets and regarded them, his expression solemn.

"I hope that you can manage without your laptop. I don't think that you're going to get it back for a day or two."

Molly nodded.

"I can use one of the others." She paused. "They didn't say much."

"I'm not sure that there was much to be said. I think the looks on their faces said it all."

Aubrey agreed. The two burly police officers had sat open-mouthed as Molly ran the footage for them. Nobody had said a word.

"I guess that they'll make copies," said Jeremy. He ran his hand through his hair. "It seems hardly credible. I mean Thomas, of all people... I've only met him a couple of times, but he seemed like such a gentle bloke. The last person to commit an act of violence."

Carlos turned to Molly.

"Do you feel sorry for him?"

Molly thought for a moment.

"No." She hesitated. "Well, sort of, yes, I suppose that I do in a way."

Carlos nodded.

"I do, too. Thomas is all right. And that Toby Carson bloke, he was, like, a horrible person and he was cheating and trying to steal George's money and that. And anyway," he added, "Thomas didn't really mean to kill him. He was just, like, upset."

"That doesn't make it all right, Carlos." Jeremy spoke gently. For all his height and attempted sophistication, Carlos, he knew, hadn't quite left the one-dimensional world of teenaged perspective.

Carlos looked away.

"I suppose so," he said, but without conviction.

"I just can't connect the Thomas that we know with the one that committed that dreadful act. It's like two different people." said Molly. "It just seems unreal."

Aubrey, from his comfortable position on Molly's lap, agreed. When there had been a spate of cat food thefts in their old neighbourhood, he had been absolutely astonished when Lionel had been unmasked as the culprit. Lionel was such a kindly old fellow. If it had been Carstairs, the soppy nerk that lived next door, he wouldn't have been at all surprised. In his opinion, Carstairs eyes had always been just a little too close together. But Lionel... although, when he thought about it afterwards, Lionel did have a belly on him the size of a small greenhouse.

Molly continued.

"It's obvious from the footage that Thomas was at the end of his tether and I guess desperate people do desperate things. But what I really don't understand is why he was in such a dreadful need of money. I mean, he earns a decent salary and his wife does too, I think, she's some sort of senior administrator with the local council. And it's not as if he's got extravagant tastes. They just live in an ordinary house."

"He gambles," said Carlos flatly.

"He what?" Molly stared at him. "What do you mean, he gambles? Gambles on what?"

"Online. He gambles online. Virtual casinos and that."

"How do you know?"

"Maxine told me. She saw it on his computer screen when she was in his office one day."

Molly's mouth tightened.

"She would. She shouldn't have been in his office. But why didn't you tell me about it?"

"Well, it's not against the law or anything," Carlos protested. "And it would have been, like, telling tales."

"I suppose so." Molly sounded reluctant. "But if we'd known how bad it was, we might have been able to help him."

"I doubt it," said Jeremy. "If he wanted a hundred grand to get himself out of a hole, it sounds like he needs more than a sympathetic ear and a nice cup of tea. Anyway, be that as it may, I suppose that there's one positive outcome from all this."

"What?" said Carlos.

"Simon's off the hook."

"You mean, like, they'll let him go and that?"

"Well, they can't really keep him now."

"I'll call Teddy."

Molly and Jeremy watched as he unfolded his long legs and leapt from the sofa. Molly sighed.

"I swear he gets taller every day."

Jeremy nodded.

"When he first came to us, he was about up to my shoulder. Now he looks me in the eye."

They both fell silent for a moment and then Molly said,

"When do you think that Simon will be released?" asked Molly.

"Pretty soon, I should think. I expect that there's paper work and so on to complete first but given what's on the video evidence there aren't any grounds for keeping him locked up. There is, of course, the awkward little matter of his confession but I shouldn't think that will count for much now."

"I wonder what will happen to him? The owner of the Lodge won't take him back, I'm pretty sure of that. And I suppose I've got to tell her about Thomas now. God knows what's going to happen."

"Don't think about that tonight, Moll. You've had more than enough for one day. Tomorrow will be soon enough. One night won't hurt and everything will look different in the morning, I promise."

Molly pulled a face.

"I doubt it."

Aubrey glanced up at her strained expression and felt a flicker of anxiety. Molly was usually so positive and cheerful, but Jeremy was right. She'd had more than enough. If she wasn't careful, she'd be ill.

"When they release Simon," she continued, "do you think that they'll just let him go straight back home?"

"Well, I don't think that they can stop him, but I hope he gets some help. He's clearly a troubled man." Jeremy sighed. "And it doesn't help that he lives alone. I'm not sure how he'll cope without even a job to go to. I hate to think of him there, all on his own."

Molly held her breath for a moment and waited for what she feared was coming next. Jeremy stood up.

"Fancy a glass of wine?"

Molly nodded and exhaled slowly. Jeremy might on occasion be too soft-hearted for his own good, but his home and family would always come first. He would never do anything to put them at risk. However sorry he might feel for Simon, the unpalatable truth was that he had a conviction for murder and that was a step too far, even for Jeremy. She wondered suddenly what the circumstances surrounding his conviction had been. When the police had told her, they had divulged very little, only that he had been involved in a post office robbery and that a man had been shot. With everything else that had been happening, she hadn't really thought beyond the basic facts. But, really, the story was difficult to reconcile with the Simon that she had known at the Lodge. Her experience of him had always been positive. Polite, slightly reserved, good at his job, he had never given cause for complaint and he was completely reliable. Of all the staff, he was about the only one who had never phoned in sick. And he'd always been brilliant about making special birthday teas for the residents, taking special care to check the spelling before he iced their name on the cake. She just couldn't reconcile it in her mind with a shooting in a post office. But then, neither could she really believe what Thomas had done, even though she had seen it with her own eyes. She smiled suddenly. If it was a school essay she could just write 'then I woke up and it was all a dream.' If only.

She sighed and reached for her mobile as the low melodic air of its ring tone filtered into the room. Please God, not more trouble at the Lodge. She'd left Martha in charge and told her to ring in the event of an emergency, but right now, she didn't even have the energy to get out of the chair, let alone drive back to the Lodge. She listened for a moment and then looked up as Jeremy came in bearing two glasses of wine.

"It's Ruth, Thomas's wife," she said, covering the handset. "He's in hospital."

Jeremy put the glasses down on the coffee table and stared at her.

"Why? What's happened?"

"The police turned up at his house and started questioning him. They must have gone straight there after leaving here. Thomas has had a heart attack."

CHAPTER THIRTY-SIX

MOLLY SLIPPED THE parking ticket into her pocket and made her way past the parked ambulances and clusters of smokers towards the brightly lit entrance. As she approached, the doors slid silently apart. She walked towards the reception desk and looked into the face of the bored-looking receptionist.

"I'm looking for the Bluebell Ward, Room 3A". She smiled slightly apologetically as she said it, although why she felt the need to propitiate the woman, she had no idea.

The receptionist stared; her expression openly hostile. Molly stared back. Surely the news about Thomas couldn't have spread that quickly?

"Through there," she said at last. "Follow the signs."

Without thanking her, Molly turned on her heel and edged her way round the trolley selling second-hand books and pushed open the swing door. The hospital corridor was long and over-lit, the bright prints placed at regular intervals appearing incongruous against the scurry of trolleys and equipment being wheeled past. A faint antiseptic smell hung on the air and made Molly feel slightly sick. It brought back a faint memory, but of what she wasn't sure. Perhaps it was when her father had been admitted to hospital with terrifying stomach pains and she and her brother and mother had stood about in frightened little clumps, wanting to know more but fearing the worst. She had still been at school then and the idea of anybody that she actually knew dying, let alone her father, had been completely incomprehensible to her. The terrifying pains had turned out to be a trapped gall stone but for weeks she had found herself staring at him when she thought that he wasn't looking, as though by force of will she could keep him safe. In much the same way, she suddenly realised, that Carlos had stared at her and Jeremy when he first came to live with them.

She stood to one side to let a porter with a wheeled trolley go past, the elderly occupant raising faded eyes in thanks, his papery hands, knotted with thick blue veins, clutching the thin blanket covering him. Gripping the carrier bag that she was holding more tightly to her body, she moved forward. Thomas must know by now that it was she who had informed the police, but she had to face him sometime.

She felt her stomach flip over at the prospect, but she was determined to go through with it, even though both Jeremy and Carlos had tried to persuade her otherwise. They had suggested that she write a note or send a card, but that would have been cowardly. She had to see him, to look him in the eye. It was, as her father would have said, the right thing to do. It was what he had said when she and her brother, holding hands, had gone and confessed to their neighbour that while racing a home-made go kart, they had crashed into his car and scratched the left wing.

She drew in her breath, closed her eyes, and compressed her lips. She was getting much the same sickening, stomach-churning feeling that she had experienced when facing their irate neighbour all those years ago, but she had to do this. She and Thomas had worked together, but they had been more than colleagues, they had been friends. She had bought him a little birthday present for his birthday last month and she had visited him when he was off sick. She couldn't just desert him now, even though he had done this dreadful thing.

She opened her eyes again as a familiar voice spoke in her ear.

"Are you all right, Molly?"

She looked up into Gordon's concerned face.

"Oh, Gordon. Yes, I'm fine. How is he?"

"Not too bad, considering. I came over as soon as I heard."

Molly started to speak and then hesitated. What exactly had Gordon heard? Did he know about the Toby Carson business? Well, if he didn't, he'd find out soon enough. But not from her.

Gordon glanced out of the window and began buttoning up his raincoat.

"I'd better be getting back. It's bin day tomorrow."

She watched as he walked off down the corridor towards the exit. It had been good of him to visit. Just ahead of her lay the sign for the Bluebell Ward.

QUIETLY OPENING THE door, she peered round it. Lying slightly propped up on his pillows and hooked to a monitor lay Thomas, his face grey and his eyes tired. His hair stood up in little grey tufts around his head, increasing the air of vulnerability hanging over him. He looked like an ageing child. She felt her heart give a slight squeeze. Creeping over, she put the carrier bag on the top of the small bedside locker, next to a jug of stale looking water.

She stared down at him for a moment.

"I've just seen Gordon. It was nice of him to come."

Thomas remained silent. The elephant in the room was growing larger by the second. She had to say something or she might as well have not come. She drew a deep breath.

"I'm sorry," she whispered. "I had to do it. Please try and understand."

Thomas regarded her for a moment, his face expressionless. He swallowed before speaking, as though giving himself time to find the words.

"It's all right," he said at last. He sighed. "I'm almost glad in a way. At least it's over." He stared back at her; his eyes blank. "At least I won't be jumping out of my skin every time the door goes."

Molly delved into the carrier bag and pulled out a large bag of toffees and some fishing magazines.

"I brought these for you," she said and then hesitated. What a stupid thing to say. Of course she'd brought them for him. She wasn't going to sit down and scoff the toffees while reading the magazines. She didn't even like fishing.

The expression on Thomas's face remained passive.

"Thank you," he said. "That's very thoughtful."

She pulled up the small plastic chair and sat down. She regarded him for a moment.

"Are you really up to visitors?"

"Oh yes. As heart attacks go, this one was Sunday league rather than Premier. Like everything else I do," he added bitterly.

From outside, the sound of heavy machinery and the occasional shout carried on the wind.

"They're building a new block," said Thomas.

"Right," said Molly. There didn't seem to be anything to say to that. She hesitated for a moment, and then ploughed on. "Thomas, you do understand, don't you? I mean, once I'd seen the camera footage... well, I had to. I didn't have a choice."

Thomas nodded.

"I know. I'd forgotten about the cameras." He paused. "I'm sorry about Simon, though. I should have come forward as soon as I knew that he'd been arrested. I suppose I thought that if I sat tight, it would somehow be all right. He'd be able to prove that he didn't do it, and then they'd let him go again. I never expected him to confess."

Molly swallowed and then said,

"What happens next? If there's anything that Jeremy or I can do…"

"I guess you know that the police started questioning me?" Molly nodded.

"Ruth told me."

"They have also very kindly visited me in hospital," he continued, "which has made me no end popular with the staff, as you may imagine. They informed me that they will continue the process when I'm sufficiently recovered. They don't seem bothered that I might abscond or anything so clearly they don't think that I pose a risk to the public. I'm not sure whether to be offended by that or not." Thomas smiled, a faint watery effort that didn't reach his eyes. "They didn't bring any toffees either. Mean sods."

"Have you got a solicitor?"

"Ruth has arranged it. He's already been in to see me."

"How is Ruth?" She paused. "I mean…"

"I know what you mean. Ruth is very… competent." He turned his head and stared out of the window, his eye following the tiny distant figures of the workmen as they laboured over the foundations of the new building. He turned back and sat up straighter, although it was clearly an effort. "Molly," his voice cracked. "It's all such a mess."

Molly leaned forward and stroked his hand, feeling the dry skin slip beneath her fingers.

"Do you want to talk about it? I mean, not if you don't want to but if it helps. I know about the gambling," she added. "Carlos told me."

"Carlos? How…" he paused and sighed. "Oh well, I don't suppose it matters. Everyone will find out now, anyway. The gambling, that wasn't really the problem. Well, it was, but other stuff was happening. Stuff I couldn't really cope with. I thought that I could, but I couldn't. The gambling was just, I don't know, a sort of release."

He turned and looked out of the window again; his voice low as he continued.

"I can remember the day it started. It was a Wednesday afternoon." He paused and looked thoughtful for a moment. "Do you ever think of days in colours?"

Molly shook her head.

"Not really, no."

"I do. And Wednesdays have always been a sort of bottle green for me. And that particular Wednesday it was very bottle and very green. It was raining. One of those dark, gloomy days that seem to just stretch on and on. I remember sitting in my office and feeling trapped. I had a stack of paperwork to do and the more I didn't do it, the more I didn't want to do it. It felt as though nothing good was ever going to happen again. Every day would just be more of the same. The most exciting thing on the horizon was the residents Christmas party and even that was months away."

Molly stared at him. The little man with the sticking up hair in his stripy cotton pyjamas, who was always so kind and cheerful with the residents. But just because he wore a chunky cardigan and ate toffees didn't mean that he didn't have hopes and dreams like everyone else. She remained silent while he continued.

"I had a girlfriend when I was young. A special girlfriend, I mean. Oh, I'd had girlfriends before." He gave a wry smile. "I didn't always look like this. But she was different. Her name was

Janey, and she trained at the same hospital as me." His face wore a faraway look. "I thought that we would be together forever. She had one of those bright faces that just lit up when she was happy, and she had the most beautiful hazel eyes. I thought," he said simply, "that she was the loveliest thing I had ever seen."

Molly held her breath for a moment.

"What happened?" she said at last.

"The usual. Junior doctor."

"What do you mean?"

"Hospital doctors chase young nurses. Or they did in those days. I don't expect that they do it now. Anyway, this one was a bit older than us, good-looking, a bit posh, drove a Jag. He was also," he added, "married with three small children."

There was silence between them for a moment, and then Thomas continued.

"He completely turned her head. Looking back, I'm not surprised. And let's be honest, good old reliable Thomas, with his second-hand Ford Cortina and polyester shirts, well, he was no competition."

"So, what happened?"

"His wife found out. Janey was transferred to another hospital. I never saw her again. I wonder sometimes whether things would have been different if we had stayed together, got married. My whole life might have been entirely different."

CHAPTER THIRTY-SEVEN

FOR SEVERAL MOMENTS, neither of them spoke. Outside, one of the workmen switched on a radio and began singing along, a burst of spontaneous joyfulness made even more incongruous in contrast to the sad little hospital room.

"But things turned out all right in the end," said Molly eventually. "I mean, you married Ruth…"

"Oh yes. I married Ruth. Or, to be more precise, Ruth married me. She was on the rebound, like me, and there I was, a sitting duck. The bloke that she'd been engaged to went off with one of the checkout girls at the local supermarket. He probably got sick of Ruth organising his life for him, so she just simply transferred her attentions to me. There's not an inch of my life that she doesn't run," he added bitterly. "She even puts my clothes out for me in the mornings. Why do you think that I'm so keen on fishing? The river bank is the one place that she doesn't follow me."

Molly suddenly remembered the neatly laid tea tray and cake when she had visited Thomas. At the time she had just thought that it was a kindly gesture, but now she thought about it, it did seem a bit odd. Thomas might be a bit on the impractical side, but he wasn't a child. He was perfectly capable of placing a couple of slices of cake on a plate.

"How did you meet?"

"She came to the hospital. Visiting her mother. We just got talking. And then she seemed to sort of seek me out and before

I knew where I was, we were meeting regularly. I didn't mind at the time. I suppose that in a way I was even flattered. She wasn't Janey, but then, nor was anybody else. We've got a son you know."

"Have you?" Molly looked surprised. "You've never mentioned him."

"He's an accountant. Very competent. Like his mother. He lives in London."

They fell silent for a moment. From outside came the sound of two doctors talking loudly, discussing a patient and when best to break the bad news. So much for confidentiality, she thought.

"So what about the gambling? I mean, how did all that start?" she asked.

"As I said, it was a Wednesday afternoon. It was raining. I remember sitting at my desk and listening to it lashing against the window. My coffee had gone cold and I couldn't be bothered to get up and make a fresh one. I didn't want to be there, but then I didn't particularly want to be anywhere else either. The thought of going home to Ruth, to that depressingly neat and tidy house with the heating always on too low and listening to yet another monologue on how she had got the better of somebody or other at work seemed unbearable. And then on my computer up popped adverts for online casinos. Bright, flashing. Attractive, fun. And I thought, why not give it a go. It would be a distraction for a few minutes. They offered free games to start with and at least it stopped me thinking about everything else. In a strange way, it was a sort of freedom."

Molly nodded, but remained quiet. Thomas continued.

"So, I opened an account. And then another one. I was making new friends, or at least that's how it felt. I had a feeling that I belonged somewhere, that I was a part of something. A sense of community I suppose you'd call it. It was like being at a party. And every site offered an incentive, a £50 bonus or 100 free spins. Before I knew where I was, I was gambling every day. I started looking forward to going to work so that I could carry on."

"You didn't do it at home then?"

"Not with Ruth around. If I take too long in the bathroom, she starts banging on the door asking what I'm doing in there. The chances of me spending any time on my own with a laptop were roughly nil."

"But what about, you know," Molly faltered. "When you lost money? Didn't Ruth notice, on your bank accounts and so on?"

Thomas smiled.

"Strangely, finance was the one of the few areas of responsibility that Ruth always left to me. More fool her," he added bitterly. "She's got some strange Victorian notion that household finances are a man's job. Like taking the bins out. So much for her feminist credentials. Funny how it's always me that has to get out there on freezing mornings when the car won't start. Anyway, I started syphoning off money from our savings accounts. I changed the passwords too, just in case she took it into her head to start poking around. But things only really started to go wrong when I began taking money out of our household account. But as long as I got to the post before she did…"

"The post?" Molly looked bewildered.

"Final demands, Molly. They have a habit of turning up with monotonous regularity." He looked suddenly weary.

"So, what did you do about them?"

"Well, those that I could ignore, I did ignore. Other than that, I kept moving money around between accounts but it was an ever-dwindling pot. I could only spread it so far. Then I started borrowing on my credit cards and when I maxed those out, I opened new ones. It was when the mortgage went into arrears that things really started hotting up."

"But why did you carry on?"

"I tried to stop. Of course I did. Every addict tries to stop. If it was that easy…"

Molly nodded. In a small way, she did understand. Most weeks she and Jeremy promised each other that they would have at least three alcohol free days. And most evenings they cracked at about six o'clock and poured themselves a glass of wine. But, she comforted herself, bad though the habit might be, at least they weren't at risk of losing their home over it.

Thomas stared ahead of him, his expression blank.

"Every morning, every single morning, I promised myself that I wouldn't log on. But it's like an itch you can't scratch. I knew that I would give in as soon as I sat at my desk."

"You must have known that you couldn't win?"

"Ah, but that's the point." Thomas smiled, a small weary stretching of the mouth. "You do think that you're going to win. That's what keeps you going. You're convinced that you're going to win the very next time. The next game, the next spin, you're going to get it all back. Next time you'll be lucky. And so, when the bills started piling up, I started betting bigger amounts. And then even bigger amounts. And sometimes I did win. Just often enough to keep me logging back in. And the thing is Molly, when I was online, getting the rush, the excitement, nothing else really mattered. And you know, if I'm honest, I think a part of me wanted everything to implode. It was like being in a car when the brakes have failed. You know it's happened, but instead of pulling over, you just drive faster. You know that you're going to crash, that you're going to hit that wall looming up in front of you, but if you can just crawl out of the wreckage, then all the problems would be solved. It would all somehow just melt away and I could start again. Without Ruth."

"Why didn't you just leave her?"

"I don't know," he said simply.

For a moment, they looked at each other. With so many words that they could have spoken, somehow none seemed appropriate.

Thomas sighed.

"Anyway, when I was gambling, I wasn't thinking about other things."

"What other things?"

"My crap life." He paused. "And the Lodge."

Molly stared at him.

"What about the Lodge?"

CHAPTER THIRTY-EIGHT

AUBREY AND VINCENT dived between the two big tumble dryers as the swing door to the laundry opened. A small dark-haired woman, her hair secured neatly into a ponytail with a plain black band, backed into the room and trundled the laundry trolley into the far corner, parking it neatly against the wall. They had come in to the Lodge earlier in the day with Molly, before she went off to visit Thomas. Taking a break from entertaining the residents by sitting on their laps and purring, they had made for the laundry for a quick restorative nap. They had discovered a couple of weeks ago that the swing door, designed so that laundry trolleys could be pulled in and out easily, could be manipulated by both of them shoving their shoulders against it. It was the perfect place for a private nap, being both warm and dry and never occupied except by one of the two laundry women.

Aubrey studied the woman as she began pulling items of clothing from another trolley, shaking them out and then loading them into one of the washing machines, pausing to adjust the temperature. She always looked so small and sad, her eyes carrying a slightly haunted look. With a worn but unlined face, it was difficult to tell how old she was. She could have been anything between thirty and sixty. Both the laundry women looked that way, now he came to think about it. They rarely spoke, not even to each other, and they never seemed to mix with the other staff, not even for a coffee break. It was like they were lost in their own little world of washing and ironing. He listened for a moment to the faint click as the machine adjusted to its load, followed by the slow swishing sound of water as it filled up and began the rhythmic vibration of washing. He liked that noise. There was something soothing and comforting about it. Next to him, Vincent had already fallen asleep again.

He looked down at his friend affectionately and then sat up straight, suddenly alert as the laundry door swung open again and a large man with a pale slab-like face and bald head entered the room. He was dressed in the blue uniform of the laundry that dealt with the sheets and towels. Around his neck hung a thick gold chain, the heavy links taut against his skin. The woman nodded towards the big trolley stuffed with the residents' bed linen and towels.

"In there."

"I need to check. One of the consignments was short last week."

His voice was flat and hard. The woman shrugged.

"Help yourself."

Aubrey watched, interested, as the man leaned over the crate and began flinging sheets and towels to the floor. Grunting, he hauled out a blue cotton pillow case which looked as though it was stuffed with something. He turned it on its side and tipped the contents to the floor. Seven plastic wrapped bags fell out, the last one splitting as it fell. The man straightened and looked around.

"Get something. Quickly." He sounded, thought Aubrey, panic-stricken.

The woman darted across to the big cabinet that held the laundry tablets and fabric softeners and pulled open the door. Reaching inside, she grabbed a plastic tub of laundry tablets and a small dust pan and brush. Emptying the laundry tablets on to the shelf, she passed the empty tub and dust pan and brush across to him. She watched in silence as the man hurriedly swept up the contents of the split bag, tipped them into the tub, and placed it back in the laundry crate along with the other plastic bags. He stared at them for a moment and then quickly piled the laundry back on top of them.

"When's the next consignment?" he asked.

"Later today."

Reaching across, he grasped the crate, turned and left the room without speaking. The woman checked the temperature on the washing machine and followed him.

Next to him, Aubrey felt Vincent stir and sit up again.

"What's happening?"

"Nothing. Some bloke just came in and took the laundry away."

Vincent stretched his paws in front of him, arching his back and yawning.

"Fancy a mosey on down to the kitchen?"

Aubrey nodded and padded across towards the door. Pausing halfway, he leaned over and stared down at the floor.

"I wonder what was in those packages?"

"What packages?"

"The bloke who collected the laundry. He took some packages out of the crate and one of them spilled out."

Vincent strolled over and joined him. Together they contemplated the grains of white powder scattered in front of them. Moving forward slightly, Aubrey dipped his head.

"Aubrey, no!"

In the split second before Vincent could stop him, Aubrey flicked his tongue out and started licking at the floor.

His heart racing, Vincent dashed across to the swing door and threw his weight against it. It was no good. However much he strained, he wasn't heavy enough on his own to open it. He looked fearfully back over his shoulder. Already Aubrey was lying prone, his beautiful green-gold eyes staring upwards.

IN THE KITCHEN, Carlos collapsed down on to one of the tall stools and rested for a moment. This was hard work, covering for Simon. He hoped Molly would find a replacement soon. Not only did he have to get the evening meal ready, but he had to prepare and clingfilm plates of sandwiches for the lunches tomorrow as well as make a large tureen of soup. Home-cooked food was one of the boasts of the Lodge, so there was no chance of getting away with opening a few tins. He was all for it really, even though he suspected that it was a ruse by the owner to save money and make sure that there were no leftovers.

He pulled his phone out of his pocket and contemplated for a moment ringing Molly, and then decided against it. She might even be home by now, anyway. He hoped that the visit to Thomas hadn't been too awful. He had seen from the expression on her face that she hadn't really wanted to go. He had also seen, as had Jeremy, that nothing that they could say would dissuade her. Molly was one of those small, softly spoken smiley people that would be so easy to underestimate. But once she had an idea in her head, she had—he knew—a will of iron. A bit like Teddy. He smiled. When he had WhatsApp'd Teddy to tell her that Simon was off the hook, she had given him one of her brilliant triumphant smiles which had quickly changed to horror.

"But what about Thomas? Carlos, we have to help him. We have to do something!"

Carlos had made non-committal noises. While he had told Teddy what he and Molly had seen, he hadn't gone into any detail. In an unconscious act of protection, he decided that there were some things that she didn't need to know. He felt sorry for Thomas, but there had been something very uncompromising about the blow to the head that he had given Toby Carson. And something even more uncompromising about the blood that had seeped out on to the carpet. This was definitely one for the grown-ups.

He stood up and glanced around again. All the prep was done for the morning. The dishwashers were running and he'd made his list for the following day. Reaching towards the damp cloth which was draped across the taps, he gave the work surfaces a final mop before pulling out the tea towel which he kept tucked into the waistband of his chef's trousers and wiping his hands on it. He might as well gather up the others as well and drop them into the laundry. He could pick up some clean ones while he was there. It would save him time tomorrow.

CHAPTER THIRTY-NINE

JEREMY, MOLLY AND CARLOS sat quietly at the kitchen table. The silence hung heavily between them, punctuated only by the soft regular click of the digital clock on the wall. Carlos stared white-faced down at his hands, his lips pressed tightly together in an effort not to cry. Upstairs, Vincent lay curled on Carlos's bed with his head under the pillow. An hour earlier Jeremy and Carlos had been standing around a big pen in which Aubrey lay unconscious, his shallow breathing as slight as the brush of a butterfly's wings, his beautiful eyes glazed over. In the pen next to him a small tortoiseshell animal with its jaw wired up—the victim of a hit and run—stared mournfully up at them.

The vet, a big red-haired man with large raw-looking hands and a faint Scottish accent, had stood with them.

"I've seen it before, you know. This isn't the first time."

"But what's happened?" asked Jeremy, bewildered. "Has he had some kind of seizure?"

The vet shook his head.

"No. It's the effect of a narcotic. Heroin possibly, there are still a few grains clinging to his fur." He brushed them away as he spoke and tipped them into a small plastic tub. "I'll know more when I get the bloods back but for the moment all we can do is try to keep him stable."

"Heroin?" asked Jeremy. "Where? I mean how…"

The vet gave them a hard look.

"You tell me."

"What? Oh really, you can't honestly think..."

The vet's expression remained impassive.

"Not all addicts hang around street corners. Some of them wear suits and ties." He stared pointedly at Jeremy's neat blue tie and let his eye travel across the dark grey suit. Unconsciously, Jeremy tugged at his tie and loosened it.

"It must have come from the Lodge," said Carlos.

Jeremy stared at him.

"The Lodge? It can't have."

"It must have," Carlos insisted. "I saw Aubrey and Vincent in one of the residents lounges after Molly left."

"You're not seriously telling me that the elderly residents at the Lodge are sitting around shooting up heroin while they're watching Emmerdale?"

"No." Carlos sounded flustered. "But I'm sure that Aubrey and Vincent didn't go in the garden or anything. I'd have seen them from the kitchen. And then I found them in the laundry."

The vet turned to him.

"What exactly happened?"

Carlos looked back at him, his long delicate eyebrows drawn together in an effort of concentration.

"I'd just finished my shift and I was clearing up. I decided to drop the dirty tea towels in the laundry and pick up some clean ones for the next day. When I got there, Vincent was standing over Aubrey and..."

"Vincent?" the vet interrupted. "Who is this Vincent?"

"He's Aubrey's friend. He's waiting in the car," Carlos added.

"So did this Vincent see what happened?" asked the vet.

"Probably," said Carlos.

"Well let's get him in and ask him then."

Jeremy sighed. Carlos still hadn't quite got out of the habit, learned during his time at Sir Frank's, of refusing to offer any more information than was strictly necessary when confronted with an unknown adult.

"I don't think that Vincent, will have much to add," he said wearily. "He's a cat."

"Anyway," continued Carlos, "Aubrey was just lying there on his back. I could see he was ill. So I rang Jeremy. And Jeremy came and picked us up and brought us here."

When he had arrived, Jeremy had hardly spoken. He had just finished a meeting and was getting ready to drive home when Carlos's call came through. He had jumped in the car and headed straight for the Lodge. Screeching to a stop outside the entrance where Carlos and Vincent were waiting for him, he had flung open the passenger door. Cradling the comatose Aubrey against his chest as Jeremy raced towards the surgery, Carlos had tried to remember the prayers he had been taught at his primary school. A jumble of words clogged up his mind in a great tangle, which, try as he might, he couldn't separate. He knew it was to do with heavenly fathers and something about trespassing, but he couldn't make the words jump into the right order. All he could think of were nursery rhymes, and he didn't think that they had the same effect. But worth a go. In his mind he began solemnly intoning Jack and Jill went up the hill. Bunched up on his feet in the foot well in a great ball of furry misery sat Vincent.

"He'll have to stay with us for the time being." The vet spoke more gently now. "But, to be honest, I wouldn't hold out too much hope. These cases don't usually have a good outcome. Even a small amount of the wrong substance can have a fatal effect. I think that you should prepare yourself. If it's easier for you, we can dispose of him here."

JEREMY GOT UP and took a can of beer from the cupboard. Slowly peeling back the ring pull, he looked across at Molly.

"All right?" he said gently, glad suddenly that he'd followed his instinct and not mentioned to her the vet's offer of disposal. She looked absolutely wiped out. The shock of the discovery about Thomas had been more than enough. And now she was reeling from the news about Aubrey.

Molly swallowed and nodded.

"I keep thinking about what the vet said about heroin. It's such a horrible thought. People taking drugs and having animals around. Don't they think about the danger that they're putting their pets in?"

"Moll," said Jeremy," I don't think that they're thinking about anything at all."

"Some of them, the dealers and that," said Carlos, "they keep dogs on purpose."

Molly looked bewildered.

"For what?"

"Protection," said Carlos.

His mind ran back to the dealers that used to hang around the Meadows and the animals that accompanied them. Big threatening beasts with huge necks, held by thick leads and bristling with aggression, the kind of animals that you'd cross the road to avoid. Even on the best interpretation, not exactly pets. More like that Baskerville dog thing he'd seen in that film he'd watched with Teddy. At the thought of Teddy, the great ogre of misery that had clamped its clammy hands around his chest when he'd seen Aubrey lying on the laundry floor started to shift slightly and a gentle, warmer feeling crept in. Aubrey would be all right. Of course he would. Wouldn't he?

Molly stood up and took a deep breath. She lifted her hands to her forehead and shook her hair back.

"There's no point in us all sitting around like this. The vet will ring as soon as there's anything to tell us. I think I'll go and do some ironing."

Carlos and Jeremy looked at each other as she left the room.

"She's upset," said Carlos.

From the cat dome where he had parked himself moments earlier, having been unable to settle on Carlos's bed and desperately wanting to hear what was being said downstairs, Vincent agreed. Molly wasn't the only one, either. Life without Aubrey was hardly worth thinking about. He'd had friends before, but never one like Aubrey, and somehow he didn't think that he'd ever have another like him. After the family went to Fallowfield, he'd almost given up hope of seeing him again. The day they'd come trundling back up the road in Jeremy's car, he had hardly been able to contain himself. Although, being Vincent, he had. Resisting the urge to leap the garden fences, he had merely strolled over and contented himself with an 'all right, Aubsie?'

If he'd ever thought about the future, it was one in which he'd had a vague idea that they would stay with Molly and Jeremy and grow old together, sleeping most of the day, reminiscing about the old days and having their food cut up for them. He curled more tightly in on himself, as if to squeeze out the thoughts that were pressing in on him. If only he'd been quicker, he could have stopped Aubrey. If only he had pushed him out of the way. If only. But he had realised, a split second too late, what the substance on the floor was. He'd seen a small plastic packet of what looked like a very similar substance passing hands on the Happy Camper caravan site and he'd seen the eager taker of it stretched out twenty minutes later on the damp grass, eyes glazed and oblivious to the rain that had started to fall. He had watched from the shadows as the weary looking ambulance men loaded the limp, inert body into the back of the vehicle.

For a moment Carlos and Jeremy remained silent, both lost in thought. Eventually Carlos spoke, his voice hesitant.

"Do you think that the vet might have made a mistake? Like about the heroin and that?"

Jeremy frowned.

"I doubt it. He said that he'd seen it before." He took a long swallow from the can and leaned back against the work surface. "I just can't think how it got into the Lodge and how Aubrey got hold of it. I'd like to kill whoever left it lying around."

His voice tightened; the sharp edge of bitterness evident.

Carlos looked at him warily. This was a side of Jeremy that they rarely saw.

"Do you think that we ought to tell the police?"

Jeremy nodded.

"Yes, without doubt. Well, when we know for sure that is. We don't know for certain yet. I don't think that Mrs. Randall would take too kindly to it if we load the old bill down on her for something that turns out not to be true. The Lodge is still having to cope with the fall-out of Simon being arrested and I don't even know if they've heard about Thomas yet."

"The residents don't know," said Carlos. "They think that he's just still off sick."

Jeremy paused for a moment as though thinking, his hand tightening around the can. He tipped his head slightly to one side.

"If Aubrey and Vincent were in the laundry when you found them, then presumably that's where the stuff was. I mean, I don't suppose that Aubrey got hold of it and then strolled over to the laundry. But how on earth did it get in there? Was it dropped by somebody, do you think?"

Carlos shrugged.

"Nobody really goes in there except the laundry women. I mean, it's, like, where the laundry women do the washing and that."

"Could a resident go in there?"

"I suppose so. It's not locked or anything. But if a resident wanted to take drugs, they could just do it in their own room."

"What about the cameras, though?"

"There aren't any cameras in the residents' bathrooms."

"Are there any in the laundry?"

Carlos thought for a moment.

"No, Gordon said that there was no point because who'd want to nick a load of dirty washing?"

"True. So, what's the routine?"

"The laundry women go to the residents rooms and collect their laundry. They take it to the laundry room and wash and iron it and then they take it back. That's it."

"How do they know what belongs to whom?" said Jeremy, momentarily distracted. "I mean, don't all the clothes get mixed up?"

"They've all got name tags in them. Even the socks."

Jeremy nodded thoughtfully.

"These laundry women, what are they like?"

Carlos shrugged.

"Women?" he suggested.

"No, I mean what sort of people are they?"

"I don't know. I've never spoken to them. I told you, they just come in and do the washing."

"But they don't do all the washing, do they?" he said. "Didn't Molly tell me something about the big items, the sheets and towels and so on, going to an outside laundry?"

Carlos nodded.

"That's right. They pick it up and deliver it back a couple of times a week."

"And is it local?"

"Sort of. I mean, I think that there's a chain of them or whatever you call it."

"Is there indeed?"

Jeremy looked thoughtful.

"Carlos, your key to the Lodge, does it open all the doors?"

Carlos nodded.

"Yes, why?"

"Let's take a trip over there. It's better than just sitting here waiting for the vet to call."

"What about Molly?"

As he spoke, Molly put her head back round the door.

"Carlos, have you…" She paused and looked at them more closely. "What?"

"Moll, we're going to take a trip down to the Lodge. Carlos thinks that might be where Aubrey found the heroin."

Molly looked doubtful.

"I'm not so sure that's a good idea."

"It can't do any harm. Anyway, I can't just sit around here doing nothing. We won't be long."

He turned behind him and grabbed the car keys that were sitting on the work surface.

"Come on, Carlos."

CHAPTER FORTY

AS THEY APPROACHED, the Lodge seemed preternaturally quiet, as though it was holding its breath. Pressing his key card against the electronic pad, Carlos stood back to let Jeremy go ahead of him. The reception area was silent, the visitors' book open on the desk.

Leading the way down the corridor, past the kitchen and the main residents' lounge in which three residents were watching the television, Carlos glanced to right and left, his expression slightly anxious. There was no reason why they shouldn't be there. But then again, there was no reason why they should. What would they say if somebody, Martha for instance, stopped them and asked them what they were doing? He glanced at Jeremy. No, it would be okay. Jeremy was married to Molly, and Molly was the assistant manager. In fact, in the absence of Thomas, she was the main manager. They could just say that Molly had asked them to come and fetch something. Or, more likely, given the mood that he was in, Jeremy would just tell them to mind their own business.

Pushing his shoulder against the big swing door, Carlos entered the laundry and flicked on the light switch. Jeremy looked around him. The room was smaller than he had imagined. In his mind he had somehow conjured up an image of the kind of laundry that used to be found on small parades of shops on the edges of towns, the kind that he had used as a student. Big, bright rooms with rows of huge washing machines and dryers with people sitting around on benches reading magazines. This room was small and functional, with just two washing machines and two dryers. Stacked against the wall were two ironing boards. On the notice board on the wall were pinned laundry lists and a chart. He walked over to it. Headed SnowBright Laundry, the chart showed a list of dates. He turned away and pulled open the biggest cupboard. On the shelves sat neat rows of laundry tablets and fabric conditioner. He pulled one of the tubs of laundry tablets towards him and prised open the lid. Leaning over, he sniffed at the contents before snapping the lid back on.

Straightening up, he turned back to Carlos.

"Have you got your phone with you?" Stupid question. Like all teenagers, and quite a few adults, Carlos had his phone permanently welded to him. "Can you check out this SnowBright Laundry?"

Carlos nodded and started tapping at his screen. Flipping it round to show Jeremy, they both stared down at it. The screen showed the logo of the company and a list of services and locations along the south coast. Jeremy chewed for a moment on his bottom lip.

"That doesn't really take us much further."

He stopped and looked around at the sound of a van door slamming just outside and then the laundry door swung open again and a small pale man with a faint shadow of acne scars stretched across his face and wearing the uniform of the SnowBright laundry entered the room. He stared at them with hard flinty eyes; his expression openly hostile.

"What are you doing in here?"

His voice was hard, with a flat estuary accent.

Jeremy's years teaching at Sir Frank's hadn't been entirely wasted. Wearing his best disappointed teacher expression, he looked the man over, casting a long, slow gaze from head to toe and back again. Jeremy wasn't a big man, but he wasn't small either and he clearly wasn't going to be pushed around by some toe rag. Carlos watched him admiringly.

"I might ask you the same question."

Jeremy's voice was cool and measured. Any minute now, thought Carlos, he'd be telling the bloke to take his hands out of his pockets when he was talking to him. He suppressed a grin and glanced out of the window. The white van with the SnowBright Laundry logo was parked up by the rear entrance. The same entrance, Carlos thought with a sudden shudder, through which Thomas had trundled the body of Toby Carson. For several seconds the man and Jeremy stared at each other and then the man smiled, a small ingratiating smile that revealed the gaps in his teeth and did nothing to improve his appearance.

"Sorry mate," he spread his hands, palms upwards. "Just gave me a bit of a start seeing you in here. Didn't expect to see no-one at this time."

Jeremy remained silent. He was doing another teacher trick, thought Carlos. He was doing his 'I can wait all day' thing. And very good at it he was, too. That time at Sir Frank's when he'd kept the whole class back after finding a pile of betting slips on the floor—it had been only a matter of minutes before each finger had pointed firmly at Petra Wade. Petra, a dull-eyed lumpy girl whose looks belied her razor-sharp brain, didn't particularly care. She'd already cleaned up on the sweepstake as to who would be the next teacher to hand in their notice. Mr. Gibson, a spectacularly inept history teacher, had resigned two days ago, an action which Petra had been able to anticipate by having insider knowledge. Specifically, that her aunt was one of the school cleaners and had read his resignation letter which had been left on the Head's desk.

The man shuffled nervously and licked his lips.

"My mate was here earlier today. He thought he'd dropped his phone somewhere. I said I'd look in on my way home."

Jeremy raised an eyebrow and remained silent. The man made an exaggerated show of looking around him.

"I can't see it nowhere though." He hesitated, clearly uncertain what to do next. "I'll be off then."

Jeremy and Carlos watched as he shuffled back out. Carlos turned to Jeremy.

"What do you think he really wanted?"

Jeremy's expression was serious.

"Not his mate's phone, that's for sure. He could have just rung and asked Martha or somebody to look for it. There's something in here." He looked around as he spoke, his eye travelling from floor to ceiling as he thought about it. "Something he came to collect. Carlos, check all the laundry tablet boxes. I'll check the other cupboard."

"Are we looking for…"

"Yes."

For several minutes, they worked in silence.

"Anything?"

Carlos shook his head.

"No. Only laundry tablets."

Jeremy scratched his head.

"There's nothing in this cupboard either except clean sheets and towels. But there must be something. It's in here somewhere, we just have to find it. The problem is, I don't know what it actually looks like."

Carlos, who did know, having seen plenty passing hands both in Sao Paulo and at the Meadows, pointed to the big laundry baskets on the floor.

"In the actual laundry, maybe?"

"Good thinking."

Kneeling down they began to fling the residents laundry from the baskets, rummaging through the socks and shirts and blouses, shaking out each item in turn. At last, Jeremy sat back on his heels.

"Nothing."

"Maybe he really did come to look for his mate's phone?" suggested Carlos.

Jeremy shook his head.

"No. There's something. I just know it."

He stood up and leaned back for a moment against one of the cupboards. He ran his eye again across the length and breadth of the small room. A small smile slowly stretched itself across his face and he reached towards one of the washing machines. Pulling open the door, he reached in and extracted two fat packages wrapped in black plastic and bound with parcel tape.

"Bingo."

CHAPTER FORTY-ONE

MOLLY LOOKED UP as the faint clack of the front door sounded. She half-rose as Jeremy came in, followed by Carlos.

"What's happening?" Her voice sounded small and frightened.

Jeremy sat down on the sofa and ruffled his hair.

"We've given our statements."

"What about the residents? Are they all right?"

"It's okay, Moll. They're not even aware that anything's happened. Gordon knows the situation and the police have got two officers up at the Lodge just in case there's any trouble."

"Do you think I should go in?"

"No," said Jeremy and Carlos in unison.

"It's okay. I told you," said Jeremy. He reached across and picked up her hand, holding it gently between his. "Gordon is looking after things. Martha is there, too. There's nothing for you to worry about."

"Nothing for me to worry about? Aubrey's lying at death's door, Thomas is facing a murder charge and you've just found God knows how much heroin stashed in a washing machine at the Lodge. And you're telling me that there's nothing to worry about?" She paused for a second. "Why a washing machine, anyway? Wasn't that a bit risky? I mean somebody might have switched it on."

"Not really," said Carlos. "The only people who went in there were the laundry women and they just did the laundry..." he glanced at Jeremy, suddenly confused. "Didn't they?"

"Don't tell me that they were in on it?" asked Molly.

"I don't know," said Jeremy. "I mean, I suppose that they must have known about it, but that doesn't necessarily mean that they were actively involved."

"Oh God," said Molly, putting her head in her hands. "I'm going to have to tell the owner. Surely this will mean the end of the Lodge. Where will all the residents go? Some of them are in their nineties. Even if we could find suitable places at short notice, the shock of having to move could kill some of them."

"About telling the owner..." Jeremy faltered.

"What?" Molly looked up again. "Do you mean she already knows?"

"Er, sort of," said Jeremy.

She stared at him.

"Surely you don't mean..."

Jeremy nodded.

"Yes, I think so."

Molly took a deep breath.

"Tell me."

"The owner, Mrs. Randall, also owns the laundry business. Don't you remember Thomas telling you? When you think about it, of all the places that you might suspect of being in the centre of running drugs about the country, it wouldn't be a care home. It's perfect. A place like the Lodge would legitimately have reason to have the regular use of a laundry and who questions laundry vans?"

"Did the police tell you this?"

"Not in so many words, but it didn't take a lot of working out. They were very interested in the owner and how many businesses she owned. My guess is that the laundry was a laundry in more senses than one."

"What do you mean?"

"I suspect that the money from the drugs was being laundered through other businesses."

"You don't know all this for sure though."

"No," Jeremy admitted. "I don't know any of this for sure. But if I had to put money on it…

"And Thomas? Do you think that Thomas knew? Do you think that he was involved?" Molly swallowed, close to tears. "If what you're saying is right, I think that he must have known," she said slowly. "That's why he was so keen not to get Mrs. Randall involved in anything. He was frightened of her." She thought for a moment. "That must have been what he meant when he talked about his crap life. Not just the gambling and the stuff about Ruth, but knowing about this thing that was happening at the Lodge."

"But if he knew, then why didn't he say anything?" said Carlos. "I mean, he wasn't the one doing anything wrong and once he told then it would be over."

"And so would his job," said Jeremy gently. "He was already up to his neck in debt and at his age his chances of finding employment again, at least at managerial level, are pretty remote. Especially if he was associated with scandal. It was probably easier for him just to turn a blind eye and keep his mouth shut." He paused and turned to Molly. "The other thing is Moll, the police said that they will want to talk to you, too. In fact, they might call tonight."

As he spoke, the sound of ringing in the hall broke through. They were each so used to their own ring tone on their mobiles that the unfamiliar noise of the landline startled them and for a moment none of them moved.

"I'll get it," said Molly eventually.

Jeremy and Carlos fell silent as they listened to the low murmur of her voice in the hall. She replaced the receiver and stood for a moment in the doorway.

"It was the vet."

Carlos stared at her; his throat dry. In his mind he began silently chanting sing a song of sixpence. What was the next line? Pockets? Birds? Pies?

Molly gave a weak smile.

"Don't panic. He's still with us. The vet said that he's hanging on."

From under the sofa, where Vincent had found more comfort than he would have believed possible, a long sigh of relief emanated. Creeping out from the shadowy safety, he padded towards Molly and wound himself around her legs. She reached down and tickled his ears before picking him up and holding him close to her.

"What exactly did he say?" asked Jeremy.

"Just that, really. That he's holding on. He thinks that if they can get him through tonight, then he's got a good chance of making it."

"And was it heroin?"

"They don't know. They haven't got the test results back yet."

She placed Vincent gently down on the floor just as a loud rat tat sounded on the front door.

JEREMY USHERED THE two plain-clothed officers into the sitting room and gestured for to them to sit down. He turned to the larger of the two, a big broad-shouldered man who despite his air of geniality was clearly the senior officer and a person to be reckoned with.

"Do you want to speak to Molly on her own? Only, if it's all right with you, I'd rather stay."

"Can I stay, too?" asked Carlos.

The officer nodded and looked at Molly's anxious face. "Don't worry, Mrs. Goodman. We're just trying to get a better picture of what is actually going on up at the Lodge."

"What *is* going on?" asked Molly.

"Can you just tell us what you know about the owner of the Lodge? A Mrs. Randall?"

"Nothing really. I've never met her. I just know that she's the owner."

The officer nodded.

"Didn't you think it was peculiar that you never met her?"

"To be honest, I never really thought about it. Any contact was by email."

"So who interviewed you when you applied for the post at the Lodge?"

"Thomas," said Molly simply.

The second officer nodded and scribbled something down in his notebook.

"And you've worked at the Lodge as assistant manager for approximately three months, is that right? And before that you worked as an administrator with the law firm Donoghue and Stevenson? How long were you there for?"

"Ten years."

The officer nodded and looked thoughtful.

"Did you ever see anything or hear anything at the Lodge that made you suspicious?"

"Of what?"

"Anything."

Molly shook her head.

"No."

"Nothing?"

"No. Really, nothing."

Jeremy leaned forward.

"What made you focus on the Lodge?"

The officer turned to him.

"Well, we've known for some time that there were some pretty big drug runs going on up and down the south coast. What we didn't know was who was organising it."

Jeremy frowned.

"Why the south coast? I mean, I thought that this kind of stuff happens in cities."

"It happens everywhere. You can buy it in the sleepiest little village if you know where to look," said the other officer. "But you're right, in that cities are usually where most of it eventually ends up. But it has to be brought in from somewhere and the south coast is very handy for nipping across the channel and back. Funnily enough, your call came in just as the Lodge turned up on our radar."

"How? What happened?"

"It was sheer chance, as these things so often are." The police officer grinned ruefully. "One of the SnowBright laundry vans tipped over on the A2 and caused a two-mile tail back. The police were called and, because of the area, one of the dog handling team turned up as well. With his dog."

"Why the dog handler?"

The officer smiled.

"In this area, large vans are always of interest to us. People smugglers," he added, "as well as drugs."

"Right." Jeremy looked thoughtful. "And the dog found… "

"Thousands of pounds worth hidden under a false floor. After some poking around we discovered that the SnowBright Laundry and Lilac Tree Lodge are owned by the same people. This Mrs. Randall."

"What did the van driver say?"

"Nothing. He's still unconscious."

Carlos, who had remained silent up until now, suddenly spoke.

"What I don't understand," said Carlos, "is how he got in."

"Who?"

"The laundry man. The one that said he was looking for his mate's phone. How did he get in?"

"The same way that we did, I should think," said Jeremy. "I expect Martha or somebody let him in." said Jeremy.

"But he came in the back way. We heard the van."

"So?"

Carlos shook his head impatiently.

"No. The back door doesn't have a key pad. It's got a proper, like, old-fashioned lock. You can get to the laundry either by going through the front way and down the corridor, past the kitchen and that, or through the back door. It's usually open in the day but it's locked up in the evening."

The police officer looked at Molly.

"Who had keys?"

She spoke slowly.

"There are only two. One was held by Thomas. I've got it now," she added. "And the other…"

"The other?"

"Is held by Gordon."

CHAPTER FORTY-TWO

AUBREY LAY WEAKLY across the rug in front of the fire, his head on the pillow, which Carlos had rushed upstairs to fetch from his bedroom. Molly had opened her mouth to object and then closed it again. It was only a pillow. There were more in the airing cupboard. Next to Aubrey, just within paw distance, lay Vincent. From the sofa, Simon, now well-fed with lasagne made by Carlos and face slightly flushed from the wine that Jeremy had poured him, sat quietly. His clean-shaven face and newly washed hair made him look handsome in the firelight.

Molly reached down and stroked Aubrey gently across the head with one finger.

"Poor old boy. Don't worry, we'll soon have you well again."

Aubrey opened one eye and gave a small rattle of a purr; it was the best that he could manage. He had never felt so ill in his whole life, not even when he'd eaten the bait that the vinegar-lipped old bitch Miss Jenkins had laid to kill the local cats in their old neighbourhood. In spite of feeling so dreadful, he couldn't help but feel a warm glow at the recollection of the expression on her face when she'd seen him strolling around her garden two days after watching him eating the bait. He'd even sat on the sill outside her bedroom, pressing his face against the window as she drew the curtains back, just to make the point how very much alive he still was.

Jeremy drained the last of his beer and turned to Simon.

"It's good to see you looking so well, Simon."

Simon gave a rueful smile.

"A bit different to the last time."

"Yes, well, it's over now. Thank goodness."

Simon shifted slightly in his chair and glanced shyly across at Molly.

"After they let me out, the next day the police sent somebody round to see if I was all right."

"Did they?" Molly looked astonished. "I'm amazed." She shot a suspicious glance at Jeremy, who was suddenly very interested in the bottom of his glass. "Well, maybe not that amazed."

"She's really nice. She's called Louise. She's not a police officer, but she works with them. Like running training courses and arranging counselling and so on if an officer needs it. She's been round a couple of times since." He paused. "We went out for a drink last night."

Aubrey watched with amusement as a faint red stain flushed up Simon's neck and tapped him on the face. He summoned the strength to nudge Vincent in the ribs, who grinned back at him.

"That's nice," said Molly, smiling at him. She paused for a moment. "I don't suppose she's told you anything about what's happening?"

"She has actually. She's good friends with some of the team who are working on the case. That's why I phoned you earlier. I thought that you would want to know."

"Are you allowed to tell us?" asked Jeremy. "I mean, we don't want to get you into trouble or anything."

"It's okay," said Simon. "Everyone will know pretty soon, anyway."

Carlos, who had been silently lying on his stomach on the floor and picking threads out of the rug, looked up.

"Is it Gordon?" he asked breathlessly.

Simon nodded.

"Louise told me that the police went straight to his cottage after leaving here. First of all, he tried to say that he gave the laundry man the key so that he could look for his mate's phone. The bloke must have told him what happened when he returned the key. He probably thought that the stuff was safe where it was for the night, nobody was likely to go into the laundry, and he could arrange another pick up in the morning. Anyway, the police said that as they were there, they might as well have a look around. They found everything. All the contacts. A stash of money. Louise said that it was thousands."

"Didn't they need one of those ticket things?" said Carlos.

"Ticket things?" asked Jeremy. "What ticket things?"

"Like to go and look in peoples' houses."

Jeremy smiled.

"You mean a search warrant."

"They told Gordon that they'd got one," said Simon. "Louise said that it was for the Lodge, but they reasoned that it covered the whole grounds, including the cottage. Anyway," he continued, "it wouldn't have mattered if they hadn't had a warrant. It wouldn't have taken them very long to get one. Louise said that first off they couldn't really find anything and then one of them had the idea of looking in the loft."

"What did they find?" asked Carlos, sitting up straight, his eyes wide.

"It was set up like a little office, so they took his laptop. He wouldn't give them his passwords but the IT forensic people got his files open."

"And?" asked Jeremy.

"It was all there. Details of all the businesses he was running, the businesses that he was laundering money through. Some of them were quite local to here. One of them was one that private school in town."

"I knew it," said Jeremy triumphantly. "I knew that there was something wrong. Every time I've been there, there's been an air of unreality. It was like being on a movie set. Not," he added ruefully, "that I've ever been on one."

Molly smiled.

"So how did Gordon work it?" she asked. "How did he manage it?"

"Through the laundry. The stuff was brought across the channel and taken to the Lodge in one of the laundry vans. Then packages were picked up by other vans and taken for distribution. The laundry at the Lodge was the perfect place to take things in and out because nobody was interested in it. In fact, it was used to control the chain. Money was laundered through other, legitimate, businesses. Well, legitimate in one sense. Every business had a key person who handled everything."

"I knew that there was a reason for not liking that headmaster. No wonder he was a bit wary about an inspection."

"Gordon was clever," continued Simon. "None of the key people knew each other or about any of the other businesses. The chances of a leak anywhere were really low."

"Who was the key person at the Lodge?" asked Jeremy.

"He didn't need one. He was there himself. It was his headquarters."

Molly frowned.

"So was Mrs. Randall involved in it? I mean," she continued, "she must have been. She owns the laundry."

Simon gave them a long, solemn stare.

"There is no Mrs. Randall. Gordon owns the Lodge. And the laundry. And Thomas is his cousin."

FOR A MOMENT the room was perfectly silent, the only sound that of a couple quarrelling outside, their animated voices fluttering back as they passed the house.

"So Thomas *was* in on it?" said Molly sadly.

"Well, yes and no. He did know about it but, according to Louise, he wasn't actively involved. Gordon wanted to keep a low profile and to be able to get away quickly if he needed to so he wanted a manager. One who would turn a blind eye. He gave Thomas the job soon after he was made redundant from his last post."

"But the strain obviously got too much for him," said Jeremy. "Hence the gambling."

"I think so," said Simon. "I suspect that Thomas is basically an honest man."

"Gordon must have been furious when Toby Carson was murdered," said Molly.

"I shouldn't think that Toby Carson was too thrilled, either," Jeremy said.

"Why did it matter to Gordon, though?" Carlos sounded confused. "I mean, he didn't even know that Toby Carson."

"Because, even though it didn't happen there, the Lodge overlooks where the body was found, so it ran the risk of focusing police interest on the Lodge." Simon spoke slowly, his voice hesitant. Aubrey looked up at him curiously. Simon didn't quite seem able to meet Jeremy's eye. All his furry little instincts told him that there was something that Simon wasn't telling. He laid his aching head down again. No doubt it would come out in due course. "And," Simon continued, "of course, as soon as the police discovered who the body was and that he had a connection to a resident, then they became even more interested. And then there was the Happy Camper camp site as well, Toby Carson lived there. Gordon must have been worried about that."

"What did the camp site have to do with it?" asked Molly.

"Gordon's business was supplying locally as well as nationally. One of the care workers was passing it through to the local dealers on the camp site."

"Who?" asked Carlos. "Who was it?"

"Maxine."

Molly nodded slowly.

"That explains a lot. No wonder she always had such a decent car. Did she know that Thomas was Gordon's cousin?"

Simon shook his head.

"No. And Thomas didn't know what Maxine was up to, either."

"So what's going to happen now?" Molly asked.

"Gordon has already been charged and so has Maxine."

"But what about the Lodge? What's going to happen to the residents? Where will they go?" asked Molly.

"I've decided to sell all the flats."

Simon spoke slowly, as if he hadn't heard Molly's question.

"So, you're moving away?" said Molly.

"Not really," said Simon. "I'm going to buy the Lodge."

CHAPTER FORTY-THREE

MOLLY HUNG UP her coat and walked through to the sitting room where Jeremy was looking through the contents of the leather document wallet that they had removed from the Happy Camper camp site. He looked up as she came in and held some sheets of paper towards her.

"I'd forgotten that we had this, but look. George Carson's original will. My guess is that it matches the one that Thomas had. And," he delved further into the wallet. "This."

Molly took the papers from him and studied the two wills for a moment.

"Do you think that he would have got away with it?"

"Probably," Jeremy admitted. "George Carson was an elderly, very ill, man. He had no near relatives except for a sister than he never saw and his half-brother. Who would have been interested? And Toby Carson didn't even have to do anything, really. Except wait for George to die."

Molly nodded and sat down. Jeremy studied her for a moment.

"Everything all right? You're late, I was getting a bit worried."

She nodded.

"Everything's fine. In one sense, it's no change. I was acting as manager in the absence of Thomas and I'm still acting as manager. The residents don't seem to be aware that anything has happened. It's funny," she mused. "It's like a little world all of its own in there. You go in and shut the door, and it's as if the outside world doesn't really exist."

"Just as well at the moment," said Jeremy. "Where are the cats, by the way?"

"I left them up at the Lodge. They can come back with Carlos when he's finished."

Molly sat down and leaned back, closing her eyes.

"I went to see Thomas again on my way home, just a quick visit."

"Molly..."

"Yes, I know." Molly opened her eyes again. "But I sort of felt that I had to. I didn't stay long, I just wanted to check that he was okay." She paused. "Did I tell you that the last time I visited him, I met Gordon in the corridor?"

Jeremy shook his head.

"No, you didn't mention it."

"I didn't really think about it at the time. I just thought he was visiting, like me."

Jeremy looked thoughtful.

"Was he warning Thomas, do you think?"

"Yes. Well, not so much warning as threatening."

"Did Thomas tell you that?"

"Yes. Apparently Gordon was going to have him torn limb from limb if he even so much as breathed a word."

"Nice," said Jeremy. "Who needs enemies when you've got family like that?"

"Thomas said that by that stage he didn't really care very much, anyway. The worst had already happened."

"Have the police interviewed him again?"

Molly nodded.

"Yes. He's told them everything that he knows about the Lodge, in spite of Gordon's threats. I suppose that there's no point in not telling them now, he hasn't really got anything to lose."

"And," Jeremy pointed out, "He's potentially got quite a lot to gain if he cooperates with them."

"He was telling me about when he and Gordon were boys. Their mothers were sisters, but he said that even then, while he always kept his head down and just got on with things, Gordon was a tearaway. Always getting into trouble over something or other but somehow always getting away with it by the skin of his teeth."

"So how did he go from being a teenage tearaway to a drugs baron?"

"With remarkable ease, it appears," said Molly. "Thomas said that Gordon was clever but didn't go to school much and after he left, he mostly did causal jobs, a bit of gardening and so on, with lots of rest breaks in between. Apparently, it drove his father mad. Gordon senior was a self-made man and did well, by all accounts. He started off as a lorry driver and saved up to buy his own truck, then bought a few more and so on until he'd built a pretty successful transport business. He wanted Gordon to join him but Gordon had other ideas."

"So how did the drug thing come about?"

"Thomas said that started when Gordon was doing bar work in pubs and clubs, although he was very clever about it. He never used any of the stuff himself. He just did deals over the bar and built up his contacts that way. When his father died, he inherited the transport business."

"Don't tell me," said Jeremy dryly. "He sold it."

Molly smiled.

"He did. He set up Randall Holdings and bought the Lodge. It was already operating as a care home. From his perspective, it was the ideal place to centre his business. He installed himself in the cottage and then got Thomas in as manager."

"And the laundry?"

"He was trying to think of a way to distribute the drugs that wouldn't arouse suspicion and that would keep him at arm's length. And he hit on the laundry idea."

"Did it actually do any laundry?"

Molly laughed.

"Oh yes, it had legitimate workers. It was just the drivers who were involved."

"So what about the other businesses?"

"He was making a lot of money but he had to launder it somehow so he bought other businesses. But they had to be legitimate, at least on the outside. The kind of places where nobody would suspect any wrongdoing."

"Hence the school," said Jeremy thoughtfully. "I wonder what will happen to it now? I mean, I don't suppose that the filthy rich will be very pleased that their little darlings were being educated by a drugs runner. I expect that the kids will be thrilled though."

"Maybe they'll find a way to hush it up. Will you have to continue with the inspection?"

"I guess so. At least until I'm told anything different."

Molly looked thoughtful.

"Do you know, it never crossed my mind that Mrs. Randall didn't exist."

"I'm not surprised," said Jeremy. "I mean, why would it? And it's the easiest thing in the world to work. It's the old jacket on the back of the chair trick. An illusion. Anyone can set up an email address in whatever name they choose. There's no checks or anything. All he had to do was set up an email account in the name of Randall and he could just filter anything that he needed to through that."

"Of course. And we were always told that Mrs. Randall was very busy and so we never questioned it."

"How much do you think that Thomas actually knew about what was going on? Did he tell you?"

"It's pretty much as we thought. He did know almost everything, but he swears that he didn't actually do anything."

"Do you believe him?"

"I do. He says that his hands were clean and his only involvement was that he just knew about it. All he had to do was keep his mouth shut."

"Doesn't that make him an accessory or something?"

"I'm not sure. I don't think so. But anyway, given that he's still facing the murder charge that's not really his biggest worry."

"Did he say anything about it? About the actual murder, I mean?" asked Jeremy curiously.

"Actually, he did." Molly looked thoughtful. "He said that it seems like a sort of dream now, like it happened to somebody else."

Jeremy raised an eyebrow.

"More like a nightmare."

"I suppose so. He said that he remembered a kind of overwhelming feeling, like a rush of despair and everything got confused, and the next thing he knew was that Toby Carson was lying on the floor with the back of his head smashed in."

"What has his solicitor said to him?"

"Apparently there may be a chance that they can rely on his mental state. Because of the gambling and the general stress he was under but there's no guarantee."

"Insanity?"

Molly shook her head.

"I don't think that would work."

"Why not?"

"Because he was so methodical in his clearing up. He knew what he'd done, and he knew it was wrong. Otherwise, he wouldn't have tried to hide it. It was one of the few big criminal cases that we had at Donoghue's. A man killed his wife and one of the partners had to talk him out of trying to plead insanity because he'd disposed of her body. Pretty efficiently, if I recall correctly."

"What did he do?" asked Jeremy, momentarily diverted.

"He was a farmer. He chopped her up and fed her to the pigs. The police traced it through some teeth that were embedded in the ground. Apparently, pigs can't digest teeth."

Jeremy shuddered.

"Blimey. Puts you right off your bacon sandwich." Molly smiled. It was, Jeremy thought with a sudden pang, the first time that she had smiled since she had come in. "So, what happened to the client at Donoghue's?"

"They went for diminished responsibility. It means that you're not insane, but you weren't really responsible for your actions at the time. If it works with Thomas, the judge can take it into account so he won't necessarily get a life sentence."

"So he's going to plead guilty then?"

"Given the video evidence, he hasn't really got much choice."

Jeremy considered for a moment.

"You still feel sorry for him, don't you?"

Molly nodded.

"I suppose that I do in a way. It must be terrible to feel trapped like he did. He must have felt at times that there was no way out. I mean, I'm not condoning what he's done, it was dreadful, but..." she trailed off.

"It's okay, Moll. I do understand. I don't know though," he grinned suddenly. "What is it about us?"

"What do you mean?"

"Well, we've got Thomas on a murder charge and we seem to have also befriended Simon, who's got a conviction for murder. Let's hope it's not catching, eh?"

CHAPTER FORTY-FOUR

"TALKING OF SIMON, he came back into work today."

"I thought that the Lodge were getting rid of him? Haven't you advertised for someone else? Although," Jeremy paused for a moment. "If he's going to buy the place, I guess that puts a different perspective on it."

"He hasn't bought it yet so at present it still belongs to Gordon. But, at the moment, given that Gordon is in custody and Thomas is in hospital, I'm the only one in a position to make a decision. And my decision is that, for the time being, he returns to work. Apart from anything else, we need him. Anyway," she continued, "I went to the kitchen just to sort of say welcome back and we had a coffee together. And a chat," she added.

"What did he say?" Jeremy asked curiously.

"He seems changed somehow, more open. He just started talking. About himself. I've never really known anything about him before. I just thought that he was naturally reserved, but it was probably because he was afraid that the story about his murder conviction would come out."

"Hardly surprising," said Jeremy.

"Anyway, he started talking about his childhood and his parents. Apparently he was brought up in the house that he owns now and his parents were quite wealthy. They owned a string of small convenience stores along the coast. He said that he was an only child and that his parents were always loving and kind. He went to university, you know."

"Did he?" Jeremy sounded surprised. "What did he study?"

"History. He didn't finish his course, though. It was the usual story. He got in with the wrong crowd and started taking drugs, stopped going to lectures and so on. From what he said, I think that his parents were supportive as soon as they realised what was going on. I mean, they tried to get treatment for him and look after him and so on but he just drifted further and further down until he was pretty much living on the streets. His mental health suffered, too."

"I'm not surprised." Jeremy hesitated for a moment. "Did he say anything about, you know…"

"Yes, he did. I deliberately didn't ask him, but he just started talking about it. He said that he was twenty-two when it happened. He was off his head at the time, and he wasn't the one to fire the gun. He said that he thought the gun was a fake and that they were only going to scare the post master into giving them money."

"Do you believe him?"

Molly nodded.

"I think that I do. But it's the joint enterprise thing. He didn't actually have to fire the gun to be charged along with the other man."

"What about him thinking that the gun was a fake?"

"The police, and the prosecution, didn't believe him. He said that he had nightmares about it all for years. He tried to send the policeman's widow some money but she wouldn't take it."

"Not sure that I blame her, really," said Jeremy.

"This new friend of his, Louise, thinks that there may be a chance of an appeal."

"On what grounds?"

"I'm not sure. I know that the law has changed but whether it would benefit him or not I don't know. Anyway, he's served his sentence now."

"How long was he actually inside for?"

"The best part of twenty years, I think."

They fell silent for a moment.

"He did say a strange thing, though," said Molly. "He said that being in prison saved his life." She smiled suddenly. "It was where he learned to cook."

IN THE LODGE kitchen, Carlos snapped the lid on the last of the leftovers and turned to Simon.

"Thanks for staying on this afternoon, Simon. It felt, like, a bit weird coming back in today. Like with everything that's happened and that. It was nice to have some company."

Simon nodded and spooned coffee into two mugs. Aubrey edged his way round the open door and flopped down on the floor between them. Might as well wait here for Vincent. He just didn't have the energy to carry on making the rounds today. Although, he had to admit, he was feeling quite a lot better. The minced chicken that Jeremy had been feeding him had definitely helped. So much so that he had actually contemplated spinning things out for a bit longer, but then decided against it. Jeremy, Molly and Carlos had been so worried about him that it didn't seem fair to make them suffer any longer than they needed to. Although the chicken was very nice...

"So what's happening?" continued Carlos. "I mean, like with the Lodge and that?"

Simon turned to face him.

"At the moment, nothing. I've spoken to a solicitor about buying it, but there's all the other stuff to sort out first. In the meantime, it's been agreed with the police that Molly will continue running it so that there's no disruption to the residents although they're bound to find out soon what's been happening. It'll be on the news."

Carlos nodded.

"Will you be allowed to buy it?" he asked, suddenly shy. "I mean, you know, are you allowed…"

"I can buy a property. It's whether I can start a business. I might have to form a company or something. That's one of the things I asked the solicitor about. I think it's more of a problem if you've been bankrupt or committed fraud or something like that but anyway, my solicitor is going to look into it."

Carlos looked at him, his expression solemn. He was, he had to admit, impressed that Simon had a solicitor.

"Do you know, like, hate Gordon for what he was doing?" he asked.

Aubrey paused in the washing of his ears and glanced up at Simon, interested.

Simon was silent for a moment, and then spoke slowly.

"There's no point," he said simply. "I've wasted enough of my life. If I let myself think about him, it would just be more negative emotion. That's what Louise says, anyway. And she's right. There are always going to be Gordons in this world. I can't go around blaming everyone else for all the mistakes I've made. It was my decision to take the stuff in the first place. Nobody made me."

"What's it like? What does it feel like?" Carlos asked, suddenly curious. "I mean," he added hastily, "if you don't mind me asking."

Simon regarded him; head tipped to one side.

"No, I don't mind." He looked thoughtful, a distant expression in his eyes. "The first time you take it, you get kind of elated, a sort of euphoria. It's like nothing you've ever felt before. Somebody once said that it was like slipping through rainbows on a warm summer day."

Aubrey stirred uncomfortably. When he'd licked that stuff off the floor, he hadn't felt elated. He'd felt like he was going to die.

"And," Simon continued, "that feeling is so good that you want it again. And again. Because the one thing that an addict always wants is more."

Carlos stared at him. Maybe that's what it had been like with his father. Maybe he hadn't really wanted to drink. Maybe he just had to. Alcohol was a drug like any other. But it didn't make everything all right though. It didn't wipe out the memories of his father rampaging around their small flat, smashing things and hurling abuse, while his mother cried and his grandfather cowered in the corner. But, maybe, a small part of him could offer some understanding if not forgiveness. He listened quietly as Simon continued.

"And it gets to the point where you'll do anything to get it. Anything. You stop caring about other people. You stop caring about family and friends. You stop caring about yourself. You know that you smell and that people pass you on the street and look at you with revulsion. You know that shooting up in a public lavatory or on some stained mattress in a scuzzy squat is disgusting but you don't care. The only thing that you care about is getting enough money together to buy the next fix. It messes with your head and it makes you lose your humanity. I still take medication even now. Proper medication," he added. "To deal with anxiety."

Carlos felt his heart bump suddenly. Teddy had told him that one of the boys in her sixth form, a boy called Mungo whose step-mother did something in the government, had taken cocaine and had offered it around in the common room. He pressed his lips tightly together. Teddy had laughed and said that she hadn't been tempted, but as soon as he got back tonight, he was going to call her and warn her. Tell her what Simon had said, in case she didn't know. Teddy might think that she was all worldly wise but the only drug takers she knew were those that sat around in designer clothes eating posh dinners. The other sort, the sort that slept in doorways soaked in their own urine, were outside of her experience.

"So how did you cope when, you know, when you were in prison and that?" he asked.

Simon smiled, a wintry smile that held no warmth.

"Everything has a price."

Carlos looked appalled.

"What? You mean, like, you can even buy it…"

"The first prison I was in, two of the screws were in on it."

"But you don't take it now, do you?"

Carlos suddenly felt anxious, the words tumbling out in a rush. Simon was his friend. He was Aubrey and Vincent's friend, too, as well as Molly and Jeremy's. They cared about him. If he was still taking heroin, then… his mouth was dry as he waited for Simon's answer.

Simon shook his head.

"No. Being sent to prison saved me really, it was the best thing that could have happened. Otherwise I don't think that I'd be here today."

"How can going to prison save you?" Carlos was confused. And so was Aubrey. Being banged up in Sunny Banks rescue centre hadn't saved him. It had driven him half-mad. And he hadn't even gone around waving a gun or anything. He hadn't done anything at all, other than to be in the wrong place at the wrong time.

"It was the last prison that I was in. One day I looked at one of the screws. I mean, really looked. And he looked clean and smart and he was laughing and joking with one of the other screws. And I thought, at the end of the day, when he's finished his shift, he's going home, probably to a nice house and wife and kids. A home-cooked meal, a pint of beer. Maybe he'll mow his lawn. And I'm here. And here is where I'll always be. Or somewhere like it, because I haven't got a shift to finish. I'm going to be somewhere like this, breathing in the stench of failure and inadequacy, until I die. Bumping along at the bottom of society." He smiled again, a proper smile this time that reached his eyes. "I couldn't even blame my upbringing. I mean, some of those poor sods in there had suffered childhoods that would make Oliver Twist look privileged. I'd had nothing but love and kindness."

He fell silent, his expression thoughtful.

"Do you know," he continued, "some of the cons inside could barely read or write. They weren't interested in books or reading. Not because they were stupid, but because it was like a sort of secret code that they couldn't open. Reading and all that stuff was for posh people. Comics were all that some of them could manage and some of them struggled even with that."

"But," said Carlos, puzzled. "How come they couldn't read or write? They must have gone to school."

"I expect they did," said Simon. "Sometimes. If you haven't got parents that are bothered about where you are and what you're doing…"

Carlos thought for a moment. It was true. The kids at Sir Frank's who mucked about in class and always came bottom in everything until they just stopped attending, generally also had the kind of parents who never came to parents' evenings. He'd heard Jeremy comment on it more than once. But school was one of the many things that Maria had always been strict about. Once when he'd bunked off she had come home early because one of the restaurants that she cleaned had been flooded, and she had caught him lounging about on the sofa and watching television. She hadn't been angry, which he had braced himself for. She had been sad, her big dark eyes full of tears, which had made far more of an impression on him.

"Carlos, you must listen to your mother. School, it is very necessary. You must go to school to learn all the things to be a famous doctor. If no school then no doctor. Tell me Carlos, do you want to be like your big fat bum-face father?"

And he had said no, he didn't want to be like his big fat bum-face father and had promised her that he wouldn't bunk off again. And he hadn't. He looked at Simon's face. It was hard to believe now that he had been as he described although, now he thought about it, that day he and Teddy went to visit him at his flat he had looked terrible and he'd looked even worse when they found him in the beach hut.

"Simon," he hesitated and then ploughed on, "When you didn't come into work that day, why didn't you phone in or anything? I mean, you could have told Molly that you weren't feeling very well."

Simon looked at him and then looked away. His voice, when he spoke, was barely audible.

"Because I saw it," he muttered.

"You saw what?"

He turned back to face Carlos.

"The body. Toby Carson. I went for a walk after finishing my shift. I like it over there, it's kind of wild and free. And I saw it."

CHAPTER FORTY-FIVE

AUBREY TUCKED HIS paws beneath him and listened. He knew that there had been something that Simon hadn't told.

"But why didn't you tell anyone?" Carlos frowned; his smooth forehead furrowed in an effort of understanding. "Why didn't you ring the police?"

Simon gave a wry smile.

"Why do you think?"

"But you knew that you hadn't done anything wrong."

Simon wrapped his fingers around his coffee mug.

"The police would start poking around. They were bound to. And then it would all come out. The post office. The shooting. I would be bound to be in the frame. I went home and," he hesitated, "I started feeling desperate, trying to think of ways out."

Carlos stared at him, horrified.

"Not…"

Simon smiled.

"No, not that. But my mind just kept going round and round When you and Teddy came, I was just about at my wit's end. I didn't know what to do. Then I thought that if I went to the beach hut, where nobody would find me, it would give me some time to think."

"And did it?"

Simon shook his head.

"No, not really. Well, it did, but not in a good way. Working at the Lodge, doing up the flats, it changed everything. I couldn't believe my luck when Thomas didn't DRB me. It felt like I was living a normal life—I was like other people. In some senses, I was being the son that my parents had wanted me to be. And then Toby Carson got murdered, and it was a bit like…" he paused and thought for a moment. "Do you remember that game of snakes and ladders?"

Carlos nodded. His grandfather had bought it for him when he was about four and they had played it for hours while his mother was at work and his father was snoring on the sofa.

"Well, I'd reached the top of the ladder and then suddenly I'd slithered down a snake and I was stuck there. It was like watching a great train steaming towards me, and there was nothing that I could do to stop it. Everything was going to be taken away. And in the end, in a way, I didn't mind. There seemed," he paused and thought for a moment, "a kind of inevitability about it. And I knew where I was in prison. I didn't have to think when I was inside."

"Weren't you afraid that you'd go back to, you know, using and stuff?"

"Yes," said Simon simply. "It's always there. Because when things get tough you know at the back of your mind that you can always go back to it. It's the friend that will make you feel better, the friend that won't ask any questions and will make everything all right. Except that it's not a friend. It's the assassin that's waiting round every corner."

Carlos nodded in what he hoped was an understanding manner, although he didn't really understand at all. His worst vice was his daily crisp habit, which he'd once tried to give up for Lent. He'd lasted for two days. But, to be fair, eating a packet of salt and vinegar didn't lead to robbing post offices and fatal shootings. He tried to think of something encouraging to say.

"When you stopped using and that, it must have been hard," Carlos said. "I mean, you did really well. I bet loads of people couldn't do what you did."

"The prison had a drugs rehabilitation scheme and I signed up for it. Eventually got myself clean. Then I started helping in the kitchens. When one of the cooks got early release, I took his place. I started to feel better about myself."

Carlos nodded. That was something that he did understand. Cooking made him feel good about himself as well. He may not become the famous doctor of his mother's dreams, but he would have his own restaurant and she would have been proud of him. He glanced out of the window. From where he was standing, he could see Gordon's cottage, the curtains closed and the empty bins parked up against the wall. He had once thought the cottage rather charming. It was the sort of place that he would have liked to have lived in himself when he was properly grown up. He didn't think so now. Now it had an almost palpable sense of evil swirling about it, like a poisonous spider in its web. He suppressed a shudder and looked back at Simon.

"I expect Gordon will get a long prison sentence. Serves him right. But," he added with a sudden teenage sense of fair play, "I suppose that he was good to Buster."

Simon smiled suddenly.

"Even bad people do good things sometimes."

"I hope that Buster's all right. I mean, he won't understand what's happened."

Aubrey hoped that Buster was all right, too. After Gordon was arrested Buster had been taken by the dog handling unit and then banged up in some rescue place. He thought for a moment of the small dog's beautiful golden fur and his happy little face.

One thing you could say for Buster, he was always pleased to see you. So pleased that occasionally he was in danger of knocking you right off your feet. Buster loved company, but if this rescue place was anything like Sunny Banks rescue centre, he'd be lucky to get any. The only real contact came at feeding time. And Vincent had told him that at one of those places he knew about, they walked the dogs about five at a time and then only for about ten minutes. Poor little Buster would burst with suppressed energy. He might be getting on all their nerves, and who knew what would happen then?

"What will happen if they can't find him some new owners?" Carlos looked suddenly stricken. "Will he be, you know, put down?"

"Don't worry," said Simon. "He's going to a good owner."

"Who?"

"Me." Simon smiled. "I'm taking him."

ACKNOWLEDGEMENTS

Huge appreciation for Sean Coleman, Meggy Roussel and the rest of the Red Dog Team for their unfailing positivity, enthusiasm and professionalism which makes them such lovely people to work with.

Thanks also to all the cat and dog rescue centres up and down the country who do such great work and gave me Aubrey in the first place.

ABOUT THE AUTHOR

I was born in London and spent my teenage years in Hertfordshire where I spent large amounts of time reading novels, watching daytime television and avoiding school.

Failing to gain any qualifications in science whatsoever, the dream of being a forensic scientist collided with reality when a careers teacher suggested that I might like to work in a shop. I don't think she meant Harrods.

Later studying law, I decided to teach rather than go into practice and have spent many years teaching mainly criminal law and criminology to young people and adults.

I enjoy reading crime novels, doing crosswords, and drinking wine. Not necessarily in that order.